Praise for *House of Yesterday*

"*House of Yesterday* is a haunting, lyrical meditation on generational trauma; a love letter to diaspora families, in all their imperfect glory; and most important of all, a shining testament to the fact that healing can come from the most unlikely of places, if only we have the courage to reach for it."

—Adib Khorram, award-winning author of
Darius the Great Is Not Okay

"A stunning exploration about a girl dealing with grief and identity. Writing in hauntingly beautiful prose, Zargarpur captures the struggle of a diaspora girl grappling with how her family's identity clashes with who she thinks she wants to be. A gorgeous debut!"

—Kat Cho, *New York Times*–bestselling author of
Once Upon a K-Prom and *Wicked Fox*

"A beautifully written tale about reckoning the rose-colored stories our family tells us as children with the often painful truths we understand as adults. Sara's unflinchingly messy and deeply heartfelt journey will remain with readers for a long time."

—Amanda Foody, *New York Times*–bestselling
coauthor of *All of Us Villains*

"*House of Yesterday* is a tender, haunting tribute to the secrets, grudges, and forgiveness that bind a family. The story is at once an open door for outsiders as well as an affirming mirror for hyphenated readers."

—Nadia Hashimi, author of
The Pearl That Broke Its Shell

HOUSE of YESTERDAY

HOUSE of YESTERDAY

YESTERDAY

Deeba Zargarpur

FARRAR STRAUS GIROUX

New York

Farrar Straus Giroux Books for Young Readers
An imprint of Macmillan Publishing Group, LLC
120 Broadway, New York, NY 10271 • fiercereads.com

Our books may be purchased in bulk for promotional, educational, or business use. Please contact your local bookseller or the Macmillan Corporate and Premium Sales Department at (800) 221-7945 ext. 5442 or by email at MacmillanSpecialMarkets@macmillan.com.

Library of Congress Cataloging-in-Publication Data
Names: Zargarpur, Deeba, author.
Title: House of yesterday / Deeba Zargarpur.
Description: First edition. | New York : Farrar Straus Giroux
Books for Young Readers, 2022. | Audience: Ages 14 to 18. |
Audience: Grades 10–12. | Summary: Struggling with her
parent's divorce and her grandmother's dementia, fifteen-year-old
Sara Rahmat tries to distract herself in a home renovation project
but instead finds the house is full of dark family secrets that give
rise to ghostly apparitions.
Identifiers: LCCN 2022017773 | ISBN 9780374388706
(hardcover) | ISBN 9781250802965 (paperback)
Subjects: CYAC: Secrets—Fiction. | Families—Fiction. |
Family life—Fiction. | Ghosts—Fiction. | Muslims—United
States—Fiction. | Afghan Americans—Fiction. | Fantasy. | LCGFT:
Fantasy novels. | Novels.
Classification: LCC PZ7.1.Z385 Ho 2022 | DDC [Fic]—dc23
LC record available at https://lccn.loc.gov/2022017773

First edition, 2022
Book design by Veronica Mang
Printed in the United States of America

ISBN 978-0-374-38870-6

1   3   5   7   9   10   8   6   4   2

For my beloved Bibi Dil jan.
I love you. Always.

HOUSE of YESTERDAY

Part One

THE DISCOVERY

"*Sara jan, do you hear this song? It's my absolute favorite. My father used to sing it to me. Let me show you how to dance to it. You move your hands like this. And never forget to smile. I could never forget that smile.*"

—A conversation with Bibi jan
One month after diagnosis

CHAPTER ONE

THERE'S A LOT TO A MEMORY.

To me, it's being seven years old and clutching the edges of a scratchy blindfold as the summer sun cascades promises of bright days ahead.

It's being ten and realizing maybe I pulled off my blindfold too quick.

It's being twelve and wishing for the dark.

It's being fifteen and not knowing how to turn the light back on.

It's the present and past wrapped up so tight until there's nothing left.

Until it's gone.

It's funny. The things people never forget.

Take my bibi jan as an example.

My grandmother will never *ever* leave her room without running dark kohl over her brows. Or approach a man without first throwing on a sheer black scarf to cover her hair and demure smile. Or let me leave the house without chastising me to cover my legs as a proper Afghan girl must do.

I take a sip from my teacup to cover my grin. Because it really is funny, these little things that stay with us. And the big things that somehow seem to slip through the cracks.

A spoon clatters from Bibi jan's hand. Bits of egg sprinkle on her worn, floral pajamas. The gleaming sapphire-and-gold necklace my grandmother wears sparkles in contrast. I grip my cup a little bit tighter when she bends from her seat to pick up the spoon from the kitchen floor. Her severe face, gaunt and swollen at the same time, turns as she takes me in for the tenth time this morning. Confusion ebbs and flows as her gaze slides right past me.

"Ki asti?" she asks.

Who are you?

My throat gets scratchy and tight, but I still plaster on my best *everything is okay* smile.

"I'm Sara." I'm careful to roll the *r* and keep the *a*'s soft. "Your granddaughter."

But my bibi jan is bobbing, her eyes searching for a lifeboat to pull her ashore.

"Ki?"

It's funny, I think as I remove my glasses. *The little details that shouldn't matter.* I shake my hair free from my bun and fluff it up. *And yet.* I bat away the watery sting as I smile again and focus on her blurry face. Her carefully brushed dark hair is pulled back into a little bun. Snow-white roots show at her hairline.

I keep breathing as she appraises me. Keep count of the seconds that pass by, running my fingers over each bead on my worn bracelet. I count and remember:

One, two, three . . .

I'm a toddler, and Bibi jan is singing me a song in her bed.

Four, five, six . . .

I'm in pre-K, and Bibi jan swats me away from the breakfast table. It's an endless game of wash-your-face-and-hands-before-eating or accept the consequences.

Seven, eight, nine . . .

I'm in kindergarten, and Baba jan has died. Bibi jan's papery hand is tight in mine at the funeral.

Ten, eleven—

"Ah, my Sara jan." She leans in close. Her Farsi sounds like a song I could never forget. It is a melody that sings to the oldest parts of my heart. "Such a beautiful girl with a beautiful name."

"Best name in the world, right, Bibi jan?" When she laughs in agreement, my smile is true and genuine. Because out of forty-one grandkids, twenty-nine great-grandkids, and three great-great-grandkids, I'm the only one that was given my grandmother's name.

I want to see the way her smile radiates, not from her mouth but from the wrinkly little corners of her eyes. So I wait a little longer before putting my glasses on. Just in case.

"Erik, don't forget, we've got to make sure the dumpsters are cleared and ready to go on Monday." My madar emerges from the hallway. She is a whirlwind of perfume and freshly manicured nails. She's talking a mile a minute as she shimmies her way around Bibi's chair into the kitchen. She throws a quick smile Bibi's way before draining her coffee mug in record time and drops it in the sink.

Mornings with Nargis Amani are unpredictable. It's a lot like rolling the dice. You never quite know which version you're going to get.

I slurp my tea quietly, hoping today's mood is forget-Sara-promised-to-go-to-work-this-morn—

Let's go, Madar mouths at me.

I sigh dramatically. Lady Luck has forsaken me yet again.

"Ki asti?" Bibi jan's spoon is midair again as she stares at my mother. Only, Bibi's voice these days is like a whisper, as if some part of her knows that she has shrunk from the great woman she used to be.

Madar doesn't hear her.

"Great. I'll be coming over later to figure out a few more things," Madar says into the phone. "See you in a few."
Click.

Bibi jan spoons another mouthful of runny egg and

misses her lips by three inches. It nearly lands on top of my foot.

"Who is she?" She squints and drums her fingers against her hips, like the answer is on the tip of her tongue.

I point at Madar and lean in close so my mouth hovers directly near Bibi jan's good ear. If this was two years ago, Bibi would joke, *I'm too young for things like hearing aids.*

"Your daughter."

Bibi jan continues to stare and shakes her head. It only takes a moment before she sits back in her seat, lost in the sea of her mind.

"Sara, we've got a bunch of houses to check on today." Madar kisses the top of Bibi jan's head before rushing out of the kitchen to the car. The Bluetooth is already ringing. Madar's mind is a million miles away.

I want to tell her, *I'm doing fine, thanks for asking.*

I wish she'd notice and say, *Bibi jan brushed her own hair today?*

I'm not that brave.

Instead, I leave my own soggy eggs untouched and hug my grandmother, run into my room to grab my camera, and rush out the door. As the door slams shut, I can't help but wince at Bibi jan's parting words that have turned me from *loved one* to *no one.*

"Ki asti?"

⌒

Exactly a year ago, Madar and I made a deal. It was the summer before freshman year and the world was semi-back-to-normal after a virus put most of the world in lockdown. During the months of social distancing, I consumed my body weight in hot fries and Sprite while binge-watching all of *Code Geass, Haikyu!!, Inuyasha*, and *Tokyo Ghoul*. Madar was convinced I'd die of processed food overdose and lack of vitamin D, which I admit was a very real possibility.

The Afghan in her was appalled at my lack of ambition when the lockdown was over, so she took it upon herself to *light the flame*, so to speak, by making me head of social media and tech support for the family house-flipping business.

In reality, I was just a glorified and (key word) *free* photographer for the houses.

Madar called it an investment in my future by taking an interest in saving the family business.

I called it making a profit on other people's misfortune, but that's a discussion for another day.

I scroll through the pictures on my camera, deleting some to clear up space. There's an embarrassing number of selfies and failed dance routines that I would rather not explain. Tap. Erase. Madar rolls her eyes in disgust as I gnaw away at my nails. I stop on a cute candid of Bibi jan tidying up her room. It makes me smile.

Our car zooms and loops along the lush winding roads of eastern Long Island, the place my mother and her family—all ten sisters and one brother—have called home for about forty years. My mother was only thirteen when they arrived.

Sometimes, I ask Madar what it was like to pick up and start over in a foreign land.

Sometimes, I wish I could do it too.

To escape and start over somewhere new.

"We were running from a war, jan," she would remind me.

As the wind roars through the open window, I find myself thinking, *I'm running from a war too.*

"Can you shut the window? It's bothering my ears." Madar takes a sharp left and my camera nearly goes flying out the window. The GPS recalculates. "It literally told me to turn here." Madar fiddles with the navigation, swerving for two seconds almost into the wrong lane. A passing car honks.

"I'd really like to digest my breakfast in peace, if that's all right with you." My camera falls between my beat-up sneakers. I leave the window open. Rebellion isn't really my thing, but I will hurl if I have to spend another second enduring Madar's driving without fresh air.

Madar soon forgets about the window when we arrive in front of a decrepit house. I blink twice. I don't recognize this one.

"Who died and left this disaster?" My brow crinkles. "This isn't the Centerport house." I notice a sign that reads SUMNER COURT.

"Slight detour. We just got this one a few days ago."
Madar shuts off the car. "Let's go inside and see what
we've got to work with."

I shrivel up in my seat. If there's one thing I hate, it's
day one photos of the houses.

"Is it safe?" I fiddle with my seat belt before stepping
out of the car. I bring my camera to my eye and rapid-fire
three pictures of the driveway, yard, and facade of the
house itself. Like a pro, if I do say so myself.

"Of course it's safe." Madar shoots a quick text before
rubbing her hands together in excitement. "We got a
great deal on this one. If we fix it fast, this could really
help us out this year. Come on."

Dandelions and other hideous weeds are living their
best lives in between the cracks of the driveway. Peeling paneling runs across once-white trim on the boarded
windows. High arches curl around the entryway, with
overgrown bushes and vines snarling around the foundation of the house. In its prime, this house could have
been beautiful.

It makes me wonder what went wrong for the former
owners to lose it.

I feel the weight of eyes through the partially boarded-up
windows of the second floor. A rusted wrought-iron fence
gate squeals, and every hair on the back of my legs rises.
I look up—there is no one there, but the feeling of being
watched lingers.

"You know, this is how all those Netflix horror films

start." I rock on the ball of my foot and decide to wait in the car. "Maybe I should just . . ." My hand is on the handle, all I need to do is—

The car beeps. Locked.

". . . or not."

"Don't be a baby," Madar calls as she huffs up the winding walkway to the front door.

A shadow falls on me as I make my way up the driveway and approach the crumbling porch. The house is massive—bordering mansion level. There's peeling gray paint scattered along the entryway and I have to jump over rotted wood to get to the front door.

My fingers catch on the rusted doorbell just as a shard of light pierces through the doorway and into the wide-open foyer. Rainbows bloom across the marble as it leads up the winding stairs to the partially exposed second floor. Silvery cobwebs drift languidly between the gaps in the railing and the solitary chandelier that sways high above.

Stay away, a lone voice—familiar yet foreign—warns as my foot hovers over the threshold. *Before it ensnares you*. I hesitate. What was that?

"What is taking you so long?" Madar's voice rings out from somewhere beyond. "Oh wow. Come look at this deck. This is going to be so beautiful once we get started."

"Um. What's the story with this house?"

"Abandoned," she calls out. "Hurry up, we have three other houses to check on today."

This is just getting better and better. "What happened to the owners?"

Madar doesn't answer back. She's already someplace else. *I can do this. I can do this.* I shake my nerves and, on the count of three, enter the house.

Call me superstitious or an idiot, but I believe there's a lingering history in these old homes. I can feel it in the way my footsteps echo against the worn tile, as my fingers brush the once-loved walls leading to a room with vaulted ceilings and a fireplace. Ever since my parents started their house-flipping business ten years ago when I was a kid, to pass the time I'd wander and twirl in old halls, putting faces and stories to the gaps in explanation from these bank-owned properties.

My parents and I used to make a game of it. *Tell us the feeling,* Padar would laugh as Madar measured rooms and made plans to realize her hopes and dreams for each house. But all that changed when Padar moved out a year and a half ago, leaving their once-plans to fade away. So now, I play pretend.

"Tell us the feeling," I mutter to the dusty great room.

There's a heaviness, like a sense of . . . melancholy lingering. I pause. Again, I feel the weight of eyes. My foot creaks on the wood floor, but all is still. *Get a grip, you've done this a hundred times before.* I swallow and continue to snap pictures.

Madar thinks collecting before-and-after pictures will get me more interested in the family business. In reality,

I think having me around on the jobsites helps distract her from the Padar-shaped hole in the business.

I continue exploring the house. Large windows line the walls, and the boards of wood covering them cast darkness in the open space of a family room. It opens into an empty kitchen, with the oven and fridge torn right out. There are French doors leading outside, and I see my mother stepping carefully on an enormous deck, testing the creaking wood as it gives with each step.

The air is denser here, like a weight that makes it hard to breathe.

A history that feels—

There's a crashing sound mixed with Madar's shrieks.

"Madar!" I bolt and jump straight through the doors onto the deck. The wood has given way, and her left foot has sunk through. I grab her hands and pull. Her jeans are torn and her calf is bleeding a little.

"Why would you come out here? This thing looks like it should have fallen down yesterday." We hobble back inside, and Madar leans against the kitchen island. There's a scowl on her face as she brushes her hair back.

"Just what I needed," she mutters, already rolling up her pant leg to her knee and inspecting the cut. "Well, it's not so bad. Just a scratch." She shrugs and her phone rings and, just like that, she's jammed it back in her ear. "Erik. Hold on a sec." She looks at me. "Go see if there are some bandages around here. I'm gonna wash it out in the sink."

I'm slack-jawed as I watch my mother rinse out her injury like it's nothing. Doesn't she care about rust or bacteria? God knows what's been lurking in those pipes.

"I wouldn't trust that water if I were you." But one glare from Madar and I'm backing away and down a hall that leads to a little bar space. I open the cabinets and nearly shriek as roaches fall out and scatter across the floor. Disgusting. "Unless you want to get an infection, we need to go to the store." I shake a baby roach off my shoe. I am so ready to head back to the car and out of this trap of a house.

There's a soft patter of footsteps followed by a few wavering beats of a drum.

"Hello?" The noise comes from behind me, leading me down a hall and into a darkened wing of the house. The beat of the drum continues. "Is anyone there?" Goose bumps run down my arms when there's no answer.

"Trespassing is a felony, you know!" I call out into the darkness. I walk into the L-shaped hall.

Still no answer.

I turn on the lights to the first room on the left—bathroom. Empty. *Click*. Picture.

At the bend, there's a room with a stained twin bed. Old clothes are strewn along the floor. Empty.

Behind me, an echo of laughter.

I twirl on my heel. "This is private property." My voice

wavers as the hall turns, leading into a pitch-black area. The drum grows louder now.

My legs tremble as I look back toward the light, where Madar is still talking on the phone. I want to bolt back. *Light of my heart, dance.* The voice I heard before sings out, again and again. The drum shakes the air as the light tinkle of another instrument joins in. I'm drawn into the darkness, one foot following another until there is nothing but me, my racing heart, and the beat of the drum.

I fiddle with the flash and auto-timer on my camera. Flash. Picture. A burst of light. Dust rains heavily from the ceiling, making me gag, but that's not what makes me scream. I jump back, my foot catches on something on the floor, and I fall hard on to the ground. My camera skitters somewhere.

Click. Flash.

The beat of the drum grows louder.

The voice continues to sing.

The light from the camera illuminates a lone figure, spinning wildly in a circle. A woman. Her hair is dark and curled. The edges of her blue-and-gold beaded dress clash furiously against her hips. A thick gold necklace studded with sapphires chokes her neck.

I shriek like a banshee. The woman stops, her face shrouded by the darkness of her hands. The drum speeds up until I realize it is not a drum but the beating of my heart, pounding furiously against my throat.

And slowly—so very slowly, the figure turns her head and moves her hand, and I'm left screaming at a haunting young face, one that I recognize only because I've seen it in pictures.

My bibi.

CHAPTER TWO

"WHAT IS GOING ON?"

Madar runs into the room. The woman vanishes instantly.

"Th-there was a woman." I shakily point to the corner, my eyes unblinking at the vacant space in front of us.

"There's no one here, Sara." Madar squints and inspects the dark room. "Nothing but bugs and dust." Her face softens when she looks back at me. She swoops in, a beacon of warmth when I don't move. "You just had a scare." She caresses the side of my face, slick with sweat, and gently coaxes me off the ground.

I know what I saw.

"She was dancing," I whisper, and fight against Madar's grip on my elbow. "She—" *She looked like Bibi.*

"Sometimes these old houses play tricks on us," Madar says. "But it's nothing, really."

"Someone was *here.*" I jerk my arm away. "I'm not a little kid. I know what I saw."

Madar ignores me and wipes dust off the back of my shirt, but her hawk eyes are fixed on the spot where the woman was dancing.

For a moment, I think she believes me. She draws in tight on herself, pinches the bridge of her nose.

"I know things are . . . different now, but you don't need to make up stories to get my attention." She hesitates. "With everything going on with your father—"

"I don't need *attention*." I harden, allowing the familiar mask of anger to cover my face as I scroll through the pictures on my camera. There has to be proof here.

Only, there's nothing. Just empty space.

"Whatever. I'm going out for some air." I stalk out of the hall and through the front doors into the suffocating sunshine. I try to yank open the car door, but it's locked. Of course. So now I'm mad and stewing in the June heat.

What does Madar know about how I feel? Or better yet, what I need? I haven't needed Madar's attention in years.

Not since Padar split up the family business and left.

Not since Madar checked out, leaving me all alone to face the wreckage of their war.

Madar emerges from the house—a haze of highlighter and sun-kissed skin. She swipes quickly at her eyes. Throws on her sunglasses.

The car unlocks.

Before she has a chance to say anything more to me, I stomp into the car. Madar settles into her seat. Her nearly silent sniffles are overpowered by the thrum of the engine. I close my eyes and pretend not to hear them.

"Sara?" Her voice is whisper soft as she backs out of the driveway. The silence is heavy between us.

But I can't.

I refuse to talk about it.

I pretend to sleep as Madar drives in silence. But something bright is reflecting in the corner of my eye.

By my feet, tangled in my camera strap, is a thin strip of ripped gold-and-blue embroidery.

⸎

Buzz. Buzz.

I'm lying on my bed, my hair fanned out messily under me. I search the pictures again, ignoring the notifications on my phone. Images flick by—the front facade, the empty living room, the kitchen, the hall—until I stop on the last picture I took. The darkened room, barely lit by the flash, but there's nothing else. Just cobwebbed office furniture and a shadowed wall.

No woman.

And yet I have part of her dress in my hand.

I toss the camera in frustration and inspect the material.

It's beautiful and looks similar to the design of an Afghan dress Madar had custom-made for me a few years ago when I danced the attan at my cousin's wedding. I sit up and fist the thread. I can't shake this feeling, and until I can place a name to that woman's face, I won't be able to sleep. Before I know it, I'm tiptoeing into Bibi jan's room. My phone lights up and buzzes in my pocket. I freeze.

Thin tendrils of moonlight swirl through the cracks of Bibi's curtains. Bibi jan is in bed and lies perfectly still on her back with her floral blanket pulled tightly up to her neck. Irina, Bibi's live-in caretaker, snores softly next to her in a twin bed across the room.

I watch the way Bibi jan's chest rises and falls before snooping my way into her closet.

Well, her closet *now*. This room was Madar's and Padar's once upon a time. Then Padar moved out, Bibi jan moved in, and here we are.

Turning on my phone flashlight, I rummage through her boxes and boxes of useless clutter until I find what I'm looking for.

Photo albums.

There has to be something here. The image of the woman, spinning round and round, replays in my head. Something about it feels so familiar. Like there's something I've seen before. I know it. I scan through until I find the albums dated 1980—around the time my family moved to Long Island. How old would that have made Bibi? My brow wrinkles. I . . . don't really know.

A cold draft fills the small space, followed by a faint *thump*. I snap my head behind me, half expecting that creepy ghost woman's eyes in between the folds of Bibi's pleated St. John shirts. *Don't be ridiculous. There's no such thing as ghosts. Also, Bibi is very much alive.* I keep telling myself this as the crinkly sheets of photo paper bend under my fingers. I'm flipping through yellowed pages, and faded photographs of my family when they were young.

There's a girl—Madar, I recognize—in a dark blue-and-white one-piece bathing suit tangled with two other darker skinned girls, my two youngest aunts, at a public pool. And another photo, of Baba jan, my grandfather, gazing pensively at the camera at a family dinner. His thinning white hair is swept to the side, his right hand raised as if to say something.

I turn the page again, and I'm bombarded with photos of a large convenience store. Madar and my uncle are smiling wide in front of the cash registers.

There are dozens of these photos, each page filled with brightly colored rows of canned goods, one sibling pushing another, spilling everything out onto the floor. Baba jan looking pissed in the background. There is blue eye shadow, god-awful poofy hair, and equally-as-large ball gowns in bright blue, fuchsia, and lime green. Madar is sprawled out over a yellow convertible with a smug smirk splashed across her face.

I don't know why, but my eyes tear up. This was life once upon a time ago—before Madar grew up, before me, before the shitstorm of now. I linger on Madar's laughing face. She has a youthful ease I've never seen before.

Madar was happy then, before Padar, before me.

I know I shouldn't think it, but sitting here, alone in the dark, I can't help but wonder if Madar could learn to be the happy girl in these photos again. After Padar. After me.

The closet door creaks open, and I jump in surprise. The photo album clatters on the carpeted floor. Like dominoes, the other albums all topple over and fall.

The closet light flickers on.

It's Bibi jan. Her watery eyes take in all of me. From my tangled hair, to my glasses that have gone askew, to my hands as I try to cover up the things of hers I've shamelessly tossed aside on the floor.

Her eyes zero in on the glinting material I've dropped.

Slowly, she wobbles onto her knees and sits next to me. I'm scrambling to clean up the mess.

"I'm sorry, Bibi jan," I mutter as I reach to snatch the ripped thread at the same time she does. Our hands meet, and for a split-second, time stops. My arm is on fire, only it's the cold kind of burning, like when you run frozen fingers under warm water. We stop breathing. Bibi jan doesn't move. Doesn't blink.

I snatch my hands to my chest. What *was* that?

Before I can ask if Bibi felt it too, she does the strangest thing. She scoops the material delicately in her hands and smiles at me.

A real, *I'm here* smile.

"Is that me?" she asks in her songlike Farsi. Her hand shakes, but she leans until both hands are grasping the album. There is a light in her face as she speaks, steady for the first time in I can't remember how long.

I forget how to answer.

"We had a huge store, just like my father did." She squints her eyes when she looks at me. "Abdulaziz. That was his name."

There are so many things I want to say. *I never knew that* and *I'm so happy you're telling me* and *How can you remember this now?* Instead, I swallow. Nod. Say "Balle, Bibi jan."

Yes, dear grandmother of mine.

She sighs when her fingers rest along a photo of her and Baba jan. She's wearing a smart pantsuit with jutting shoulder pads and low heels, posing next to the opening sign of *Fresh Start Mart.*

"You know, Sara jan, I have twelve children."

I furrow my brow. Twelve? "I think you mean eleven, Bibi jan. Ten girls and—"

"One boy and *eleven* girls." She holds up her fingers to count as she says each name, in order. "Farzana, Firoza, Gulnoor, Afsoon—" She hesitates. "M-maluda . . . Firoza." A little thin line nestles between her brows as she stares at her shaking fingers and starts over. "Farzana, Firoza, G—"

I wrap my hands around hers as she struggles and hold her tight. With my own fingers, I finish what she couldn't and we say the names together. "Zelaikha, Zenat, Nargis, Mojgan, and Nazaneen."

Ten daughters. All accounted for. I wish I could hold this moment for her, keep it tight in her heart, like how she'll always be in mine. If only it were that simple.

Bibi leans her head on my shoulder, and we sit in silence. The light in her face fades. There's the familiar dimness to her eyes, and she asks, "What am I doing here? What's with this mess?"

"Let's get you back to bed, Bibi jan." I help her up, watch her empty hands as she wobbles back to her bed. Irina is still snoring. I get on my hands and knees and clean up the mess of albums. I search for the gold-and-blue material. It's nowhere to be found. Maybe Bibi pocketed it when I wasn't looking.

I'm putting away the last album when a photo comes loose and flutters to the ground. It's horribly bent up, folded too many times, which is so odd for my grandma to do.

I unfold the image and jump back with a gasp. The photo falls face up.

It's the woman in the house.

Wearing the same dress and necklace.

That sapphire-and-gold necklace.

Bibi jan's necklace.

And she's in *that* house.

It is *Bibi*, I realize without a shadow of a doubt.

I can't stop staring at her face. There is a sorrow in her eyes, a haunted smile that extends past her face and into her shoulders as she poses.

I know the signs before it happens. The dots in my vision, the rapid, short breaths as my heart pumps a beat too quick. *Don't panic.* My fingers numb, and my phone continues to buzz, and all I can think about is that look on her face. I try to focus. Use my counting technique to calm down. My fingers pass over the beads in my bracelet and I count.

One, two, three . . .

I'm in pre-K surrounded by macaroni and glue, with Madar laughing by my side. There's a noodle stuck on her cheek.

Four, five, six . . .

I'm graduating fifth grade, and there are two empty seats where my parents should be. The ceremony comes and goes, yet the seats remain vacant.

Seven, eight, nine . . .

Rich, dark blood seeps into the cracks in the marble floor of our house. A crash comes from the hall. I don't know what to do.

This isn't working.

My phone buzzes again, and this time I pick it up.

Padar: I have something I need to tell you.

Padar: Why don't you answer me?

Padar: What time should I pick you up tomorrow?

Padar: This is getting ridiculous Sara

I linger on *something I need to tell you.* I can't explain why, but it makes me want to puke.

I pocket the photo and run, as fast as I can, out of the house, into the blanket of night air. Crickets chirp happily, and I want to squash them. I walk down the driveway, feeling the sharp sting of rocks beneath my bare feet. The stars gaze weakly through the smog of lights. I look up, wondering what I must look like to them.

I just need to walk it off. I'm near the mailbox at the end of the driveway when a dark figure flickers across the street. I step on a fallen burr and curse at the sharp pain in my foot.

"Hey, are you okay?"

I freeze as a sudden sense of déjà vu takes over. Like I'm thirteen again, and it's that night, and I'm running, running, running.

A hand waves in front of me, bringing me back to the now.

It's *him*.

"Do you make it a habit of stalking people, Sam?" I snap.

Bright blue eyes blink in surprise. His cropped blond hair glows softly in the night, and I hate the way I notice little details like that.

Here's the thing about Sam. We've been neighbors since his family moved across the street when I was six. We *used* to be friends—scratch that, we used to be best friends. All that changed a year and a half ago when Sam stuck his nose where he shouldn't have, and I haven't spoken to him since.

"Well, *you* were the one who was out here staring at me like a zombie." He fiddles with the sleeve of his T-shirt while his eyes linger on the bracelet on my wrist. "And, as a *concerned neighbor*, you know I felt I had to see what was up."

"Well, as a *concerned neighbor*, maybe you should learn how to mind your own business."

"Well, as a *friend*—"

"We're not friends."

"Sara." His stare looks a lot like hurt. "You can't mean that."

The problem is I do. My heart twists as I turn on my heel and stalk back into the house. My phone continues to buzz in my pocket.

"You know you can't avoid me forever!" he calls out. After a moment, I hear an exaggerated sigh and the rumble of a trash can being pushed.

"Watch me," I mutter to no one. Doesn't he get it by now? I'm the master at disappearing. I learned from the best.

Just ask Padar.

Plus, I have more important things to worry about. Like figuring out why the hell I saw a vision of my grandma in that creepy house in the first place.

CHAPTER THREE

THERE'S SOMEONE I WANT YOU TO MEET.

Padar's message throbs like an ugly case of cystic acne just waiting to pop. I leave the message on read and throw my phone on the grass. Lying on my back, I anger-stare at the clouds that pass by in our front yard. I can only handle one mystery at a time, and introducing this *someone* is like dropping a hive of agitated bees in my lap and expecting me to smile and say *thank you so much, Padar jan, just what I wanted, how did you know!*

I imagine a cloud-shaped version of my dad being squashed by a falling piano down a flight of stairs. But every time I blink, the clouds turn into visions of summer mornings in the garage, where I'm helping Padar carry plank after plank to his workbench. It was the summer Padar and Madar surprised me with a very American tree house, complete with tunnel and hideaway fort. Padar chipped away at that project for weeks, and on late nights when my parents thought I was asleep in bed,

I'd watch the two of them with their heads bent, sipping tea and leaning against each other next to the mess of hardware and broken wooden planks, counting their blessings to be *here*, in a place that finally felt like home.

I was just a kid then, when the only things that bothered me were the bugs that settled in after a few months and the splinters from Padar not properly sealing the wood.

I never thought those nights had an expiration date.

I never thought we'd be here.

My glasses fog—from the sun, I swear—when I sit up. I know I should answer Padar's messages. It would be the *right* thing to do.

I clutch the worn photo of Bibi in my hand.

Padar's nonsense will have to wait.

Behind me, the front door swings open, and Madar is balancing piles of folders in the nook of one arm, her phone blaring on top, and her coffee mug is sloshing in her other hand. Curiously, her hair is up in a messy ponytail. She has a cap pulled low over her eyes. When she looks up at me, I nearly do a double take.

Madar looks *awful*.

And Madar never looks awful.

Normally, I'm the troll in our teeny family. I'm not being self-deprecating, it's the truth. I come from a family of non-aging Afghan-Uzbek vampires. My mother is proof enough of that.

"What are you doing out here so early?" Madar asks. She takes a long sip from her cup and waves at Khala Farzana and Khala Gulnoor, who are doing their usual powerwalk around the neighborhood.

"Photosynthesizing."

Madar just blinks. Maybe it's too early for jokes.

"I wanted to ask you about yesterday." I nudge the camera at my hip. My hands are sweating as Madar stares at me. "I swear I saw something, so I thought I would do some digging in Bibi's things—"

"You *what*?"

"—and I found this." I jut my arm out and dangle the offending photo like it's on fire. "That's *her*. In that house!"

Madar snatches the photo and inspects it. Her tired eyes narrow before she turns on her heel and spills her folders into the back seat of her car. She sighs. "Sara, this doesn't prove anything. It could be any house."

"But it's the same room as yesterday!"

"All the houses built around then had those awful parquet floors." She's chewing on her thoughts as she slips her phone in her back pocket. "You know, maybe it's not a great idea for you to help out with the Sumner house."

"What? Why not?" I scramble for an excuse when she hands the picture back.

"Doesn't seem like—"

There's a loud and obnoxious honk. Madar startles

before a wobbly grin spreads across her face. A sleek black SUV pulls into our driveway. There are five pairs of arms waving through the tinted windows and the sounds of whooping and cheering. Close behind are two more cars. Muffled shrieks from excited children and blaring synthesized Uzbek music create a ripple in the sound barrier of our neighborhood.

The Amani family cavalry has arrived in true Afghan-Uzbek fashion: random and unannounced.

Khala Farzana and Khala Gulnoor are doubling back on their powerwalk—their arms are pumping furiously as they zip their way over to our front yard, like magnets attracted to the pull of their own kind. Their hips shake to the electronic beat and Gulsanam Mamazoitova's silky voice.

I brace myself for impact in 3, 2, 1—

"USE THE SIDE GATE TO THE POOL! DO NOT STAMPEDE THROUGH THE FRONT DOOR!" My khala Nazaneen's kids tumble out of their SUV like an avalanche. Her two youngest children—Harun and Madina—hightail it to the backyard with their beach towels draped over their shoulders like capes. A small army of munchkin cousins follow in their wake.

"Salaam, janem, it's good to see you." Khala Gulnoor is kissing each sister as they stumble out of their cars.

"Don't forget to kiss your aunts properly, and let's drop the mopey attitude, girls." Khala Mojgan scolds her two teenage daughters—Amena and Ayesha—when they try to slink out of the back seat of their car empty-handed.

"Nazaneen jan, you have to give me the recipe for that cake you made last week." Khala Farzana smiles pleasantly as she takes trays of sweets in her arms. They make their way toward my mother, who—is she crying?

My youngest aunt, Khala Nazaneen, leads the charge as the Amani sisters trample their way over our grass and embrace my mother in a hug.

"Today we celebrate us," she whispers in my mother's ear. "And forget about the rest."

It hits me, when I watch my aunts convince Madar to take the day off work and shove bags of hamburger buns and condiments in my arms, that Madar somehow knows about Padar's *someone*. Which means my aunts know.

But it's all wrong. As I stand there, gripping the bags, I want to shout, *this someone is just a blip*. The separation is just a bump in the road. Don't they get it? The dance between Madar, Padar, and me?

Sometimes we spin apart, but in the end, dancers always get back together.

The dance hasn't ended yet.

"Don't get distracted," I mutter as I enter the backyard. "That's all this is, a distraction." Because if my aunts could somehow get this intel, then maybe there's more to why I saw my bibi in the abandoned house than what my mother is letting on.

⚬⚬⚬

"The vampire finally emerges from her lair," Mattin remarks when he sees me. He kicks off his shoes as he takes a seat on the tanning chair next to me. He pushes back his black bangs from his eyes as he slathers globs of sunscreen on his arms. "It's been a while, cuz."

"Yeah, I think it was Eid the last time you graced us with your presence," Aman jokes as he drags another chair closer to us and flops on it, propping his feet on the edge of Mattin's chair. Mattin kicks his twin brother's feet. Aman scoffs and shoves Mattin's shoulder. They enter a shoving-and-sunscreen-throwing war. Boys.

"Glad to know you two are still idiots." Amena peeks through her sunglasses with a sour look on her face that screams *do I really want to sit here?* She chooses to hike up her skirt and sit by the lip of the pool. She kicks her feet in the water. "What a buzzkill, I thought there weren't going to be any boys here. I wore my bikini for nothing."

"You could always swim in shorts and a big T-shirt," I say, absently playing with my bracelet.

Amena looks offended. "And ruin my hard-earned tan

with those atrocious lines? No thank you. I choose to sweat."

Mattin and Aman roll their eyes at each other.

"Love you too, cuz." Aman waves at Ayesha, who bypasses us entirely and cannonballs directly into the pool with said big T-shirt and shorts. "Seems like she's got the right idea." He launches in after her, leaving us in a tense silence.

"Sooo." Amena twists and points a manicured finger at me. "I'm ready for an apology for ditching us last week, along with the forty dollars I wasted on you, by the way."

"I had to work," I lie. "Busy with the houses, you know how it is. Thrilling stuff. Must have lost track of time."

Mattin and Amena stare at me like I've grown two heads.

"Don't you hate working in the houses?" Amena asks.

"Like, absolutely loathe it. Would rather exchange the soul of your first born," Mattin agrees.

"Uh . . ."

Maybe I should explain. Mattin, Aman, Amena, and I were born pretty close together (but I'm the youngest). When you have so many aunts, cousins tend to be born in batches, like cookies. And there are about six of us that fall into the angsty teen range right now. In theory, we should all be close. And we used to be. Unfortunately, Padar and Madar's fighting got in the way of a lot of things.

"Oh, Sara, are you talking about the new house? Here,

come sit, all of you," Khala Nazaneen shouts from the shade of an umbrella on the other side of the pool. "It's family time, so everyone sit at the table and socialize."

"But I'm sooo comfortable here . . ." Mattin groans, lying out on his back.

"*Now!*"

There's something about a pissed-off aunt that you don't want to mess with. We're all scrambling around the dessert-laden table and somehow I am squashed in between Mattin and Amena.

"There aren't enough chairs." Amena flips her light brown hair over her shoulder as she squeezes her butt into the same chair I am currently sitting in. "Make room. Helloo!"

I ignore her because I couldn't have asked for a better moment. With six of the ten Amani sisters milling about, I'm sure to get some answers about Bibi. I'm sure of it.

"What do you know about the house?" I ask.

"It's beautiful; Firoza jan and I drove past it earlier today." Khala Nazaneen bites into a warm sambosa. "It seems familiar though, doesn't it, Nargis?"

I lean in really close at *familiar*.

Madar leans back in her chair, fanning herself. "Yeah, it reminds me of that first house we moved into, back in the day."

"The one in Queens? I never lived in that house." Khala Nazaneen wags her finger. "That must have been a good two years before I got here."

I knew my family came in waves after the Saur Revolution in 1978, when the president of Afghanistan and his entire cabinet were killed in the presidential palace. From what I can vaguely remember—no one really likes to talk about it, and I can't really blame them—my grandfather decided it was best to leave the country, but it was never meant to be permanent. When he was alive, he used to say, *One day, we'll go home.*

It's been over forty years since then, and my aunts have never set foot in the place they once called home.

"I still remember the day we left. The great *vacation* to America." Madar is forlorn as she looks off into the distance. "Dada's voice. *Pack light, just one suitcase. It's just for a week. Don't you want to see what America is all about?* You know, I left all my notebooks. My pictures. My friends' notes. Everything."

"I would have been pissed if that was me," Mattin jumps in. "Like, joke's on you, it's not vacation. It's permanent."

"You couldn't blame him, could you? I would have done the same thing." Khala Nazaneen sighs, big and heavy. "I had hoped that, one day, we could have taken you kids to see it. I kept telling myself to wait, what's the harm in another year, but now, with the Taliban, it feels like the past has repeated itself all over again and the window to go back has shut."

There's a blanket of silence that settles over us and I wonder what it feels like to live through a revolution in

1978, to see your home repeatedly invaded by foreign powers, to feel the guilt of surviving while so many others did not.

I try to imagine it, but I can't.

I've always been safe.

"It's like if you close your eyes hard enough, you can almost hear the music Dada used to play in the backyard and smell the fruit he always kept in his pockets." Madar and Khala Nazaneen share a look I can't understand.

"Those were the days," Khala Nazaneen agrees. "Those two years in Afghanistan alone with Mojgan were tough. But at least I had her."

I'm gnawing on my lip. "What about Bibi jan? Who did she come with?"

"She was the first one to come here. All by herself." Khala Nazaneen turns to Madar. "Can you believe that? Our poor mother. Working alone like that."

"I know." Madar nods. "I can't imagine it."

First.

The image of the woman flashes like a warning.

"What year did she come?" My forearms are flush against the metal table.

Madar counts on her hands. "Well, I suppose around 1979 or 1980. My father wanted us out as soon as possible. It had to be around then because I came a bit later, in the '80s with your uncle."

"And this is where we take our leave . . ." Amena

mumbles as she and Mattin slip undetected from the table. "You coming? I can only handle so much depressing conversation in a day."

I wave her away. Little sirens are going off in my head because this information proves I'm right.

"So what you're saying is that it's *possible* Bibi could have lived in a house no one knows anything about?" I throw the picture on the table.

"Sara," Madar hisses. "Not again."

"What's this?" Khala Nazaneen's eyes go wide as she loosens her blue hijab and lets it lie on her shoulders.

"Sara somehow is convinced our mother was in Sumner because of some shadows." Madar tries to snatch the picture away but Khala Nazaneen gets to it first.

"Farzana jan would know." She waves at my eldest aunt, who is holding on to Bibi jan's arm as they slowly make their way to the patio. "Hey, kids, Grandma's coming out. Get a chair for her. Let's go."

Bibi is all smiles as we make room for her. Her laugh is like tinkling bells as Khala Nazaneen kisses her cheeks and a sopping wet Ayesha drags a chair for Bibi to sit on. Aman magically already has a serving tray of fresh green tea.

If our family was a solar system, then my grandparents were the sun we all revolved around. They had set the example on how a family should behave, should love, should stick together no matter what.

The khalas nod in approval. We grandkids share a knowing look: When Bibi enters, nothing else matters.

Well, except for one thing.

"Khala Farzana, do you think Bibi lived in the Sumner house? A long time ago?"

She settles into her chair, smoothing out her curling flyaways. "The new house? Let me see a picture." She squints at Madar's cell phone screen and brings it closer to her face. "I mean, I'm not entirely sure. I know an Uzbek couple, the ones who helped with Bibi's immigration paperwork when she first came, lived around the area. Bibi did some housework for them in exchange for a place to stay."

"So it's possible is what you're saying?"

"It's possible, yes," Khala Farzana says.

Madar has a troubled expression.

"You're awfully curious about all of this. I don't think my children have ever asked me about that time." Khala Nazaneen steeples her fingers against her chin. She glances at Bibi. "Have you ever given any thought to writing it down?"

"Like . . . a history of the Amani family?"

Khala Nazaneen gazes tenderly at Bibi. "It would be something. We've grown so distant, with that dreadful virus. Could be something to bring us together, don't you think, Nargis?"

"Maybe it's a sign with everything going on in Afghanistan lately." Madar's warm hand covers mine. "Maybe we've taken her for granted, her story and even our own.

Someone should be asking questions about our history before it's gone."

"Oh wait . . ." I hedge. "I never said I'd—"

"We always said we would with Dada jan, when he was sick." Khala Farzana agrees. A wistful sort of regret settles on her shoulders. "He used to tell us so many stories. So many pieces of who we are, lost."

All eyes are on me. I feel a lot like an ant under a magnifying glass being left out to cook under the heat of their expectations.

Bibi jan's wrinkled hand slowly reaches for the photo. She frowns immediately and drops it, as if it pains her to touch it. She draws in a rattled breath. "You know, I have one son—Ali—and eleven daughters." She counts on her fingers. "Farzana, Firoza, Gulnoor, Afsoon—"

"Ten daughters, Bibi jan," Khala Nazaneen sweetly interrupts.

Bibi jan shakes her head as she restarts, determined to get the count right.

"—Maluda, Zelaikha, Zenat, Nargis—"

"That's me!" Madar points at herself.

"—Mojgan, Nazaneen, and Malika." Bibi finishes, looking straight at me.

I freeze. So does everyone else.

"Mashallah." Khala Farzana smiles, but discretely whispers to Madar, "Has she been taking her medication?"

"You know how it is." Madar sighs. "She's getting confused more often these days."

But Bibi's eyes never leave mine.

"All right! Enough talk, let's get this party started." Khala Mojgan comes out of the house with a set of speakers blasting fast-paced music. Everyone laughs as she shimmies in her glittering bathing suit cover-up. Amena trails grumpily behind her.

Bibi's confession is long forgotten.

Except.

"Come on, Sara." Amena drags me away from the table. "I'm dying of boredom. Let's do something. 7–Eleven on me."

I take one last look at Bibi. Goose bumps litter my legs at the way she stares at me.

Like she wants me to know.

Like she wants me to remember for her.

Amena drags me away before I have the chance to ask, *What happened to you in that house? What is it that's only now trying to break free?*

After this conversation, there's one thing I'm sure of: The only way to get answers is to go back.

Back to the source.

CHAPTER FOUR

SUMNER LOOMS LIKE A FORTRESS AHEAD OF US. I'M
quick to unbuckle my seat belt and open the car door.

Madar's hand is quick to catch me.

"Sara, you'd tell me if something was going on with
your father, right?" She's back to normal now. Her face
is effortlessly flawless with her dewy-makeup look. Her
eyelashes flutter as she gazes at me.

I avert my eyes because looking at Madar is a lot like
looking at the sun—blindingly beautiful. I'm reminded of
the girl splayed out confidently on a convertible. The girl
who looked like she had never known sadness. Although,
I can't help but wonder, underneath the layers of makeup
products, if another girl lingers in Madar.

A girl I'm not brave enough to know yet.

"Yeah, Madar. There's nothing important to know."
Because there isn't anything important to mention. *Someone* could be a new business partner or a long-lost rela-
tive coming to stay with Padar. There's no point jumping

to conclusions and worrying Madar for nothing. After all, this is exactly what my parents do. It's part of the dance. They spin away, but somehow, they always make it back to each other.

Watching Madar stare me down, like she doesn't quite believe me, makes me dash out of the car. I force myself to focus on Sumner. I'm not here to talk about my parents.

The windows appear like eyeless sockets from the first level. Looks like the crew took out the boards and the glass. The front landing creaks and sways. Vines of ivy wind up around the pillars framing the doorway, and I inch my way past. If there's one thing I don't need, it's an outbreak of angry, itch-my-eyeballs-off poison ivy.

My mom's usual crew is already here. Erik and his band of construction workers spread out across the massive first floor.

"Oh, hey." A tanned and muscular-in-a-ropey-way guy wipes sweat from under his cap and waves. "Look who finally decided to show up."

"Hey, yourself, Erik." I duck my head as two guys barrel through with the railing from the stairway. *Wow, they move fast.* Without the boarded windows, light floods the space, and glints off the mirrored walls. I adjust the lens on my camera and snap more progress photos. "Yeah, just here to capture the magic, you know?"

"Well, we've got a ton of work, so." He reaches into his toolbox and plops a mask, gloves, and protective glasses in my arms.

"Wait, what's this for?"

"We need muscle, not pictures. Maybe you can help the new kid demolish a few things." His brown eyes narrow at my tank top. "Hm. You don't have a long-sleeved shirt in the car?"

"I'm not really a manual labor kinda girl. Also, what's wrong with my shirt?"

"Never mind." Erik laughs and shakes his head. "We've started taking down the cabinets in the kitchen, but you can help clear out the bathroom down the hall." We're walking and talking, but goose bumps rise on my arms the moment I realize he's taking me down *that* hallway. I grip my camera tightly, suddenly wanting to hightail it out of there.

"Uh, are you sure there isn't something upstairs I could smash? Or . . ."

Flashes of Bibi's pale face, with shadows slashed across her cheeks, are front and center. I shudder and suddenly feel like the walls are closing in, as if something is watching me from the darkened corners.

"You'll be fine." Erik slaps my shoulder before pushing me forward. "We always start the novices on the easy stuff anyway."

"Who are you calling a—"

Erik's already gone. I sigh and toss the glasses. I mean, really? Glasses on glasses? I think not. I fit the mask over my mouth and brave my way to the bathroom. With the windows open and letting in light, it seems like a normal house, so why do I feel like there's someone just out of reach, flitting from the corner of my vision?

I lift my camera, point, and shoot. The flash goes off just as someone exits the bathroom. Oops.

A loud clank and a muffled *motherfuaargh* erupts as a hammer falls to the floor. I stop five steps away. A boy has his back to me, sweating bullets. The planes of his back tense as he breathes heavy and rubs his eyes.

I may or may not take this moment to stare.

"What are you trying to do? Blind me?" He spins on his heel. Before I have a chance to stop gawking, we lock eyes.

Oh no.

Oh *no*.

This has to be a joke.

It can't be—

"Must you always find new ways to torture me, neighbor?" Sam's mouth cocks into a half smile as he rubs his face. He's so sweaty, his shirt is nearly see-through.

Surprised, I do what any normal girl does when confronted with her former childhood best friend. I pelt my dusty gloves at his face and scream, "Have you no decency? This is a place of work!"

"What are you talking about?" Sam looks bewildered and swats the gloves away.

"I can't work like this." I immediately do an about-face.

"I think your gloves got something in my eye!"

"Good!" I shout without looking back. I clench my fists at my sides and take a deep breath when the kitchen comes back in view. A part of me feels triumphant, like I've slayed the demon that's plagued me for years. But another part of me, the part that remembers I have manners, feels a little bad.

I almost turn around to apologize.

Except I hear the pitter-patter of small feet.

And was that a little kid's cry?

I look down another hallway (there are So. Many. Hallways.) and see that it's the one that has the cockroach-filled bar. There are no windows down this hall, so the light only shines halfway down. I push my glasses up my nose with my index finger, squint a little—

And see movement.

A flash of dark hair turning the corner.

A little girl in a floral dress.

"Hey!" I sprint down the hall and find myself in an empty dining room. Another flash, to the left. I follow, calling out to her.

She turns, this time into a door. I brace myself, expecting her to smash face-first into the door, but she doesn't.

She vanishes *into* it, taking her laughter into the basement.

All the hairs on my body have fallen off in fear. I have died and there is no reviving what is left of my corpse. I take one step back, then another.

Light of my heart, dance. A voice stirs deep within me,

echoing until it feels like a physical tug on my fingertips. Like a calling I cannot refuse. My legs move forward on their own while my mind shrieks, *This is how you die!* And yet, my body doesn't listen, as if it's no longer my own.

I step into the basement.

CHAPTER FIVE

I'VE WATCHED THIS MOMENT A HUNDRED TIMES.

The girl in the horror movie, naively opening the door that leads into an eternal dark abyss. She calls out, and despite all the warning signs, despite every viewer screaming at the screen "Don't go down there!"—she goes.

I am that girl.

The first thing that hits me is the wave of humidity and damp smell of mildew. The second is the murderer-cloaking darkness.

I flip the light switch, and a single, flickering light bulb buzzes to life. It sways tauntingly and illuminates the dozens of spiderwebs littering the low ceilings. The basement looks like a moment caught in time, as if the previous owners never bothered to pack their things. It's almost as if they just walked out one day and never came back.

I wonder if it looked like this when Bibi was here.

Old Lego sets and tiny racecars litter the chewed-up rainbow rug. A giant stuffed teddy bear takes up an entire corner of the room. A painfully old television set with two cracked leather couches, and—

A shape flickers in the corner of my vision. My glasses fog up and I swear the temperature just dropped thirty degrees. Goose bumps crawl up the back of my neck. I jerk back, lose my balance, and crash down into the landing.

The back of my head throbs. I open my eyes to see a blurry darkness. My glasses must have fallen somewhere. I pray I didn't break the camera. A bright halo of light swings back and forth, and one set of blurry eyeballs blinks curiously at me.

I scream and frantically butt-scuttle away, hitting the back wall. A thread of spiderweb attaches to my mouth and I gag.

"Get away from me!" I swipe at it, but my hand only catches air.

The blurry shape moves closer. I squeeze my eyes shut, saying every prayer I can to God, begging Him to forgive me for my sins and for being a shit to Madar and ignoring Padar, and promising to be different if all of this goes away.

"You dropped your glasses." A girl's voice speaks coolly. I have to open my eyes to make sure I'm hearing correctly. Squinting, I can see the rough shape of my glasses. I snatch them back and put them on. A tiny crack has spiderwebbed in one of the lenses.

Standing in front of me is the little girl with black hair down to her shoulders. And she does *not* look happy to see me.

The girl's brows furrow as she grips her little hands into fists. "Why are you chasing me?"

"I—" It seems so obvious why. "You shouldn't be playing in a construction zone and scaring the crew." I wipe the grime from my palms on my tank top, so thankful that all this trouble was for a little kid and not a psychotic killer.

"This is *my* house." The girl in her sunflower dress takes a brave step closer. Her orange shoe lands in a pile of dust, but her foot just goes through it, disturbing nothing. "*I* live here. And you're a stranger and Aya always tells me to trap strangers in the basement and run upstairs."

"Are you saying you lured me here? On purpose?" There's an ache in my back. "I could have gotten seriously hurt."

"It's not my fault old people are so easy to trick." She smiles in triumph, but it doesn't reach her eyes. "And better a stranger gets hurt than me."

"Hold on a second." There are so many things wrong with what this kid just said. "You said you live here?" The basement is in shambles. There's no possible way she's telling the truth. The stench of mold is so strong, I'm 100% sure there's some sort of lung-infesting bacteria ready to infect us. I wince as I sit up. My jeans are torn, and it looks like my elbow is bleeding a bit.

"Yeah, what's it to you?" She jumps as I stand. "Don't move! Or else!"

"You can't smell it? Or see everything covered in bugs and dust?"

"Are you trying to say Aya is dirty? Maybe you hit your head harder than I thought." Though she acts brash, I notice the way she scans the basement. As if unsure. She's directly under the swinging light. There's something . . . off about the way the light cuts through her.

An iciness slides into my throat. "I'm not going to hurt you. Just trying to get some answers." I slowly take one step toward her. "Who is . . . Aya? We can try to find her." I study her, but there's a pit in my stomach as I remember Bibi's eerie gaze. "Let's just both go upstairs and get some adults involved and get all this sorted ou—"

I swipe for her, but she's all knobby knees and quick feet.

"Get away from me!" she shrieks as she runs. Not fast enough, though. Through the scramble, the photo falls from my pocket.

"I'm doing you a favor, kid—" My fingers close around her small arm. The moment my skin touches hers, there's a rush of icy fear that seeps in. And sorrow. A sorrow I've never felt before.

It's agony. It takes over as ice builds, block by block,

from my arms to my waist, until it's sitting right under my throat. I try to scream, but my lungs burn like I'm drowning, like there's no air left in this world. The basement bursts into bright light, flickering, flickering, between the lone swinging light bulb and a new kind of place. A warmer space, with a TV that works and new couches filled with blankets and pillows, neat playsets filled with toys, and the girl blending in perfectly. Like I've jumped back forty years.

What the hell?

The feeling is over the second the girl wrenches away from me. I'm back in the dank basement. The light bulb swings faster now, and with each pass, I see it.

The girl, with her chest heaving up and down as she zeroes in on the photo, who looks so real until the light catches her and it's like she's made of stardust. Sparkling and clear, like a moment stuck in time.

"It's her," she whispers. She bends down to take the photo. Her little fingers hover, like she's afraid to touch it.

I freeze.

"How do you know my grandmother?" I really look at her this time. The round curve to her eyes, the way her nose, not quite hooked like mine, flares out at her nostrils. Her face has a softness to it, like my khala Nazaneen. Could it be her? Or perhaps . . .

Malika?

"Your grandmother?" Her head snaps up. The light swings fiercely as her doe eyes darken. "No way!" She moves to snatch the picture, but I'm faster.

"That's mine." I whip my body out of her reach. I definitely don't need to experience that feeling a second time. "Didn't your mother teach you not to take what isn't yours?"

"Give it back!" Her face scrunches, and the light swings faster. Her anger swirls, cutting into the loneliness, and my entire body shivers. "If you don't—" Her tiny mouth opens wider and she screams.

"Please, stop!" I cover my ears as the bulb swings faster, grows brighter.

It shatters.

There's a commotion upstairs. Loud, banging footsteps. A harsh light floods the entrance to the basement, and I have to cover my eyes.

What the hell just happened?

The basement door swings wide open and thuds heavily against the wall.

"Oh, shit. Sorry." Sam's voice rings out. "I'll, uh, fix this hole."

Beyond him, I hear another noise, the sound of two voices arguing faintly.

Sam stomps down the stairs, tugging his mask over his mouth. His plastic glasses are covered in specks of dust. "There you are. What are you—You should really be wearing a mask if you're down here, you know."

My heart is running like a madman. I can't control my breathing. It's like I need to keep gulping air, otherwise I'll get sucked back down into that abyss, that sadness.

"Whoa, whoa, whoa. Take it easy." Sam rushes to calm me down. "You'll pass out if you keep breathing like that."

"Where'd she go?" I whirl around, scan left and right. But she's gone.

"Where'd who go?" Sam pulls off his gloves.

"She was right *here*." I ignore him and walk around, knocking over toy cars and moth-eaten dolls. I walk near the boiler and make a big circle until I'm back where the stairs meet. Sam is down at the bottom. There's an unease in his stance.

"Did you really not hear anything?" My sneakers crunch on the broken glass.

"No? Are you okay?" he asks.

"Never better," I mutter, and move to brush my way past him. First, I see the dancing woman. Now, this girl. I can't be down here. I need to clear my head. Need to think.

"Uh, wait!" His clean hand holds my arm in place. "I think we should stay down here awhile. Admire the . . ." Whatever excuse he's about to cook up dies on his lips. "Were you down here all this time? Jeez." He quickly pulls his mask off and fits it over my head.

"That is disgusting." I try to shove him away, but he's

faster than me. "I do not want to be infected by your breath particles."

"Better my breath particles than inhaling mold spores, which—" He points to a very suspicious wet spot in the ceiling. "We should probably tell Erik about that if he doesn't already know."

"It's probably just a leaking pipe. No big deal." The mask smells like sweet mint, and I *hate* mint. There's a tense silence between us as Sam really takes a look around. I do too. I notice things I didn't realize in the dark. Fist-sized holes pepper the walls. Sam walks to the closest one, his fingers brushing the hole. A memory in his mind.

Then he looks straight at me, and I know we're thinking back to the same moment.

To Madar and Padar's arguing, the crash of glass against marble, Padar's fist breaking the drywall.

To thirteen-year-old me running through the front yard, just wanting to escape.

To Sam's wide eyes as he chases me across the grass that night, pleading for me to *wait, Sara, wait.* Like his pleas could fix what was already put in motion.

If only life worked that way.

My fingers tremble, and little spots wiggle in front of my eyes.

"Hey." My knees give out right when Sam bolts over to keep me upright. "Take deep breaths. It's fine. You'll be fine." He tries to calm me down.

"Yeah. Thanks." I need to move. I need to get out of here. I need to—

"The feeling in this basement reminds me of that night too. It feels . . . angry," he says slowly, as if speaking to a spooked cat. "I know it must have been really hard having to deal with your parents like that. But then you iced me out. And I can't figure out why."

I can't look at Sam. I feel his stare, feel the question that's burned every time I avoid looking at his house when I grab the mail. Even now, he still doesn't get it.

"If it's because I saw—"

"I don't care that you saw my parents fighting." I move out of his grasp and stand on my own two feet. "Practically the whole world has seen them fight."

"Then why?"

I don't have time to answer. Shouts from upstairs answer for me.

"I knew you'd be behind this." Padar's voice. "You think I have the time to drive the entire island to look for her?"

"Excuse me? It's not my fault you can't properly communicate with a fifteen-year-old!"

"And I wonder who told her to ignore me?"

Oh, for the love of—

"Nothing will happen," Sam reassures, but his face says otherwise.

"I don't need your help. I can handle myself. They're my parents, after all."

"Sara, you don't need to act tough all the time. It's okay to—"

"I said no thanks. Really, I got this."

Sam sighs as he watches me shove my way up the stairs.

I'm at the top when I pretend not to hear "I miss you, Sara," because he didn't get it then, and he doesn't get it now, and that pisses me off even more than Madar and Padar's petty arguments.

Noise floods the main floor before I know it. Back to reality.

Erik's crew continues working, but I know this dance, the looks that they give me when I walk by, thinking I can't see. Pity. I can practically hear their thoughts. *Poor girl, having to deal with those parents.*

"What are you looking at?" I bark at one of the guys who stares at me a moment too long. He shrugs. I want to tell them it wasn't always like this, but Madar and Padar's arguing grows louder the closer I get to the entrance.

Padar's shiny new Alfa Romeo SUV is parked by the mailbox. They're yelling at each other: Madar from the front porch, Padar from the driveway.

This is my fault. I should have responded to his texts.

Madar pulls out her phone. "You are violating the restraining order." She dials and her phone glints in the sun. "Don't think I won't report this."

"Are you crazy?" Padar shouts with his hands in the air. "I just want to talk to my daughter!"

My head throbs as I walk past Madar. Time to play

peacemaker. "Stop. It's his day to pick me up." I'm the rope in their constant tug of war. The thread that holds them together when they want to fall apart. I robotically hug Madar goodbye and let my battle armor slip in place, a mask I can never afford to lose. Madar clings a tick longer, but I wish she wouldn't.

I'd trade all the hugs in the world to rewind to before we fell apart, to rewind to the days when we lived in eternal sunshine, to a place before the fighting existed.

"I'll see you in a few days." She kisses my forehead and I look at anything but her. I throw her a quick wave while I walk toward Padar. As my feet crunch on the gravel, I rip off Sam's mask and let it flutter to the ground.

I walk straight past Padar.

"That's the hello I get?" His fingers twitch, like he wants to stop me but knows he can't. "I've been trying to get in touch with you for days."

"Yeah, well. Here I am." I imagine my armor gleaming brilliantly in the summer sun as I take one last look at the house. My fingers are only working faster against the beads on my wrist. It isn't supposed to be like this. My parents shouldn't be drifting further apart.

Don't think about that, a little voice slithers in my ear.

Instead, I scan the dusty windows, the darkness that peeks through chewed up curtains. I wish for a flash of straight black hair or a glimmer of gold and sapphire. I feel for Bibi's photo, tucked safely in the space between my phone and case.

"Let's go." Padar honks his horn. Slams his door.

I glance one more time, and whisper, "Tell us the feeling," to the windows. There's no one there. But I wish there was.

I'd take ghosts over Padar's wrath any day.

CHAPTER SIX

STEAM WINDS UP AND SLICKS THE TILES OF THE bathroom. I sink deeper into the tub, watching the bathwater swirl around my elbows as I do my millionth Google search on the Sumner house.

Being at Padar's condo has given me a lot of time to think, considering the cat and mouse game we have with each other these days.

I go over what I know.

The house was built in the 1970s and has had a handful of owners over time.

Bibi jan would have been there in the late '70s. Or early '80s. I assume she was in her forties, but her real age is anyone's guess. No one knows my grandmother's actual birthday. We just sort of guess, which is hard, considering how well she has aged.

And then there's the little girl who looks so familiar, who has a face I can almost place.

At first glance, she reminded me of Khala Nazaneen, but—

If my khala Nazaneen came years after my mother, then that would have made her nine. Too old to be the girl I saw. And if I'm being completely honest, a part of me thinks back to the spilled photo albums, to Bibi jan's miscount of her children and if it really was a mistake or the truth.

We've taken it for granted, her story. It's time for someone to start asking questions about our history. You.

I drop my head to rest against the tub. What am I thinking? It can't possibly be true. Still, after days away from the house, I can't shake the overwhelming sorrow I felt looking at the girl. It was like a physical force drawing me to her.

Like it was going to consume me.

Rap-tap-tap.

"Sara, you've been in there for a while." Padar's muffled voice through the triple locked bathroom door breaks my concentration.

"I'm relaxing. There's a thing called privacy, you know!" Water sloshes against the wooden holder my phone is propped on.

"I need to use the restroom." He knocks again, more urgently.

Time for desperate measures.

"I'm naked!" I fish through the suds for the drain. "Do I need to spell it out for you? N-A-K—"

Padar sighs before walking away. As his footsteps

recede, I relax and rest my forearms on the lip of the tub and wait for the water to drain.

I don't actually like baths. They make me feel like I'm stewing in a soup. But a bath is the only thing that ensures at least an hour away from Padar in this cramped two-bedroom apartment. Only now I feel like a jerk, so I hoist myself out of the water and dry off.

This would be easier if I had my camera to go over the evidence. I wish I hadn't left it at the house. I settle onto the couch, my head too wrapped up in Sumner to notice my dad say, "Watch the water on the stove." He makes a beeline for the bathroom.

Lightning flashes through the living room window as rain drums on the ceiling. Drums that warp into a soft voice singing, *Light of my heart*, followed by a little girl screaming in the reflection of the glass.

I jump backward, and nearly knock over the remotes on the coffee table.

"It's not real, it's not real," I whisper quickly. "Just a flash of lightning." But as I get settled again, the fluorescent lighting in Padar's galley kitchen flickers overhead like it's winking in Morse code. I stand up and inch my way to the kitchen. The lights continue to wink. It reminds me of days with Amena, Aman, and Mattin. When we'd pretend it was us against invisible enemy forces and we'd transform my grandparents' living room into a base, filled with forts and stacked blankets. I used to look for messages in between gaps in those pillow forts.

Back when Baba jan was alive. Sometimes he'd join us, but never once did he yell at us for making a mess. Most times, he and Bibi jan would simply sit, holding hands, watching us. I don't know why, but it brings me back to the gold-and-blue embroidery that vanished and the ice-cold feeling of being swallowed up twice now.

What happened to you, Bibi?

The light stops flickering, and I'm left with only my wandering thoughts. The logical part of me wants me to forget it. I *did* hit my head. Yet, there is a part of me that wants to believe.

My phone buzzes on the counter.

Sam: Renovation hiatus on Sumner for a week.

Sam: Black mold everywhere!!!

Sam: Told you to wear a mask.

Mold.

Could I have made it up in a post-mold-spore-inhalation daze?

A quick search of symptoms of mold exposure shows me hallucinating little girls in basements is not one of them.

Sara: What is it you really want to say? You know my mom can just tell me about the mold.

Sam: Astute as ever.

Sara: Well?

Sam: Don't be mad, but I have your camera. You forgot it in the basement.

The toilet flushes and Padar comes back in, wiping his hands on his shirt. "I was thinking we'd watch a movie with dinner."

"I was thinking I'd eat dinner in my room." I'm rapidly typing away a response when Padar scowls.

"Who are you texting so late?"

"Just a friend from school," I lie before hitting send. The fact that I can't simply say *a boy* is a can of worms I'd rather not unearth today.

At this, Padar frowns. "You know, your cousins keep asking about you. I think it'd be nice for us all to get together. What do you think? Maybe we can talk about what I texted you a few days a—"

Water crackles on the stove. It's boiled over.

"I thought I told you to watch the water." And just like that, Padar goes back into his orbit. "You're not eating in your room. Pick the movie while I clean this up. Maybe we should just microwave some cup ramen and call it a night."

"Whatever."

"Sara." I know that tone. It's a warning, but I can't be like him and pretend everything is okay when we've so clearly deviated from our regularly scheduled programming.

I settle in on the couch and sneak one last text before switching it to silent.

Sara: Leave it at my house. And don't you dare go looking through it.

Sam: . . .

Sara: You can't be serious.

Sam: I just . . . I'm sorry I looked but I have to ask. Who is the girl in the picture?

Sara: What girl?

Sam: The last photo you took. In the basement. I think it's a girl. Can you just get out for a bit? I need you to confirm that I'm not losing my mind here.

Holy. Shit.

⎯⎯⎯✒⎯⎯⎯

We decided to meet at midnight, but it's nearly 1:35 A.M. when I roll up to a tiny parking lot. The movie I was forced to endure ended up running longer than I thought, and Padar took forever to fall asleep. He always leaves his keys on the table beside the front door. All it took was some fluffing of pillows and I was out.

The rain is coming down in sheets and it's impossible to see more than five inches in front of my face. I grip my umbrella and make a beeline toward our agreed meeting spot.

The Throgs Neck Bridge looks fuzzy in the distance. A steady stream of traffic, even now, floats by. I pull my raincoat around me more tightly against the panic I feel walking along the trail.

I don't see Sam. Or anyone, really.

Thunder shakes the ground as I spot a bench. My shoes

squelch in the mud as I try to wipe as much excess water as possible before sitting. Sam better get here fast. I'm not sure how much more I can take, out here in the rain. I scroll through my messages. Sam's got an iPhone so I can't tell if he's read the message or not. I kick a rock as the wind picks up.

This was a stupid idea. Maybe I should have waited until I got back to Madar's.

I should be scared to be out here alone. If this was a movie, there'd be some soundtrack to give me a clue as to what was coming next, but it's not, and here I am, huddled on a rough bench, counting the passing cars, wondering.

Who is the girl? I have full-body shivers.

If he really sees the girl on my camera, then that confirms it, right?

I haven't been imagining it.

She's really real.

Lightning arcs against the sky.

"They say a bolt of lightning is actually a soul released from purgatory," a voice whispers by my ear.

I nearly jump out of my skin and fall face-first on the wet ground. "Don't do that!" My umbrella is snatched away by the wind. The rain does not relent. I am soaked.

Sam is cherry red as he waves his hands frantically in front of him. "I'm sorry, I thought I was being clever." Rain is dripping off his ears and nose as he tightens the string around his hood.

I swat away his hand. My forehead stings, and I'm sure I've got mud up my nose. "How is sneaking up on a girl in the middle of the night clever?"

"Consider it payback for making me meet up with you so late. Truce?" Sam sticks out his hand. His hair glows as usual, even with the rain, but he's got bruising under his eyes. I don't take his hand.

"This is ridiculous. Let's talk in my car."

"Wait. You *drove*?" Sam's boots squelch against the trail. "You don't have a learner's permit."

"So?"

"You can't drive, Sara!"

"Can't, not allowed." I wag my finger. "Semantics at best."

Sam sighs.

We've trekked back to the lot. Sam's car is parked a few spots away. Once we're inside my dad's car, I blast the heat and squeeze the excess water out of my hair. Thank god I wasn't wearing makeup.

"So." I turn to face him.

Sam throws off his raincoat and stashes it in the back seat. There's a lump in his sweatshirt. My camera.

"That's how you chose to protect it?" I screech when he hands it over. "With some useless *double layering*? Do you know how much this thing costs??"

"More than my life, I know. I know. Jeez." He rubs his arms uncomfortably. "Just. Can you look already?" A serious expression crosses his face.

Curiosity should be my middle name because I'm already searching through (and secretly thanking past me for deleting all those embarrassing selfies). "What picture? There's nothing here but the norm—"

There.

Right after the picture of Sam's startled face and sweat-drenched shirt is another photo. It's dark but the flash was clear enough to outline a figure.

And a face.

"H-how?" Her angry eyes fill the darkness as she looks straight at the camera. Most of her body is gone, but her face is as clear as the stars that dot the sky. I stare wide-eyed at Sam.

"That's what I was going to ask you, Sara." He gets quiet as he looks at his muddy fingers. "Because it couldn't have been long before I came to get you. And you were alone."

I can't stop staring because here's my proof.

I wasn't mistaken. Or hallucinating.

This is real.

"I wish I knew." My thoughts are whizzing left, right, diagonally over my head, and trying to find the words is too overwhelming, so I focus on the little halos of white from the parking lot lights.

"Then start at the beginning," Sam encourages. His warm hand obscures the screen. "And we'll go from there."

"You'll think I've lost my mind." I squeeze my legs tight to my chest, crushing my camera. "My mom was with me the first time it happened and she basically told me that."

"Lucky for you, I'm not your mom." He laughs awkwardly with his eyes pinched shut. His hand scratches his hair and I'm too aware of the way his Adam's apple bobs when he's nervous or scared.

"Come on, Sara." His fingers drum against the dashboard. "I can tell you've been turning this over for a while now. Since I saw you basically teleporting out of your body last week on your driveway."

"I was staring at the stars, having a beautiful, peaceful moment until you ruined it."

"Call it what you want, but you need to let it out." He twists so his back is against the door. He wiggles his shoes off his feet before sitting cross legged on the leather seat.

My chest pinches just looking at him because I know he's right.

"Something happened with my grandma a long time ago. Something I need to get to the bottom of," I begin. Not quite from the beginning, but in the only way I know how. I show him the crumpled picture. I tell him about the ripped dress. The memory that came back to Bibi jan when we touched it. The little girl in the basement.

Through the skylight, I look up at the stream of rain and see an outline of a shimmering dress thrashing against the sky. "I think . . . that there's something haunting the house. Something that came alive when we bought it."

"You think it has to do with that girl?" Sam asks.

"Maybe." I stare at the image of the angry girl. "I think . . . she could be Malika."

"Well. There's only one way to find out, right?" There's a determined glint in Sam's eyes. "You have to go back and find her."

"But what if it's not her? What if—"

"Then we'll find out the truth together." Sam takes my cold hands in his. His fingers press my bracelet into my skin. "It's what friends do for each other, right?"

I hesitate. Because for a moment, it feels like no time has passed between us, and I'm taken back to a year and a half ago. To that night when, for a moment, everything felt possible. Until it wasn't.

"I want to go tonight," I blurt in a breathless whisper.

"Let's go, then. *I* will drive and—"

Bright blue and red lights flare up all around us. A siren wails horribly in the air and we jerk apart.

Coming fast in a police car are two cops and my father's furious face, like thinking about that night conjured him from thin air. He must have found my location from my phone. I quickly turn my phone off.

No, no, no!

"Give me your keys," I hiss at Sam. "*Now!*"

"Wait, why?"

"It'll be faster if I drive. On three, we run."

"Sara, don't be ridiculous. We can't run from the police." Sam's face is wild and I know him too well. I know he's too freaked out, and ready to come out of the car with his hands up. He's too good of a guy to make a run for it. "We'll pick another night to go, okay?"

"There isn't another night." I groan in frustration. I can't explain why, this fluttering panic in my chest whenever I think of the girl. She reminds me so much of a trapped butterfly, furiously flying in a glass cage with no air. And I know exactly how that feels. "If you won't go, then I need you to take the fall for this, okay? Just lie to my dad, say I tricked you, but I need to go to that house tonight."

"I can't afford to get into that kind of trouble, Sara," Sam hedges.

When I realize negotiation won't get me anywhere, I make an executive decision.

I steal his raincoat from the back seat and make a run for it.

"Sara, hey!" But he's too late. I'm already out of reach.

The wind is beating furiously against my back as I fumble for the key and start the car. My hair is plastered to my skin, and I don't dare adjust the rearview mirror to steal a peek at myself.

I don't need to look at my reflection to know I'm a shitty friend. And breaking a ton of laws. "I'm sorry, Sam," I mutter as I peel out of the lot and onto the highway heading east. "But this is something I need to do now."

CHAPTER SEVEN

THUNDER BOOMS AS I PARK. SLUDGE FROM THE RAIN makes it hard to walk along the street. Sumner looms in the near distance, like a presence waiting in the shadows. I try not to think about that and focus on the gate.

A thick chain is wrapped around the bars, shuddering against the wind.

"*Of course* there's a lock." I bang my fist against the lock. It doesn't budge.

Thunder rumbles as it waits for my next move. Trees sway menacingly as the house watches. Darkness curls around the edges of Sumner.

There has to be a way in. I look around the gate, but it's fully covered and it's too high to climb. I smack one of the BEWARE OF DOG signs Erik must have recycled from the last house. When did they have the time to put up a new gate?

The rain has me freezing. I curse and run back to the

car for my phone. It's too dark to see anything. With my phone turned back on in airplane mode, I enable the flashlight. A strip of light beams against the grass. Up the hill to the side of the house. Into the second floor windows.

Lightning.

A silhouette.

I stumble backward, losing my balance. My butt makes contact with soft mud, and dirt smears all over my pants.

I want to scream. Is this karma for leaving Sam behind? Is this what I get for throwing him under the bus?

There's no way I'm getting in like this. My cheeks burn in embarrassment as I trudge through the downpour, my raincoat a useless mess. I'll have to come back with supplies. Bolt cutters or a key. A key would be best.

I wipe as much water as I can off my glasses when—

Crrrrrrhhhhhtttttt.

The front gate opens. Sumner stands innocently, casting itself slightly out of the shadows of rain clouds as if to say *welcome back*.

I slip and roll my ankle in surprise.

That's impossible. I shake away wet hair plastered to my cheeks and hobble over to the gate. Maybe I saw it wrong. My cell phone light is getting weaker as I get closer. As the chains swing against the gates, I notice there is no lock.

Rain batters down on me as my heart tugs at my throat.

Don't go in, it begs. But as I push open the gate and make my way up the cracked driveway, there's something else. Another force whispering, *Stay*.

"It's just a house, nothing more," I mutter, reaching the front porch. There are sheets covering the doors and windows. "It can't hurt you." I peek through the sheets. "You're doing this for Bibi. You can do this."

It's pitch-black. The falling shadows of raindrops are the only movement inside. The front door is locked, so I search for another way in and double back to the drive-way, where the garage is. On the side of the garage, there is a tiny window. The glass is worn and cracked. I make my way over. Cover my hand with my sleeve and mutter, "Here goes nothing." I break the rest of the window and go feet first into the hole.

There's almost no light now, except for the thin strip of light from my phone. I bump into something and my phone flashlight flickers. Of course it does.

I decide not to waste any time and make my way toward the garage door that opens to the basement.

"Hello?" I tentatively whisper-shout when I'm finally in the basement. "If anyone is here, please say something."

The silence is disappointing. Even more disappointing is when my phone gives out. For the first time, I realize that I'm alone. In the dark. Fear winds itself around my ankles and up my legs as it hits me. You know when you're so scared you can't move and start to recount every single horror movie you've ever seen? That's where I am at the moment. I feel like my cat, on high alert at the smallest sound.

"It'd be really nice if you'd say something, Bibi." My voice trembles as my foot hits a stair. Oh thank god, I found the stairs. I hold on to the railing like a lifeline. I race up the steps, not caring about the muddy footprints I've left behind. I just need to get somewhere else. Get rid of the crushing feeling in my chest before it happens. Before I royally freak out and can't breathe.

The grand entryway flickers with shadows as the original chandelier sways, casting its own spidery reflection in the mirrors. The wood groans as I step closer to the front door. This is what I would call a complete failure. There's no one here. For better or worse, maybe this is the universe's way of telling me to leave well enough alone. Maybe that's the problem. Maybe I'm not supposed to go looking.

I'm unlocking the front door when the hall groans again. I look back into the darkness. "Bibi jan?" The chandelier stops swaying. The shadows halt.

I wait a second before turning the doorknob. The entire hall sighs as a soft melody sings from upstairs. I look behind me and scan the stairs leading up to the second floor. It's a soft, sad sound. A tinkling that feels like . . . regret.

And weeping.

Not the song. I hear an actual *person* crying.

I feel it so deeply as it winds around my bones, coaxing me to follow.

My hand slips from the knob, and I make my way up the stairs, transfixed. The railing has been completely removed, disconnecting the top from the bottom.

"Is anyone there?" I call out as I reach the top. "Are you hurt?"

The song softens, as do the sobs. They come from the left, leading me toward the master bedroom. The double doors are closed. I take another step, and the song stops. My hand hovers over the doorknob and, despite being frozen by rain and fear, despite the ache in my ankle, the moment I turn the handle, I feel something entirely new.

Something warm.

I push the door open. Let it swing slowly away from me. Moonlight cuts into the darkened room. In the corner is the back of a woman. She startles and turns. Her tear-streaked face, blackened with mascara, leaves me paralyzed.

She makes her way soundlessly toward me. Until she's close enough to touch. Her hollow face breaks as she squints, her translucent palm reaching for me.

Whisper soft, she asks, "Malika?" Then her palm touches my cheek. A blinding pain cuts through me. It's unlike anything I've ever felt before.

Worse than the cold from Malika the other day.

It feels like my mind is being split in half, withering away until there's nothing left.

Is this what it feels like to die?

Of all the ways to die, this certainly wasn't how I had imagined it would go. I thought I'd at least make it to twenty. Twenty seemed like a good, full time to go. Any older than that, and it just feels like a black void of adulthood.

"Why are you screaming, janem?" A familiar singsong voice in Farsi asks.

The pain evaporates all at once when she moves her hand. I breathe heavy as the house comes back into focus.

"Bibi jan?" I whisper, clutching my hands in fists by my sides. I am too afraid to touch her.

She stands, confused, in her heavy dress. The necklace—thick with jewels—chokes her neck and, for a brief moment, I want to ask her if it hurts. If she can feel the bite of metal sink into her skin.

"You're not Malika?" Her blackened tear tracks intensify on her youthful face. She looks like she's about to disappear, like she's nothing more than a figment of my imagination.

"Wait!" I splay my hands out. How do you grab a . . . whatever she is? "I've seen her."

This catches her attention. "You have?"

"Yes, she was looking for you." I swallow, my throat constricting as she solidifies. "You must have seen her, she was in the basement last time I checked." Not entirely true, considering that's where I just was and I, indeed, did not see her.

"Can you take me there, girl?" Her bright eyes implore and my heart breaks in two. The way her expression glazes past me, longing for someone else. Like she doesn't recognize me. Like she doesn't know I exist.

"You don't remember me?" I whisper honey-lodged words. "At all?"

She stills, floating an inch off the ground. Her delicate eyebrows furrow just a bit. "Have we met before?"

I want to laugh at the irony. At the metal spike shackling my chest. The pain in humor. "I've known you my entire life, Bibi jan."

"Bibi? You must be mistaken," she says with a delicate air, with a voice that is pulled from a past life I only know from grainy home videos and faded photographs Madar used to show me. Of who my grandmother used to be. "I only have one child here. And she's far too young to be a mother herself. Are you . . . Why are you crying? Have I upset you?"

"Only one?" I pry. "You can't remember the others?" The children my bibi counts, religiously, every damn day.

"Others?"

"Before you came to this house. Can't you remember your life from before?"

"Before . . ." A far-off look settles on her face as she paces the room. There's a question on her lips. The air swirls around her, growing more frigid as she moves throughout the room.

"Hey, let's . . . try to find Malika while you think on

it." I turn on my heel and lead her out of the room. It's all too much to take in. It seems I can't escape it. Even here, I'm reminded of the family I'm slowly losing.

"Oh, thank you." She smears the trail of tears with her palms and brightly follows behind me. "I cannot tell you how much this means to me. God will reward you for your kindness."

"Yes, I'm sure He will." I grit the words out as I stand at the top of the stairs. Throw her one last look—she looks so young—and motion for her to follow. "Right down here." Only, I forget the railing is missing and my hand slips. I lose my balance.

"Oh no!" Falling forward is a lot like slowing time. For whatever reason, the brain decides it needs to speed up, to make us feel every second of the fall, to anticipate the impact.

Bibi's hand darts out. There's a stricken look on her face.

Her grip holds firm.

She *saved* me.

We stay suspended like this for a second. Her chest moving up and down rapidly; mine sputtering to be revived. Her dark eyes lock on mine as warmth blooms from her fingertips into my wrist. It seeps into my skin, inch by inch. She pulls me up with surprising strength and lets go.

"Th-thank you." I collapse on my knees, drawing deep breaths. Bibi jan crouches next to me, her eyes bright with curiosity. She studies the slope of my cheekbones. The slight bump in my nose. The shape of my eyes.

"Nargis," she whispers. "I have . . ." She struggles to find the words.

"Ten daughters." I finish the sentence for her. "And one son."

"Eleven." Her voice grows stronger as she gazes at me. Something new blooms in her eyes. Love. Recognition. "I have eleven. And you—"

"I'm not her." I shake away the swell of waves wanting to push me adrift. I will not cry. "I'm her daughter. My name is Sara."

She startles at this. "Her daughter? But she's only a young girl herself. Not much younger than you."

"Don't you know what year it is?" I ask.

"I—" There is a heartbreaking grasping in her expression as she tries to remember something she lost along the way. In all these years that have passed. Unless . . . maybe it hasn't.

It's like she's an actual memory of Bibi jan's past. A figure stuck in the time she lived in these halls. She can't remember me, or Madar how she is now, because it hasn't happened to her yet.

"You're saying my daughter named you after me?" I can see the unfamiliarity tinged in her voice as she struggles to make sense of what I am in front of her.

I nearly laugh.

"Something like that." I tentatively smile. "She thought—"

A crash from down the hall.

Footsteps, running.

Huffing and puffing.

I'm on high alert and look for something to protect us. "Bibi jan, stay back!" I move myself in front of her, determined to protect her from the intruder. Something soft touches my shoulder, and the warmth spreads again.

"There's no need." She moves past me.

A figure bursts into the entryway. A little girl with puffy sleeves in a sunflower dress.

"It's you." Her eyes well. Malika runs to her but stops short.

They circle one another, constantly staring but never daring to touch.

Why?

Pink starts to filter through the horizon, and I know the bright glow of dawn is only a few moments from breaking through the windows. Memory Bibi—as I have now dubbed her—smiles sadly, with two rows of gleaming white teeth. I try to smile back, but it feels more like a grimace. She starts to hum that song again. *Light of my heart, dance. In melodies without worry. In hopes without regret.* Only now, I realize it sounds more like a lullaby. *We sing for the light.* Slowly, she disappears out of the room, twirling, taking the song with her. *So until dawn, my light, we dance.*

Malika lingers. Her eyes, deep with shadows, take a tentative step away from the sunshine that bleeds across the floor. She's waiting for something.

"What is it?" I ask. "What is it you want?"

As the sun rises higher and warm light cascades across Malika's face, as if illuminating her, she whispers, "To be found before it's too late."

"Are you lost?" I ask. "Am I meant to find you? But where?"

My questions goes unanswered.

Sunlight sweeps the empty space where Malika was. I am left standing alone, suddenly finding it very hard to remember anything at all.

Except for one word that has attached itself to my bones.

Lost.

Part Two

THE SECRET

"Bibi jan, I think I did something bad."

"Why do you say that? Oh, my dear, dry your eyes. Tell me what worries you."

"I've been keeping a secret. And Madar told me secrets ruin everything. I'm afraid that— Is it my fault?"

"What happened to your parents will never be your fault, janem. Do you understand?"

"But Madar said—"

"Listen to me, janem. Yes, secrets can hurt, but sometimes, secrets are the very things that hold us together. In my life, I've learned that, perhaps, secrets are the only things that keep us from falling apart."

—A conversation with Bibi jan
Six years after diagnosis

CHAPTER EIGHT

IT'S LIKE I BLINK, AND SOMEHOW I'M BACK AT Padar's apartment complex.

Hazy swirls of pink and gold shine down on me as I quietly slip inside. The smell of coffee brewing is like a welcome friend. From Padar's room I hear the soft splatter of the shower running.

I'm absolutely exhausted and it's a miracle I make it to my desk. I throw my glasses aside and massage my temples. Little flakes of hardened mud trail everywhere. Padar will be pissed, but I can't bring myself to care because Malika's angry little eyes haven't left me.

"Find me before it's too late," I mutter while face-planting on my desk. Where? How? I try to remember what Memory Bibi said in Sumner—maybe there's a clue—but the more I try to focus on her, the blurrier the night becomes, like it was nothing more than a dream.

Only, I know I wasn't dreaming.

I know why Bibi appeared to me in that house.

To find out the truth.

To find her eleventh daughter.

Padar grunts in surprise. "Why is there dirt everyw—" He rounds the corner into my room, and I sit up ramrod straight. Flashes of red and blue lights come right back to me in embarrassing clarity. Sam's shouts. Me peeling out of the parking lot.

Padar holds his wet hair back in frustration. "Do you have any idea what you put me through last night?"

"I can explain—"

Padar cuts me off with a clipped laugh. "Explain? Your *little friend* made everything crystal clear to me when I had to drive all the way to your mother's neighborhood to drop him off."

I wince because I really do feel bad about it. "What did Sam say? Did he—"

"I don't give a damn what he said. What I give a damn about is why my daughter is out at all hours of the night, doing god knows what, stealing my car when she is not allowed to drive!" Padar paces in and out of my room. His hands keep flexing, like he's trying to hold it together.

"If you didn't want me to drive, then you shouldn't have taught me," I mutter under my breath.

"What did you say?"

"I—"

I bite my tongue. It's probably best not to push it. I'm

already skating on thin ice. When Padar gets worked up like this, sometimes the best thing to do is let him pace it out.

His phone buzzes in his pocket, and I swear to god, one look and his face softens.

"Hey." It's such a soft *hey*, my right eyeball twitches. "I was just thinking about you." He leans against the wall, his entire demeanor changing. Talk about Jekyll and Hyde.

His smile unrolls something deep in my chest. It chases away any shred of sleep I was hoping to get this morning.

Padar rubs his face. "We're in the middle of discussing last night. Yes, I know. You always give the best advice."

I grip my fists a little bit harder because this isn't right. A blip shouldn't give advice, shouldn't check in, shouldn't know the delicate events between Padar and me. I feel last night's ramen coming right back up my throat because all I can see is Madar. The hollows around Madar's bare face. The way she feels like utter shit.

And Padar is *smiling*.

This is beyond wrong.

"I prefer not to be talked about like I'm not here," I say loudly. "Especially with strangers who I know absolutely NOTHING about."

Padar shoots a glare at me, and I swallow.

"I've got to go," he says quickly. "Okay, I love you too."

It's like someone has pulled the pin on a grenade.

"Sara, I am trying my best not to lose it on you." Padar slips his phone in his pants pocket. "Your behavior last night was alarming. Where were you all night? Why do you look like you buried a body?"

"I—" My excuses go out the window. It feels like my armor has wrapped itself around my mouth.

"Did something happen with that boy? Is that why you ran?" Padar crosses his arms in frustration. He rubs his face. "I don't have time for these games, Sara."

I'm having a hard time processing Padar's line of questioning when I'm still stuck on that *I love you too.*

Because I still remember when those words were only meant for Madar and me. Because I still feel like no one else deserves them more than Madar. Because saying *I love you* to anyone else is wrong. Because I can still count the moments when we were happy.

One, two, three . . .

It's Madar, Padar, and me in our old town house. Madar is wrapped in Padar's arms and I'm lying in between them, safe.

"I think I might have to reconsider the terms with the judge because it's obvious your mother isn't holding up her end of the bargain."

Four, five, six . . .

It's my birthday, and Padar places a blindfold over my eyes while Madar videotapes. I'm laughing so hard, so excited to see the surprise.

"I should have known accepting joint custody was a mistake."

Seven, eight, nine . . .

I'm dragging my blanket, my favorite one, looking for Padar to tell me a story, only to find Madar alone in bed, crying.

"Who knows how many times this has happened on your mother's watch, who knows—"

My armor fails. All I feel in this moment is an undeniable rage. I stand so quickly, my head spins.

"I'm sorry for taking the car, but stop acting like you're perfect in this situation." I stare at him incredulously as a crater shifts and moves in my chest. "Calling the cops for a missing car? That's so dramatic. Maybe I needed a few hours to myself because I can't stand it here. Instead of blaming my mom, maybe *you* should look in the mirror and ask yourself some hard questions."

"First of all, I didn't call the authorities because of a missing car," Padar says, quietly. "I called because I had a *missing daughter* who left the front door wide open and wasn't answering her phone. So forgive me for calling in a favor and disturbing your little escapade."

"Oh."

"And secondly, I don't think you have any ground to stand on, not after that stunt you pulled last year."

"That's not fair." I blink and blink and blink because I'll cry if I stop. "That has nothing to do with this and you know it."

"You opened the box, Sara jan," Padar continues. "There are consequences when you break the rules."

Memories swim in my mind. Jagged, scary moments that had me running at thirteen. Running while Padar yelled *how could you do this*. Running while seeing fist-sized holes in the walls.

I force myself out of that moment.

"Consequences like what? Saying *I love you* to another woman when you aren't even divorced yet?" I throw the words at him. "Did you suddenly forget you already have a family?"

Padar's hand instinctively goes up, and I flinch.

The veins in his temple bulge. We are frozen in our dance for power, hurling words that are meant to cut. Padar is the first to raise his white flag.

"Sara jan, this isn't how I wanted to start this conversation." Padar lowers his hand as I retreat. "You know it wasn't always like this. I wasn't always like this."

"I know." The sweet sunshine of my childhood casts a halo around me, and I think we've finally made a breakthrough. That he has realized this is the part of the dance where he spins back in.

Padar takes a step back, away from the light. Once upon a time, we basked as father and mother and daughter along the streets of New York City. Once upon a time, we were happy.

As Padar stares at me, I can't help but think: *When did we stop being that?*

"I'm sorry that it took this long for me to start this talk with you, but I wanted to be sure this is what I wanted before having it." He bites the inside of his mouth. Rubs the lines on his face. "You know your mother and I are separated. We have been for a while now and when adults separate, well, things can change to the point where it's impossible to go back to how it used to be."

"But separation doesn't mean divorce," I say. "It's always worked out in the past, so I don't get why we're talking about this."

"Because this time is *different* for me. Forget the past situations, Sara. They don't matter," Padar explains. "I really need you to understand that."

"It matters to *me*." Doesn't he get what those words mean? What questions they open up? I want to shoot back, *Will your love for me fade too? Will you forget me too?* Given the direction of this conversation, I keep these questions locked in my head, too much a coward to risk an answer I won't like.

"The point is this isn't up for debate. I'm willing to forget last night because I understand this situation is hard on you, but I can't have you acting out when all I'm trying to do is move us in a direction that has all our best interests at heart. This is reality, Sara, and I need you to grow up and accept it." Padar clears his throat and adjusts the collar of his shirt. "I need to go to work now, but when I get back, we are going to continue this discussion, okay?" He hesitates when I don't say anything. He moves awkwardly, like he's half debating either walking away or leaning in to hug me. In the end, he shakes his head and chooses walking away.

"Great talk," I mutter under my breath.

Padar briskly walks to the entryway, puts on his shoes, and leaves. There's a small click as the front door locks. I count to one hundred in my head. I don't know what he intends by *moving us in a direction that has our best interests at heart*, but if this blip is any indication of changing into something un-blip-like, I—

If this is our new normal, then who are we, as a family? If Padar has broken away from the dance, what's stopping all of us from spinning farther apart?

What's stopping him from replacing us altogether?

I've always viewed Padar's condo as temporary. That Bibi's presence was an of-the-moment accommodation. But what if it's not? What if it's permanent?

I stand up. The longer I sit here, the more I'll start to believe it. I run into Padar's room and rummage through the bottom drawer of his nightstand until I find my way out—his spare credit card.

Finally, an easy solution.

"Thanks for the gas money, Padar." As I leave the apartment, I drop those ugly ideas of *permanence* and *moving forward* where they belong.

Very far away from me.

"Just knock on the door, hand over the keys, and walk away," I tell myself in the rearview mirror. Bruised eyes stare back at me. "Just knock and—" My bracelet clashes against the steering wheel as I idle in front of Sam's house.

My phone is completely nonfunctional and, if I'm being completely honest here, it'd be so much easier to just leave the car in his driveway and walk away from this entire mess. Walk away from last night. I know I could do it. Disappear again.

"Aw, okay, fine." I push the rearview mirror up and get out of the car. "Even I'm not that much of an asshole." I knock on the front door before I lose my nerve. The wind picks up and I shiver into my T-shirt.

I hear scuffling and heavy footsteps coming from the stairs. The door whooshes open and a gust of cold AC pushes my hair back.

"No thanks, we're not interested in whatever bullshit you have to sell." Sam moves to shut the door in my face. "Just leave the keys under the mat."

My foot is quicker, and the lock doesn't click. I push my way through the front door just as Sam is heading up the stairs.

Time to face the music, Sara.

"I admit, last night wasn't my finest hour, but if you'd just stop for a second. I—I want to—I mean . . ."

Sam turns, his hands gripping the oak banister. "You want to what?"

It's happening again. The words I want to say turn to stone as my mind jumbles them in my mouth. "I need to—" *Say sorry.* But everything is spinning, and suddenly Sam's blurry face contorts with worry.

"You know you should really stop staying up all night." Sam rushes next to me and helps me sit down on the cool tile floor in his living room. "Here. Why don't you lie on the couch." I lean against their gray couch. If I'm being honest, Sam's house looks like an Ikea showroom— ultramodern and a little bit cold. I can't imagine anyone wanting to lie on these couches. They remind me of the knockoff Lego sets I used to play with as a kid.

"I'd rather . . . just sit on the floor for a sec, if that's fine." If we're going to continue with the honest train here, perched right next to the Lego couch are dozens of picture frames of Sam and his parents. His cousins. Grandparents. A complete, unbroken set.

The normalcy of it all makes my chest twist in ways I can't explain.

The silence only adds to the twisting.

Sam is the first to break.

His mouth twists as he takes in a pained breath. "Why did you do it?" I feel the way his eyes survey my ruined clothes, the dirt caked on my shoes. "Why did you go alone?"

I scoff because here's the other thing about Sam. He doesn't care about silly pretenses like *why'd you throw me under the bus* or *you better not have dented the front bumper*. He goes in for the kill—because he already knows why. It's part of growing up together. He just wants to hear me say it.

"Look, my dad showed up and I panicked. That's all." I pick at the beads on my wrist. "Like I said, I wasn't thinking." I look away because I don't want to see the way Sam's face falls.

"Right." He balances on the heels of his socked feet. "Well, if one of us is going to be truthful here, I guess it's going to be me. Which, shocker." Sam stands and lends me a hand. "You look like hell, Sara. I suppose if you don't want to face the inquisition at your mom's, you might want to clean up here before you go."

"Thanks, Sam." I knot my fingers together. Sam waves his hands like it's no big deal, but the way he beelines straight for the kitchen, far away from the bathroom, speaks volumes. I hurry up the stairs and dart into the bathroom. Locking the door, I sink to my knees and wrap my arms around them real tight. I try to quiet my mind, but it's too full of *moving forward. Consequences.*

Even here, I can't escape Padar's words.

Breathe. One thing at a time. I turn the shower as hot as it can go and peel off my clothes. The water burns as it runs rivulets through my hair and across my shoulders and arms. The hot water should hurt more, but I can't feel it. I lift my face up, know that the contours of my skin will raise red. I push out my conversation with Padar and pull in Malika's last words. My hand ghosts over where Memory Bibi touched my arm. I squeeze my eyes shut and focus only on that night. Remember Malika. The way she circled Bibi like she was the prey. The way they danced around each other in the dark, so much like Padar and Madar and me. This dance to a never-ending song I can't help but listen to.

Light of my heart, the melody sings softly through the stream of water. *Without worry. Without regret.*

In the impossibility of the moment, I huddle down and allow myself to cry.

When the moment passes, I turn off the water and dry my face. I wipe away the fog on the mirror and take a good look at myself. I watch the space between me and my reflection. I watch until my eyes clear, and when all my emotions are safely locked away and under control, I remember Malika and shift my focus to the ways *lost* can become *found*.

CHAPTER NINE

SOMETIMES, WHEN I'M FEELING OVERWHELMED, I turn back the clock and rewind. That's what I find myself doing now. Rewinding to when I was a fussy kid at bedtime, and Padar would tell me a story about love. First, he'd bring us two steaming mugs of chamomile tea peppered with cinnamon and my favorite fuzzy blanket. I'd burrow real close and gaze at the glowing stars Madar and I had stuck on my ceiling the summer before. This was before the treehouse, a soft spot in my memories when everything was perfect.

Padar would say, *Once there was and once there wasn't a beautiful girl named Laili and her best friend, Majnun, who loved each other from the moment they first met as children.*

Majnun proclaimed his devotion for Laili from rooftops, but like all great love stories, fate had other plans for Majnun and his Laili—plans that kept them apart. Forever.

As a kid, I was in awe of the great Majnun and Laili. I held on to that story when the clock started again, when I got older and life became imperfect, more complicated. I held on through each rise and fall of the chorus, through each stanza break. I held on, even when it hurt.

Way back then, I thought the story meant *never let go*.

Now, I'm wondering if I missed the point of Padar's stories entirely. What if this was a lesson? A warning of what it means to love or a sign of what to expect when you are loved by a person, whether it be a father or a mother or a sibling.

Or a friend.

My hand flips on a light switch in Sam's kitchen. Lying before me are two mugs and two plates—one with a single egg and spinach, the other an Eggo waffle. My two favorite breakfasts. Sam is sitting on the quartz counter, his head dipped back and eyes shut, like he's working through a problem in his head.

I know what you're thinking. How could I be so callous to Sam? The only explanation I can give is this: There's more to Sam and me than just last night. He opens his eyes and we stare at each other with nothing and everything to say. I know the twisting in my chest— the ugly, bent-up feeling that's taken hold in the absence I put between us—is only getting bigger. Even when we sit side by side. Even when he watches me take a bite of egg and waffle, take a sip of both tea and coffee. I know we've never felt further apart. But this is routine, how the dance always goes.

As always, Sam is the first to break.

"I'm pissed at you."

"I know." I hold the Chihiro mug in my hands and stare at the ripples in my tea. "You kept my spare pj's under—"

"—under the sink, in the corner to the left." Sam kicks his foot against the kitchen island. "Yeah, well, my mom must have forgotten it was there. So, lucky you, I guess."

Dozens of memories pop up. The morning light filters through the white curtains and casts a halo around Sam's shoulders. I see Sam and me in second grade with his mom creating volcanos on this countertop. Madar in the background, talking urgently on her phone. Afternoons spent sprawled on the tiled floor, with flashcards and textbooks fanned around us. Dinners with his family, when Padar failed to show up again and Madar spent the night aimlessly driving. Sitting side by side on his porch, just Sam and me, knocking knees, saying nothing, staring at the cloudy night as the shadowy silhouettes in my kitchen window angrily danced.

I keep sipping, chewing, swallowing. Keep ignoring the fact that I feel more like a stranger than ever.

"I'm pissed because I didn't know," Sam admits like a secret, "if you were okay. Last night. You iced me out for a year and a half without an explanation. I didn't know what happened to you then and it felt like déjà vu all over again. And I wish." He finally looks at me. "I wish you'd—" *Be the same girl again. Before that night.*

I wish I had an answer for why it's so hard to talk back. The longer he stares, the harder it is to want to stay. It would be so easy to grab my things and run out the front door and get as far as I—

Sam gently pries the mug from my shaking hands, as if to say *I won't hold you here if you want to go.* His turquoise eyes reflect a memory I wish he'd never seen. The night that twisted our friendship and his kind words into a jealousy that formed shadows around my heart. Because how can I tell him that I want everything he has?

In the nine years I've known Sam's family, I've never once seen his parents fight, let alone raise their voices. They've never forgotten a birthday or a graduation or a single chorus recital. They don't combat their son's frustration with sharp retorts like *you think you have it bad* or *you have no idea what real suffering is.* Sam's parents try to understand him, even if that means putting their own feelings to the side (a concept that is practically unheard of in my family these days).

The ugly truth is I'd trade my broken family for his perfect one in a heartbeat. Even if it meant he'd suffer. Even if it twisted his heart when he looked at me.

I can never tell him this.

"Tell me something else then, Sara." He sets down the

mug and grips both my cold hands in his. "What did you see inside that house last night?"

"The truth." I tuck my voice away, afraid of the secret that might carry across the street, into my waiting mother's ears, into the ears of all my bibi jan's daughters who live in this neighborhood. "The girl in the house. She is the eleventh daughter."

"Whoa."

I nearly snort and knead my hands together into the wet mess of my hair. Braid and re-braid over and over. "That's your insightful response? I tell you something that has the potential to change the fabric of my family forever and *that's* what you come up with?"

"It got you to talk more than three words to me, didn't it?" Sam clears away my half-eaten plates. "So yeah. I stand by *whoa*." The water creates a buffer of white noise. It's comforting, the steady whoosh. "What's the next step?" Dishes clack against the drying rack.

"I suppose I have to find her." I spin around on my stool. "But I don't even know where to start. Every time I try to bring it up to my mom, she just looks at me like I'm making it up for attention."

"How do you know she's not, you know, dead?" It's an honest question that makes my skin crawl. There's a flutter of annoyance in my throat. I clear it.

"Because I saw my grandmother in there too, and last time I checked, she wasn't *dead*, Sam." I jump off the stool. My mind feels like the inside of a fuzzy blanket. I need to go home. Need to check on Bibi jan. Need to get far away from Sam's flushed face.

"I'm sorry, I didn't mean it like that." Suds drip down his elbows as he walks toward me. "I just—doesn't it make you wonder why your grandmother kept her a secret in the first place? If she had wanted your family to know, wouldn't she have said something?"

"What are you insinuating here?" I snap. "That she left a defenseless child all by herself?"

"You can't strike it out as a possi—"

"My grandmother would never leave a child behind. Not of her own free will." Bibi jan is the grounding center of my mother's family. A person like her would never do something so unforgiveable. "Something happened in that house that separated them, and I'm going to get to the bottom of it, preferably without your unnecessary comments."

"I'm only trying to help you, Sara. I didn't mean anything by it. Just freethinking here."

I whirl on my heel. "And who asked you to help me, Sam? Who asked you to butt into my business? Because it wasn't me."

"It wasn't *you*? Are you being serious right now?" he asks. "Then why are you here?"

"To clear the air and return your car, which I did."

"You could have just left the keys in the driveway if that's all you wanted, and we both know that." Sam searches my face as he tries to figure me out. I blink nervously when a light dawns in his eyes. "Did something happen with your dad?"

"We're not going there." I gather my things from the counter and quickly start to shuffle out of Sam's kitchen. "I returned your keys, so we're even now. I gotta go."

"Sara, what happened?"

"I said we're not going there, so why can't you just butt out?" Without looking back, I advance into the harsh, summer sunlight. I'm just far enough away to hear, "We're nowhere close to being even," right before his front door closes shut. I swing open my own front door to the startled gasp of Irina as she shuffles Bibi jan toward the sunroom.

"Aren't you supposed to be back next week?" she asks.

I ignore her and face-plant on my comforter. I throw my pillows on the floor. Close the curtains. Lock the door. Stare up at the glowing plastic stars and finally fall asleep.

～

Thunder bangs heavily against our roof as I sink deeper into the couch. My cat's fluffy tail lurks nearby as she pauses, listening to the storm outside. She scrunches her face.

"You and me both, cat," I mutter while fiddling with my computer. "You and me both."

With a fresh head, I've realized the only way I'll be able to figure out what happened to Malika is to map it out. Step by step, I'll retrace that time until I find her. Find out the different ways a mother could be separated from her child. It's not much of a lead, but it's something. My cat jumps up and walks all over my keyboard until she curls up in my lap. I scratch her ears absently, wondering just how far back in Bibi's story I need to go.

The bullet points I've got about her Trek to America are woefully sparse. Khala Farzana had mentioned something about a young Uzbek couple living in that house. She must know something more. A name. A date. The next lead.

In the meantime, I've started searching public records for a Malika Amani in New York. So far, nothing pops up.

"Rain again?" Madar comes out of her room, wrapped up tight in her favorite sweater. She sleepily gazes out the window. "It's like the entire sky is falling." Pellets of rain drum steadily. There's a brief flash of lightning. "Surprised Aya is sleeping through it."

"She's a champ. And also half-deaf." If there was ever a moment I could just think alone, now would be it. I fake stretch. "But going to bed sounds like a grea—"

"What are you working on?" Madar's face brightens as she settles in next to me, locking me into the couch. "Oh, so you *are* recording our story. Let me see what you've got so far."

"Umm. It's not much yet. Just names and stuff." I click

out of the doc. My background is an old picture of Padar, Madar, and me at Hershey Park. She stares at it for a second.

Silence stretches between us.

"Why did you call her Aya?" A little flag waves in the back of my mind.

"Did I? I must be tired. I haven't called her that in years. It's like if you started calling me mommy again." Madar looks bemused as she lays her head against the couch, a faraway memory on her mind. "When we were kids in Kabul, that's what we used to call our mom. Aya." Madar laughs a little. "I used to get picked on so much because of it."

"Why?"

"Because the Afghans where we lived said *madar*, not *aya*. Our speech made us different. Not quite Afghan. Not quite Uzbek. All I really wanted back then was to blend in."

"I can relate to that." It's hard to tell her that when I'm at school, I revert to Mom and Dad and Grandma for that exact reason. Terms like Madar and Bibi jan are reserved for home use only.

"You should write it down." She waves her finger at my screen. "It's a great detail to remember."

"Yeah." I don't though. A part of me feels a little embarrassed I had no idea what *aya* meant. It's not like I'm clueless about my mixed heritage, but if I'm being honest, if I really had to tell you what it meant to be

Afghan-Uzbek, I wouldn't have much to say past the hyphen. It's like that part of me was just erased.

"How come you never taught me how to speak Uzbek?" I ask.

"They never taught me." Madar shrugs. "And for whatever reason, I never questioned it. By the time I finally did, we were already resettled here, and I chose the language that made the most sense to learn. English."

"Oh."

"It was a long time ago," Madar continues, "but sometimes it feels like it all happened yesterday." She doesn't expand on the topic, she never does, but I know she's thinking about what happened with the Taliban, and the mass migration of Afghans leaving the country. It hit my entire family hard, but my mother especially so. To distract herself from the situation with Padar, it felt like Madar needed to throw herself into something, anything, to keep herself going. So she threw herself into assisting Afghan refugees in any way she could for a few months.

Even if that meant leaving me to sit in the quiet spaces of her absence.

Unexpectedly, Madar curls around me and pulls me closer. I reluctantly squirm, but I'm too tired to put up a fight. "So. Want to tell me what happened at your dad's?"

I should have seen this coming. It's the Nargis Amani classic tactic. Where Padar approaches tough topics with bluntness and frustration, Madar swoops in all sugar to lure me in.

"There's nothing you don't already know," I mumble. "I'm sure he already told you."

"Yes, well, your father loves to exaggerate." Madar sighs. "And blame me, of course."

I shrug, and a silence falls between us. I tense, waiting for the fight, for the reprimand.

Madar smooths my baby hairs from my forehead. "Your father jumps to conclusions because he's a man. But I know you. I know you're not that kind of girl."

What kind of girl am I? It riles me up to think if I *was* that kind of girl, a girl who goes around with a boy in the middle of the night, then what would Madar think?

The doorbell rings. Followed by rapid knocks.

Madar turns, surprised, but there's a smile on her lips. Ever since my parents separated, unannounced aunt visits have increased tenfold.

"Look, Sara. I'm not like your father. If you want to be friends with the neighbor boy, then you have to do it properly. No middle of the night talks. And no more driving. Not until you're sixteen," Madar says as she strides to the door. Before she unlocks it, she looks my way. "You don't want to make mistakes, janem. You don't want people to talk. Understood?"

Khala Farzana stands in the doorway, drenched but triumphantly smiling with a clear container of freshly baked cream rolls and sugar sambosas. From the shadows of the couch, I watch the two sisters embrace and laugh as they help each other to the kitchen. Something complicated and bent lingers behind my tongue. A chill settles as I swallow.

The falling rain beats like distant drums again as the melody of that lullaby seeps into the kitchen. Little shadows twirl around Madar and Khala Farzana's ankles as they busy themselves in a familiar rhythm. The electric kettle buzzes. Drawers open. Silverware clangs. The recessed lighting flickers as Madar looks up.

"Strange," she says while reaching for teacups. Malika's reflection flashes against the glass of the cabinet. The shadows have tangled even more and, without warning, they pull. Madar loses her balance, and the cups shatter on the ground.

"Are you okay?" I leap up off the couch. When I blink, the rain is just rain. The lights are steady and there are no shadows. No reflections of Malika.

"Must have tripped over the cat or something," Madar mutters while cupping her face in her hands.

"Don't worry, I'll clean up the mess," Khala Farzana says in Farsi. "You just relax, Nargis jan."

I try to swallow the chill away, but the knotted feeling in my throat is too large. I've never known what it's like to have a sister, a person who is bound to you in the most intimate of ways. I think of Malika's loneliness and wonder how it would feel to discover an army of them.

Could all those people fill the gaps in a heart?

I eye Madar, staring off into the distance.

Or would the loneliness remain?

CHAPTER TEN

TIME SLOGS FORWARD IN A HAZE RIDDLED WITH
dreams of chasing screams in hallways, only to be consumed by a blanket of darkness. I'm running toward—or
is it away from?—something. Or someone.

Ever since I came back from Sumner, I've had bad nights,
with dreams blending into the shadows of my room. I
shuffle down the hall and make a beeline for the fridge.
My bun flops in my face, and somehow it feels the most
appropriate. Sometimes, I just want to be a wilted bun,
drink out of my Haku mug, and call it a day.

"We'll see you in two days." Madar waves at Irina as
she's about to hop into an Uber. "Enjoy your time off.
Tell your father I say hello." She shuts the door quickly
and yanks on the fuzzy blanket I've draped over my
shoulders. "Hold on there a second, speedy."

Normally, I'd fire back with something witty. But I'm
so tired.

Madar frowns. Her manicured hand pushes away my

bun and checks my temperature. "Hm. You're warm."
Now her hands are on my cheeks. "And pale."

I shiver and draw the blanket closer. "I'm *fine*." A tickling in the back of my throat comes on, and I have to jump away just as a coughing fit emerges.

Madar gives me a look that screams, *Why do you continue making things harder on yourself?*

"Have you been taking your vitamin C?"

"Yes?" No.

For whatever reason, Madar has been a bit obsessed with vitamin C. Weirdly, nothing else. Just that. She swears all you need is a dose of citrus and a shot of turmeric to live a long and healthy life.

"I've got to run, but can you take your grandmother to Khala Farzana's house?" It's more of a statement than a question from Madar. She's already halfway to the car, mid-wave at Khala Firoza down the street when she looks back to confirm that I understood what she meant.

"Yeah, yeah." I hustle back to my room and throw on whatever semi-clean leggings I can find. This is exactly the opportunity I need. Only, there's a series of drawers thudding and muffled shouts coming from Bibi jan's room.

"I know he took it!" A pair of pants goes flying, and I quickly dodge them. "My most expensive bracelets!" Bibi throws an accusatory glare my way.

I quietly lean against the wall and watch her melt down. I wait until she calms. Bibi always gets agitated when Irina leaves but she relaxes when she sees me. The doctors say it's a normal side effect of her dementia. The best thing you can do is be patient, and validate what they feel. Anything to lessen the confusion. So I count to three and give her my best megawatt smile.

"Bibi jan, let's go to your other house. Maybe you left it there." Like magic, Bibi jan transforms back into herself. Her knuckles loosen on her drawers, and her face relaxes.

"Yes, let me get my cane," she says as I extend my arm for her. She kisses my cheek. "Such a good girl."

We stroll along the neighborhood street. Bibi jan clutches her sheer white scarf as she points out each house. "That's our house. We bought it first." It's actually my khala Firoza's house. "And that one too." She proudly puffs her chest (it's actually my mom's second cousin's home). Our neighborhood is peppered with family, both extended and nuclear, like everyone just decided to up and move together during the war.

It's like they created their own slice of the past, nestled safely in a Long Island suburb. I'm told we're lucky to not have our community fragmented and scattered across America. I'm told other asylum-seeking communities did not have the same experience.

But there's a little bit of the truth missing in those things I'm told. Not everyone is accounted for. Someone critical is still missing. Holding Bibi's arm, my mind drifts back to Sumner, to Memory Bibi's tear-streaked face. In the chaos of the night, I hadn't asked the important questions.

Questions I can ask now.

"Bibi jan, how many children do you have?" I ask as we round the corner. The smooth pavement of our neighborhood paints a picturesque scene—a quiet street lined with trees. Only, now, they seem to be caving in on us, narrowing, looming, taking up the entire sky until the last ray of sunlight winks out.

"Farzana, Firoza"—she counts on each finger—"Mojgan, and Nazaneen."

"You must love your children to remember so many," I continue.

"Of course, who am I without them?" Bibi responds.

"I know you'd do anything for them." Like scope out a new country first. "And I know it's hard for you to remember, but I need you to try and tell me about Malika." My heart skips a beat. "What happened to your last daughter? Who took her from you?"

Bibi jan startles as her delicate brows crowd together. Her papery thin fingers bite into the soft flesh of my arm. She doesn't say a word, but her eyes go glassy. I know that look. She's lost, sailing away.

"Ow!" I try to pry her hand off. "Bibi jan, you're hurting me."

"I want to go home," Bibi's voice wobbles. She loosens her grip.

I'm about to ask her another question, but we're

already rounding the corner into Khala Farzana's driveway. Like the dutiful eldest daughter she is, Khala Farzana is already waiting for us, with a spread of breakfast treats prepared on her outdoor patio.

"I was wondering what happened to you both." Her embrace is like sunshine, even though she's covered head to toe in smudges of dirt from her gardening. She guides Bibi jan to the table and delicately serves her shir chai. Normally, I'd head home, but I hang back and watch the way she discretely pours Bibi's medication into her porridge.

Eldest daughter and mother. How would their relationship change if my aunt knew there was another daughter? Would she try to find her? Would sadness tinge the edges of her smile when she sees her mother?

"Sara jan, is there something you need?" Khala Farzana wipes her forehead with the back of her hand. "Did your mom need anything else?"

"N-no." I look out at the array of flowers landscaping her front yard. "I . . . it's kinda quiet at my house. Is it okay if I stay here a bit?"

"Of course, qandam." She sighs while surveying the bags of fertilizer and plants that need to be potted. "There's more shir chai inside if you want some. I'll just be here keeping an eye on Grandma."

"I can help, if you'd like." I try to lift a bag of fertilizer. "And maybe, I don't know. Talk about some things."

"Oh?" She raises a brow while gesturing where the bag

should go. She squats down and digs holes for her rows and rows of tulips. "Questions like what?"

Bibi jan slurps her breakfast while smiling at us both. A serene haze crosses her face as she looks up at a nest of birds, my past questions about Malika completely forgotten.

"For . . . a project I'm working on for Eid," I lie. "I . . . thought about what you said about writing Bibi jan's story down. I wanted to surprise my mom, so if you could just keep this between us—"

Khala Farzana beams as she wipes her hands on her overalls. "You really are a sweet girl. I always knew this, from the day you were born." She sighs while sitting down in the grass. "Come, it's okay if we take a break."

I lie down next to her and stare up at the sky. There are no clouds today, just sun and a harshness to the heat in the air. I swallow. "Isn't that what it's always like when you have kids? Babies always seem to be, I dunno, cute."

"It depends. All children are different. You all seem to come with your own personalities right from the very beginning." Khala Farzana laughs. She pushes back her short brown hair, lays a hand on her belly, as if touching a memory. "When I was pregnant for the first time, with Zaynab, your bibi jan was also expecting your Khala Nazaneen."

I recoil. "Isn't that weird, to be pregnant the same time as your *mom*?"

"A little bit. But there was something poetic to it as

well. My first time being a mother, my mother's last time giving life. I'm sure there's a line of poetry that could more eloquently express what I'm trying to say." Khala Farzana gets teary-eyed as she looks at Bibi jan. "She was always lecturing me. Eat sweets. Keep warm at all times. One day"—she barks out a laugh—"they convinced me that if I laid in bed with a dead chicken on me, I'd for sure have a boy."

"Excuse me?" I sit up immediately, appalled for so many reasons. "A dead chicken? In your bed?"

"In retrospect, yes, it was ridiculous," she says, "but I was young. And your grandmother and I were from a different era. We were fools to think we had any control over what was already meant to be. It didn't matter how many sweets we ate or how warm we kept ourselves, in the end, those babies were always meant to be girls." Khala Farzana pushes back the sticky baby hairs from my cheek.

"Is that why Bibi jan had so many kids? Because she wanted boys?" A wild thought slips through my mind, a horrible thought. What if Bibi wanted Khala Nazaneen to be the last girl?

"After Khala Nazaneen was born, I think that's when my mother finally stopped trying for more boys. She was getting too old to be having more children." Khala Farzana struggles to get up, so I help her. We slowly make our way back to Bibi jan. Khala Farzana takes a seat next to her and wraps her arm around her.

"Why do you think that was?" I hang back and balance on the balls of my feet.

"Maybe she finally stopped chasing an impossible dream." She smooths out the back of my grandma's shirt. "Maybe she was finally ready to be a mother to the girls she already had. Are you okay? You look a bit green."

"I—I'm fine." I try not to let my face slip, but I don't understand. If anyone knew my bibi jan the best, the longest, it would be Khala Farzana. But she's not letting on any hint of knowing that Bibi was pregnant one last time.

"Do you think Bibi jan would have wanted another child, if she . . . I dunno, accidentally got pregnant or something? After Khala Nazaneen?" I twist my fingers in my bracelet as my spirits sink over Khala Farzana's confused expression.

A cloud crosses her face as she stares down at her mother. She holds Bibi jan's weathered hands and kisses them. "No," she says. "She definitely wouldn't have wanted another."

"Why do you say that?"

"Sara jan, how do I put this delicately?" Khala Farzana purses her lips. She looks almost embarrassed to say it, but she says, "The grandmother you grew up with was not the same mother I grew up with. It took her . . . a long time to become the doting woman she is . . . was."

"But—"

Bibi's glass clatters to the ground, spilling her water

all over her pants and shoes. "I'm sorry, let me—" She shakily tries to bend over in her chair to reach the glass.

"Don't worry, it was an accident." Khala Farzana's demeanor changes instantly as a mask of sunshine and warmth locks in over her as she picks up the glass and dabs at Bibi's ruined clothes. "Qandolak, poor thing. Let's get her inside and changed."

"Thank you, F-f- . . ." Bibi jan's eyes crinkle together and she laughs. Red colors her cheeks as she takes Khala Farzana's hand into her own. "Ki asti?"

"Who am I?" Khala Farzana's tinkling laugh guides the pair inside. When they enter the house, my aunt kisses the top of Bibi jan's head, smooths the snowy white peaks of her flyaways.

I stare at the sky, watch as a cloud floats over the sun, casting shadows on the front patio.

Who are you? swirls and swarms in my head. Because I thought I knew exactly who my grandmother was. So then, why are the words warping, becoming a new flood of questions?

Who were you, Bibi jan? Before me? Before your daughters? Before the story of the Amani family began?

Who were you?

CHAPTER ELEVEN

IN THE LORE OF THE AMANI FAMILY, THERE HAS always been one constant: the tales of Bibi jan and Baba jan.

The first wave of stories came in the wake of Baba jan's death, when suddenly it became tradition for Bibi to end a lunch date, or iftari, with a story, almost like a prayer, to immortalize my grandfather's life in our memories. He became the example on the proper way to raise a family, to love a wife, to start over in a new country, to *be*.

The second wave came in the aftermath of Bibi jan's diagnosis, when doctors informed us of my grandmother's dementia. She held on as long as she could, but when the years rolled by, and the stories became fragmented or lost in Bibi's recollections, a sister would jump in, and without knowing it herself, the torch had been passed to the point where Bibi jan began to fade into the background and listen to her daughters recollect the story of her life.

Of her grand, beautiful, selfless life.

Except.

The grandmother you grew up with was not the same mother I grew up with.

I turn the words over and over in my head. When I need a quiet spot to think, I slip out through my bedroom window and make my way up on the roof. This is where I am now. Sitting and wondering and turning Khala Farzana's words, Malika's request, Memory Bibi's tears.

What does it all mean?

Across the street, Sam's house is dark, save for his bedroom light. A part of me wants to let Sam in on the new information I've found out. At least, that's what I've learned from so many TV shows and movies. I know you're supposed to fill your best friends in on everything.

But this *everything* . . . if it passes from my lips to Sam's ears, I'm afraid of what would come next. The logic turning in Sam's analytical head. *Maybe she's dead. Maybe your grandmother isn't who you believed her to be. Maybe she had something to do with it.* I stand up and wrap my blanket tighter around my shoulders. No, I can't let the doubts warp Bibi jan for me. I crawl through my window back inside when the squeezing starts again. Take a deep breath and start counting.

One, two, three . . .

I'm sitting in a room in Bibi and Baba jan's old house.

The smell of citrus fills the air as Baba jan spins me higher and higher.

Four, five, six . . .

I'm sneaking into Bibi jan's sacred closet and wearing her most prized jewels. Emeralds and sapphires and opals sparkle all around me as I pretend for a moment they belong to me.

Seven, eight, nine . . .

I'm crying when Bibi jan snatches her prettiest necklace—the gold and sapphire one—from my neck. She yells, short and clipped, *never again do you touch this* as she tucks it away in a dark drawer.

Wake up. It's now, and I hold my breath because, wouldn't you know it, I need to see that necklace again. I quietly tiptoe into Bibi jan's room, slip past the wink of moonlight and rummage in her closet. I fumble in the darkness because it'd probably be best not to have a repeat of the other week. My shoulders shake as I sink into the carpeted floor and open the lid of the St. John's box Bibi had wedged all the way in the back corner of her closet under three blankets and a pair of sleeping clothes. *To keep away from the man that steals in the middle of the night*, she says.

I don't know what I was expecting to feel when I lift the necklace up. It's cool to the touch. In the darkness, the sapphires look like the color of the ocean, and the closer I look, the more it feels like drowning.

I couldn't tell you why I take the necklace, or why I slip away into the night toward Sumner. It's like when you see the girl, again, standing by the gates of the house that looms ominous against a pale moon, you want to tell her, *don't you remember what happened last time?*

That's the fickle thing about memory.

You can never quite remember if you do.

———⌇———

This time, I bring the keys in my bag. And ride my bike instead of stealing a car again.

I shiver as the moonlight guides my path. There's a snap, and I look nervously over my shoulder. Last time, I had a phone to call for help. Now, I'm walking into Sumner truly alone.

Somehow, that thought doesn't scare me at all.

The front porch looks forlorn—almost somber—in the weary way it droops, as if it was exhausted by time. The spokes in my bike click with each step. I carefully lean it against the rotting wood and make my way up, brushing past the enormous web that has sewn itself on the front door like a shield. Unlike last time, I have a key—stolen from my mother's purse as she slept. A twinge of guilt guides my hand as I push the creaky door wide open and take a step inside.

For a long moment, there is nothing but the weight of a breath being held.

"Hello?" I grip the necklace like a lifeline.

My footsteps creak, and goose bumps race down my legs. The air feels . . . different tonight. Like the soft wail of a violin note, like something is . . . unfurling a carpet in welcome.

"Bibi jan?" I call out tentatively. Tarps are hanging everywhere, and the smell of decontamination is putrid. I cover my nose with my hoodie sleeve. Sam's face flashes for a moment, a scowl painted on his lips. Maybe I should have brought a mask with me.

The halls grow colder the farther I venture in. I circle the first floor once, then twice before heading toward the basement. And still nothing.

How do I get you to come out? I throw the necklace onto a toolbox and lean against the stair's banister. I still feel a bit woozy. Then I look out the window.

And freeze.

The overgrown lawn and quiet street lined with lights are gone. The homes across the street are replaced with a style of home I've never seen in person before. Behind them are the shadows of large, looming mountains.

My heart thumps as I race to the window.

Where am I?

"Sara jan." A deep voice calls out.

I turn, my stomach plummeting as I clutch my chest. There is a towering man dressed in elegant ceremonial clothing. I squint because he looks so vaguely familiar in a way I can't put my finger on.

"Yes?" The tiniest voice—a girl's voice—trembles. Only, the sound feels like it's coming from me. I clasp my hands over my mouth in shock as the figure floats closer and closer toward me. His dark eyes are never once blinking, the shadows slashed across his face only deepening.

My heart is trilling in my mouth as it screams *get away from me!* Fear makes me feel like I've turned into cement. No matter how I want to move my legs and run out onto the street, to call for Aya and pound against the neighbor's doors, I can't.

Wait. *Aya?*

"I know this isn't what you want, my dear." The figure is right in front of me now. His shape is amorphous, always changing. His body is in constant motion, as is his face. A thousand expressions flit across it. From anger to laughter to roaring fury to extreme sadness. They all swirl together and clash wildly as he crouches over me and raises his hands like he wants to hug me but doesn't know how to let himself. The gesture reminds me so much of Padar.

The reminder of my dad triggers a war to rage in my chest, and the thread of loss squeezes until it hurts to breathe. I fall on my knees, gasping as sweat drips off my cheeks. I cry out in agony, but the voice again is that girl's. Looking at my hands, they are trembling and it's directed toward some*one*. But it isn't toward this man.

Toward this man there is . . . sadness. And confusion. And a broken heart.

The feeling continues when he lifts my chin with his fingers, his touch plummeting me into the same frozen unknown, into the building pressure of ice in my body until there is nothing and everything—pain and numbness—at once.

My vision blurs, and his watery eyes go out of focus in his ever-swirling stream of facial expressions. I can't take it anymore. Somehow, I get my numb legs to move and collapse to the right, away from his touch.

I breathe big, gulping breaths. *What just happened?* I get more confused when I look back at the man—only now, he is not alone. Occupying the spot I was just in is a young girl, who looks to be barely thirteen. Tiny and frail, but also magnificent. Her lithe form is clad in a glimmering emerald dress, woven with the prettiest gold choking her wrists and ankles. Iridescent tears trail her round cheeks as the man continues to stare at her, as if for the last time.

"His name is Amir, you've met him. He is a fine and honorable young man," he says.

Amir. My grandfather's name? I do a double take between the girl and the man. What exactly is playing out here?

The girl shakes her head, jerking away from the man's touch. Her hands squeeze into fists. A burning desire swirls around her, which makes my heart ache for her, but I don't know why. Her brown eyes harden. "This isn't what I want, Dada."

"My sweet Sara jan. It is what is best for the family. He's a good man. We've known this family for years. He will be perfect for you." Her father twists as if opening a box. When he comes back around, he has something delicate in his hands.

A gold-and-sapphire necklace.

The necklace.

"I know in time, you will come to feel differently." Sara stiffens as he leans over and clasps it delicately around her neck. "You are lucky, my daughter."

Suddenly, this young girl looks shackled, like a prize to be sent off. Her hands tentatively come up to her neck at the weight of gold and power that has now latched on to her.

But I feel it, the intensity of her sadness, the feeling of betrayal. She has a storm swirling ever larger within her. Curiously, she smiles. Bows her head slightly.

I want to scream at her, at both of them, *how could you do this to a child?* This isn't right. Tell your father *this isn't what you want!* The problem is my voice is not my own. It is hers.

She throws me a reproachful stare—like she's saying *help me.*

She can see me?

Get out of here! My brain is begging, but I'm caught in her haunted stare, in her face that is so unfamiliar except for the fact that I have seen a version of this face every day, this face that has loved me and hugged me. And I know, but she doesn't yet, that one day, this face will be surrounded by children of her own and grandchildren and she will be *happy*.

Another thought swirls in my head. *Is she happy?*

Because right now, this face is telling me the exact opposite.

This girl is screaming to escape.

The man—I suspect he is my great-grandfather—kisses the top of her head, and just like when he arrived, he dissipates into a swirling mass of smoke. We watch as it drifts up and into the ceiling until it's gone.

The silence is weighted.

Finally, she gets up and searches the room. She reminds me of a fluttering butterfly, unsure of where she will land next. I squint through the darkness. It looks like she's . . . packing.

"Hey, where are you going?" I ask.

"Somewhere far away," she snaps at me. I see the things she chooses to pack—she's going to run away.

"Wait." I chase her upstairs, follow the rapid clicks of her shoes because the well in my chest has burst. A thousand questions want to spill out. As I follow her in and out of the rooms, I notice while the house is the same, the decorations are . . . otherworldly, as if from a different life. A different time.

Somehow, I'm caught in the middle of a memory. Of Bibi jan's childhood.

The night my grandparents married.

This doesn't make any sense, because the image of my grandparents is a happy one.

"You can't just leave." I try to grip her arm to slow her down, but she's fast. She spins away from me. When she stops, she clutches her small bag to her chest.

"I don't want this." Her eyes are so bright. She looks around at the room and shakes her head. "I don't belong here. Don't you see? I want to go home. Back to where I'm supposed to be."

I scratch my head because it seems stupid of me to say no, I don't actually know where we are. I mean, I know my grandparents were married in Afghanistan, but that's like saying my parents were married in the United States of America. I don't really *know* the finer details. I frown.

". . . Where is home?"

"Not here!" she says. "I need to go back to where my friends are. Where my mommy is." At this, her voice breaks, and hot tears span my own cheeks. "Where I need to be."

She runs straight for me, and I brace myself for impact. My arms go up but she vanishes.

When I open my eyes again, it's just me and the darkness.

Though I am not unmarked. The girl's anger is all around me. It burns in my chest, as if she flew right into me, nestling her fire in my own heart. As if to say *hold on to who I used to be.*

When dawn comes, the necklace is nowhere to be found.

CHAPTER TWELVE

FOR AS LONG AS I CAN REMEMBER, THE STORY goes like this:

Once there was a young girl who was captivated by a handsome boy with eyes the color of a foggy sky. They met under the shade of a mulberry tree. One day, the boy presented the girl with a flower and tucked it into her hair.

As the days passed, one flower became two, then twenty, then two hundred.

Soon, a lifetime had passed and still, every year, on the anniversary of that first meeting, the boy—now an old man—gave his beloved a flower, tucking it securely into her hair until the day he bid her goodbye. Forever.

I'm hunched over my laptop in my kitchen nook, gnawing on my thumb. The washing machine clacks down the hall. I listen to the *tha-thunk-tha-thunk*. This story has been passed down, from my mother's mouth to my ears, and recounted to me a million times when I was growing up. It is the love story of my grandparents, the Amani family origin story.

It was, perhaps, the best tale in the saga of my grandfather's life because it gave his children a guiding light, a firsthand example of what it means to love and how to be loved. I used to wrap myself in these stories when Madar and Padar's love story turned sour. I thought, somehow, the fairy tale would rub off on me.

Now, I'm not so sure.

If I'm being honest, I don't think that love story exists.

I think all it is, is a story.

A fabrication of *once upon a time* and *happily ever after*.

But why?

Madar shuffles into the kitchen with Bibi jan in tow. She guides my grandmother to her chair before making a beeline for the fridge. Bibi's eyes are more swollen than usual. Her hand touches her bare neck. Little threads of wispy darkness curl and float around her fingers until they form a chain around her neck.

I blink.

The shadows disappear.

"The dead have awoken," Madar jokes as she rummages through the fridge. "Have you told your dad what time to pick you up today?"

"Huh? Why would I be going there?"

"It's Father's Day, Sara." Madar turns on the gas stove

and lays the world's teeniest frying pan on it. "How could you forget?"

"Oh." There's no way it's already mid-June. I pat my sweats for my phone, but—wait. Right, it's dead. Dead like the stories I held on to like a balm. I eye Bibi jan. If her origin story was a lie, what about the rest of it?

Do I really know anything about my grandmother?

"This is way too much." Bibi jan swats the plate away. There's only a single runny egg on it. She moves to stand up. "I'm not hungry anyway." Her words are halted and stuttering. Less song, and more broken record. "Where is Irina?"

"Please, eat a little for me?" Madar smiles wide and smooths Bibi's flyaways. "We'll eat together." She sits down in the seat next to Bibi and sips her own cup of tea. "At least drink something." Madar nudges a cup of tea—it is the only thing my grandmother will drink religiously—dosed in medication.

Bibi's eyes sparkle for a moment as she stares at Madar. "Such a beautiful girl," she says as she sits and sips at her tea. Under normal circumstances, I would capture the moment, lock it away as a mental file that will never corrupt.

We are not under normal circumstances, and the last place I want to go right now is Padar's apartment.

"Maybe," I say slowly, "it's better if I stay here. This year." I can't bring myself to look at Madar or Bibi jan.

"I feel a little feverish. Can you just tell him it's better if I stay here?"

"Sick or not, I'm sure he'd wa—"

There's this feeling of slipping in my head. The only way to not fall is to hold on to the first thing my mind can find. Anger.

"It's not like either of you care where I go. Don't you have some party to plan or get ready for anyway?"

"Today of all days, Sara? Really?" Madar's eyes flash. Her jaw is working to say something more. Whatever she was about to say, she chooses to get up instead.

I look out the window, curl up on myself. The backyard is lined with tiki torches and flowers. Farther away, the pool glistens in the summer sun. I know what this day means to my mother and my aunts and uncle. I know they miss Baba jan. I miss him too. But what Madar doesn't know is I'm teaching her my ultimate battle technique: The best way to steal away the sadness is to channel it into something that makes you mad.

Then the tears go away.

You're welcome. I pour myself a cup of tea when Madar's door slams shut. I settle in next to Bibi jan. We don't speak to each other. She's somewhere else again as she hums to herself. My cat slithers next to me and paces until she finds a suitable spot on my lap. I scratch her ears as the kitchen blurs into abandoned halls and cobwebbed chandeliers. Moonlight replaces the morning sun. I blink and blink, but the image is resolute.

I turn to Bibi. Her hand lays on her collarbone. The smoke slithers and winds its way from her neck to her fingertips to her wrist. I want to ask her, *What happened all those years ago? Did you run? Did you fail? Are you happy?*

Instead, Bibi turns her watery gaze at me. Says, "Ki asti?"

"Who am I?" I whisper back. "Who are you?"

Bibi jan just blinks.

So, I do what I do best. I take off my glasses. I fluff up my hair. I say, *my name is Sara jan.*

Here's the thing about Amani family gatherings: They are organized chaos.

It always starts the same. Well-intentioned discussions. Careful party prep. Thorough group chats. Then, the day of arrives and, well.

"I *told* you to bring the kishmish and paneer." Madar pinches the bridge of her nose.

"I didn't have time to make it, and the little Afghan market was sold out. So now you'll have to settle for chabli kabob." Khala Gulnoor laughs as she bumps into Khala Nazaneen's littlest children, Harun and Madina, who weave in between them in an explosion of giggles.

With ten aunts and one uncle, our small home can

barely fit everyone. Add in significant others and children, and our house is close to bursting at the seams.

Normally, I would love this moment.

Now, all I can see is a barely teenage grandmother running for her life.

It is tradition during family events that anyone who falls under the angsty teen category makes a beeline for my bedroom and stays there until the adults remember we're missing and hiding from socialization. This is where we are now. Smooshed in my room. I flop onto my bed, trying to get a good spot. "Guys, truly, I am going to die and need to lie here forever, please."

"Ow, watch it," Mattin grumbles as I elbow him in the armpit. He's hogging both pillows, sprawled out while Amena and Ayesha—my khala Mojgan's daughters—shove each other for space at the foot of my queen size bed. Aman is leaning against one of the bedposts, combing a hand through his hair.

Ayesha rolls her eyes. "Don't know who you're trying to impress here, Aman."

Aman's cheeks redden. "I'm just standing casually."

"You mean casually posing while looking off into the distance," Amena mocks with a grin.

Mattin snorts. "He's been something else since that girl at school told him she liked the way he grew out his bangs."

A sudden chorus of oohs and a girl, huh and laughter follows Aman out of the room. "I'm gonna go get some food, you jerks."

"Bring me some baked ziti," Amena calls out. Mattin pushes her with his feet and she rolls over on the floor. "If you messed up an inch of my foundation, I swear to god, Mattin."

My eyes roll to the back of my head, and I drag my hands over my face. "Can anyone explain to me why you're all in *my* room?"

"Don't be like that." Ayesha picks through her straight brown hair in my mirror. Her green eyes catch my reflection. "Your room is the only safe space away from the khalas."

Amena flips her hair back and nods. She wipes the corner of her eye, making sure her eyeliner is still in place. "Which, by the way, shouldn't we be asking *you* why you're here? Shouldn't you be at your dad's?"

"Yeah." Three sets of eyes are glued on me.

"It's my house." I can feel myself sweating on my comforter. "I can do what I want."

"I'm not saying I don't want you here. I mean, you're better company than Amena—" Ayesha stops mid-brush as she turns to me. "And don't take this the wrong way, but isn't this like, the day one spends with their father?"

Don't say something rude, Sara. Don't sa—

"Yeah, well you're one to talk. I don't see *your* dad here."

Everyone in the room freezes.

Ah, shit. I want to swallow the words the moment I say them. But since that's not possible, I sit up and double down my stare at Ayesha.

"That's not funny," she mutters tensely. Her knuckles whiten around my brush. "And I take it back—you're shit company."

Amena abruptly gets up and smooths her cream-colored dress. She lays a hand on her sister's shoulder. Motions toward the door. "Well, can't say it's been a pleasure seeing you again, Sara. Hope you get your shit straightened out."

They leave without another word, knocking into a bewildered Aman and his five expertly balanced plates. "Hey, where you guys going?"

Mattin sighs and rolls over on his stomach. He props himself up on his elbows to watch as I grab my nearest pillow and scream into it.

"You know that was messed up."

"Whatever," I mutter into the pillow. I need a few more seconds. I don't want them to see how red my face is.

"What'd you say now?" Aman sits cross-legged on the bed and cracks open a can of soda.

"She brought up their dad." Mattin shares a knowing look with Aman.

"Ouch."

"Well, they started it." I cast the pillow aside and cross my arms while hunching in on myself. "If I want to be here for Father's Day, why should I care what anyone thinks?"

"I get it," Mattin says, "but their dad left them without a word and moved halfway across the world. I'm sure if they could, they'd, you know." *Be with their dad too.* He doesn't need to finish the sentence for me to understand what he's trying to say. "If anything, I'd think they'd understand what you're going through the most."

I hate it when Mattin is right. But how can I tell Mattin that if the roles were reversed, the last thing I'd want is for someone else to remind me of what's missing?

Mattin doesn't push for an answer, and I'm grateful when he steals one of Aman's plates and bites into a piece of chicken.

"That plate was *mine*," Aman grumbles.

There's a soft knock at the door. It's Khala Nazaneen, dressed in a brilliant blue dress. Her matching scarf glimmers against her narrowed eyes. The Khala dagger stare. We all cower back for a second. "We're cutting the cake. Come. *Now*," she hisses before rushing back to the main dining room.

"If I was on my death bed, you think that'd be a good enough excuse to not go out there?" I dramatically throw a hand over my face.

Mattin nudges my hand. "Come on. It's not that bad. Just a few minutes and you can return back to your lair."

I blow my hair out of my eyes as he extends a hand to lift me up. "I'm holding you to it."

We trudge on over to the packed dining room. All the fathers have lined up, side by side, each gripping the other's forearm. In the center there is a black-and-white photo of my grandfather, Baba jan, as a youth, looking regal. His gray eyes are fixed on me, no matter where I move, like he knows I know *the truth*.

The table in front of the men is covered with sweets—plump berries, freshly iced cream roll cakes sprinkled with pistachio, rows of perfect cookies for tea, and in the center, a modest cake with *Happy Father's Day* scrawled over it. One large candle sits in the center.

I'm crowded in with my khalas all clamoring over each other, trying to get the best angle for the picture. I slide next to Bibi jan, who is gripping her cane as she looks on. I take advantage of the moment to point at my grandfather's picture. "Who is that?"

Her watery eyes trail over to Baba jan's photograph and she scrunches her overly highlighted forehead. Finally, she says, "I don't know."

"You and me both, Grandma." I sigh and hold on tight to her hand when she gives it to me, shuffling with her out of the sweltering room right as Madar clamors with Khala Nazaneen to take the perfect picture of the men cutting the cake as everyone cheers, *Happy Father's Day!*

My momo Ali shouts, "Wait!" and gestures at my mother and Khala Mojgan to join in, because *they're both mother and father too*. I stop briefly to see Madar shy her way to her brother. Her eyes shine bright as he lays a hand on her shoulder, guiding her to the knife. Elbows clash into noses and ribs as my cousins run around and under the table to congratulate their fathers.

The bent-up feeling returns, and it feels like the happy

family image in front of me has cracked. How many Father's Days have passed, knowing that my grandmother was a child bride? I want to scream, *What if our happy family is a lie? What if all of this is not the love story we think it is?*

My chest gets tight as I lead Bibi jan away from the chaos. Amena and Ayesha are sprawled out on the family room couch. Amena glares at me over her phone, but Ayesha scoots over and makes room for Bibi jan and me.

"The first is always the worst," Ayesha says while patting my shoulder.

I want to say *sorry for before* and *how do you deal with it year after year.* Instead, I just nod, and we fall into an awkward silence.

Bibi jan eyes the collage of photos hanging over the fireplace. After a moment, she points at one photo in particular. "That's me. And my husband. And our son." I can't stop staring and thinking about what Khala Farzana said. *She wouldn't have wanted another.*

Amena and Ayesha nod and smile, but their eyes dart to me. They are too proud to admit that they don't speak Farsi. I translate under my breath and hope that suffices as an apology.

I want to ask Bibi what happened next. Did she run away? Did she ever make it back home? How did she end up here? Even though Amena and Ayesha wouldn't understand the words, it still feels like something private that I shouldn't share. Not yet.

When Bibi launches into telling us again about her ten daughters and one son, Ayesha leans in close to me. Her mascara is smudged as her eyes redden. "You don't know how lucky you are," she whispers thickly, "to have a choice."

We stare at each other for a second, and I know this is *the* moment. I know with every fiber of my being she wants to talk, and our fight is behind us. So why do I turn into a sweating stone statue? Why do I scoff, roll my eyes, and get up?

"Don't waste your breath, Ayesha," I hear Amena mutter as I escape to the front door. "She's an unfeeling robot."

I quietly make my way outside. The warm night air does nothing to soothe my nerves. I shiver as if it's the middle of winter. The stars wink, mocking me.

Across the street, all the lights are on at Sam's house. I have a reckless thought to crash his parade and demand *why haven't you tried to reach out to me? Don't you know this is what we do?*

But today isn't about me, and even worse than the reckless thoughts is the fear of walking into his house and feeling like my parents, feeling like a storm that crashes in and ruins everything.

So I choose to stay outside and focus on the stars. I start to count.

One, two, three . . .

I've got a snot bomb coming out of my nose, and

Padar's face is cherry red as he holds in his laughter. I chase him around the rug, and he's crawling on all fours, laughing for mercy against the fearsome booger monster.

Four, five, six . . .

I'm half-asleep, curled up in Padar's makeshift studio as he sings to me an old Ahmad Zahir song while playing his accordion keyboard.

Seven, eight, nine . . .

I'm hiding behind Madar as Padar packs up his music room, never to sing again.

A hand on my back startles me. I jerk away quickly. It's Madar.

"Hey," she says in that sugar-sweet way only a mom can. She smells like her usual floral perfume. Her face is perfection, as always. She's too beautiful to look at. Her arm snakes around my shoulders, and I stiffen. She sighs.

"It's hard for me, too," she says. "I miss my father every day, you know. And it's okay if you miss yours too."

I stubbornly keep staring at the stars, grasping for my battle armor, but today, somehow, it's out of reach. My throat tightens as I swallow back the past—both mine and Bibi jan's.

"Would you miss him . . ." The words are like glue, but I say them anyway. "Even if he wasn't who you thought he was?" If you knew that he took on a child for a bride. If it were you.

Would you still miss him?

Would it be allowed to still miss him?

"People are very rarely who we think them to be, Sara jan," Madar says. "But that doesn't mean you should punish yourself for not being able to switch off your feelings because of it. And it's okay to change your mind. I would never think less of you for that." Her sadness lingers between us, and I can't get Ayesha's words out of my head. *You don't know how lucky you are to have a choice.*

I don't know why I ask, "Can you drive me to Padar's?" but I do.

I don't know why she says, "Of course, my love," but she does.

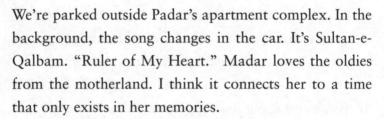

We're parked outside Padar's apartment complex. In the background, the song changes in the car. It's Sultan-e-Qalbam. "Ruler of My Heart." Madar loves the oldies from the motherland. I think it connects her to a time that only exists in her memories.

But I freeze when *this* song comes on.

It was their song. The song Padar would hum so, so quietly in between late-night car rides after long renovation days at houses far away, when my parents thought I was fast asleep.

Hearing this song now makes me feel like it should be bottled up and stored safely in Yesterday. Without Padar with us, it feels wrong to hear it in Today.

Madar puts on a brave face, as the music continues to play. She smiles, though her eyes say otherwise. She says, "I'll see you soon."

I'm woozy on my feet as I knock on Padar's front door. When he opens it, there's a look of surprise on his face. "You came." I'm taken aback by how . . . haggard he looks. Like he hasn't slept in days.

Meekly, I stand at the door with a partially melted cupcake in hand. "I, uh, would have lit a candle, if I had any."

Padar opens the door wide as his lips lift up. He runs a hand through his hair and says, "It's perfect." We don't talk about the last time I was here or the fact that I stole his credit card and ran away. We especially don't talk about why Padar chose to sit alone in his apartment, when he could have joined in on a Father's Day celebration elsewhere. Instead, we sweep it all under the rug and sit on top of it. Padar places the cupcake on his coffee table in the TV room. We crowd around it. I notice his laptop is open on the couch, and it looks like he's up working on some sort of event.

We pretend to light a candle, pretend to ignore the awkwardness between us. My father closes his eyes and makes a wish. I hear him whisper, "To new beginnings." I want to tell him about the song. About the feeling in Sumner house, but that whispered confession halts me in my tracks.

Before he can blow out the fake candle, I blurt out,

"What new beginnings?" I hate the sinking feeling in my chest when he opens his eyes and stares at me. Like he's saying goodbye. To what?

This is the first time I've seen Padar just as nervous as me. Even more surprising is what he says next. "Ever since I moved out, I've had time to really think about what I wanted the rest of my life to look like, but more importantly, I had to think about what the rest of *your* life was going to look like. And I'm ashamed when I look back at everything you had to endure because of your mother and me." He swallows while blinking back tears. "So, I had to make the tough choice. For all of us."

I sit, unmoving. "Which is?"

"You know what it is."

I blink and blink and blink because I don't want to believe it. I *can't* believe it. And for whatever reason, Padar still can't bring himself to just *say it*.

Maybe Padar senses the way my entire world is unraveling in my head. Maybe he feels like I am too fragile a thing to push any further. Maybe that's why he kisses the top of my head and says, "I promise this will all look different in the morning. Please remember that when the delivery is made."

"This is more than a blip," I whisper. Not so much a question, but Padar still gives one final answer.

"Yes."

CHAPTER THIRTEEN

PROMISES ARE FUNNY THINGS. THEY'RE LITTLE words that peel off and attach to the sticky parts of our hearts. Like somehow, slapping an *I promise this will all look different in the morning* onto a situation is supposed to fix everything. Which, okay, sure, I'm sometimes guilty of it too. For example, I promised Malika I'd find her, but in this exact moment, I am doing the opposite of finding her.

Instead, I am ripping bad carpet out of one of Madar's flip homes, wondering with each nail that scrapes against my fingertips why it is that God chose to implode my family. I imagine it's what I deserve for thinking the worst of Bibi jan and Baba jan. For meddling in something that I should have left alone. What's the expression adults say when they don't want to explain anything? *Ignorance is bliss?*

Each pinch of the nails strikes a painful reminder of

Padar's promise on Father's Day and all the other scattered promises he tucked away in bedtime stories and kisses goodnight. I chuck the strips of carpet into a lumpy pile with more force than necessary. They land with a dusty *thwack*.

I wish I knew then that *promise* was just another word for *lie*.

Nothing is better.

Nothing looks different.

"You doing okay in here?" Erik leans against the doorframe. His lips smack as he chews his gum. "We can send in Sam if those nails are giving you trouble." I hear a slight groan a little ways off.

"Um, no. I think I've got this handled." My face reddens when Erik gives me a thumbs-up and guides Sam upstairs. I catch a glimpse of his retreating back, deciding we need more space.

"That son of a—" There's a thud, followed by a scream.

Erik, Sam, and I freeze and crane our heads around to where the noise is coming from. My mouth runs dry when there's another thud and then a muffled sob. Sam and I lock eyes for just a moment before I peel out of the room to run down the hall.

"Sara, wait!" Sam's familiar call is hot on my heels, but I'm not here anymore. All I can think about is *please remember when the delivery is made*. All I can do is count the seconds before I discover what it is.

One, two, three . . .

I'm in a white dress, flowers in my hair, watching Madar and Padar dance on their ten-year anniversary, whispering promises of *only a lifetime to go.*

Four, five, six . . .

I'm in my bed, pretending to watch Netflix, when I hear the first crash of glass against marble that night. I crack open my door and wander down the hall.

Seven, eight, nine . . .

I stand in the doorway, afraid to round the bend into the kitchen, where my parents' shadows angrily dance. Bits of glass cut into my toes. I take one step. Then another.

"Madar?" I am thirteen years old again as I step into our kitchen. Madar's back is to me, but her entire body is shaking. There is a trail of blood lining a path from shattered glass to where my mother stands. "What's going on?"

I blink and I realize we are not in our kitchen. We are in a flip house my parents bought together but now work on separately. There is no blood. No glass. Just paper. Lots and lots of paper strewn about. I bend to pick one up.

"He had to do it *here*, of all places. Through a *courier*." Madar grabs a hammer from a toolbox on the ground and chucks it at the drywall. "He didn't even have the decency to hand them to me face-to-face. How"—Madar is not calming down—"dare he do it like this." She curls into a ball, cradles her head in her hands. "Why like this?"

"What do you need me to do?" Sam's hand is on my shoulder.

My insides bend and twist when I read the pages. "Get the crew out of here, please," I whisper. Sam nods, and he's gone. I hear footsteps clearing out. Soon, it's just Madar and me. Dust filters through the open windows, letting in the sounds of birds.

Madar continues to destroy the renovation site. I don't stop her. I stand by and watch as she lets go of all her grief. In my life, I've learned that Nargis Amani can be many things—a mother, a businesswoman, a sister—but at this moment, she is a girl with a broken heart. And I am a girl with a broken heart. So what the hell am I supposed to do? How the hell is this *for me*, Padar?

"Did you know it would happen today? When you last saw him, did he say anything to you?" Madar still refuses to show me her face. A part of me is glad she can't see mine because I've always been a shit liar. I remember Padar's eyes squeezed shut. His wish. *I promise.*

I am too afraid to answer, to hurt her more.

I let the divorce papers flutter from my hands and walk a coward's walk out of the room.

"Of course" is all Madar says.

After a few moments of intense internal debate, I do

the only thing that makes sense—I take my mom's phone and call my aunt.

───✦───

Khala Mojgan's car pulls into the driveway. I wave timidly as she hurries out and hugs me.

"Where is she?" she asks.

I point, and she disappears into the house. Amena and Ayesha stand next to their car. Ayesha throws me a quick wave. I know it's a white flag. I rub my arm self-consciously and wave back.

"Wanna go for a ride?" Amena asks nonchalantly while picking at her nails. "I think we're heading to Northport. We can sit on some benches, feed bread to some geese or whatever shit people do next to the water." She looks up, as if she's annoyed that I've created a detour in her plans. But then her mouth twists into a small smile.

"You're actually not supposed to feed geese bread, Amena." Ayesha opens the car door and slides right in. "And of course she's coming. It was never a question."

Amena mutters "yeah, yeah, yeah," while gesturing for me to follow.

I take one last look behind me, see that Khala Mojgan's putting all the papers neatly into a folder, and join my cousins in the car. All three of us are squeezed into the back seat. Madar emerges in the doorway with Khala Mojgan rubbing her back.

"I take it the delivery was made here?" Amena wiggles so she's sitting forward. Her delicate arms loop around the passenger headrest.

"Yep."

"Dads are the Worst." I can hear the capital letter in her voice. Ayesha kicks her beat-up sneakers onto the center console as our moms get in the car. "Salaam, Khala jan," Amena and Ayesha sing in quiet unison. Madar doesn't respond. She just stares out the window, a deep grief etched on her face. She's got that far-off expression she always gets when it's about to be waterworks city.

I would literally do anything to escape the awkward tension of this car ride.

"It sounds like a funeral in here," I mutter while throwing my hair up in a bun, elbowing Ayesha in the shoulder. "Can we get some music going or something?"

Khala Mojgan eyes me from her rearview mirror before turning on a playlist. To my horror, a slow, synthetic beat hums through the car as we wind down narrow, shadowed backstreets.

"This somehow seems worse," Ayesha whispers to Amena and me as the chorus of "I Wanna Know What Love Is," paints the scenery with an ancient '80s vibe. Amena whips out her phone and connects to Bluetooth to change the song to something more appropriate (aka something from this century).

Weirdly, the old song pulls Madar out of her thoughts. She turns to look at Khala Mojgan. "You know what night this song reminds me of?" She grips the folder tightly, so as not to lose any papers to the whoosh of wind from our open windows.

"You mean the night you and Zenat bribed Nazaneen and me to pretend to be you in your beds so you two could sneak out to go to prom?" Khala Mojgan snorts. She takes a turn and the forest opens up to a horizon of water. "I have a scar on my ear for covering for you two."

"You what?" The three of us gape in unison, breaking the somber mood.

"And yet I can't go to my own junior prom," Amena gripes with her face squashed next to the headrest holder.

"It was different then." Khala Mojgan huffs. "We had a good reason."

Amena rolls her eyes. "There's always a *reason*."

Madar smiles delicately. There's a glimmer in her eyes as she swipes at them. "It wasn't even our prom. It was just a moment to get away from it all. From life."

Khala Mojgan reaches and holds Madar's hand. Again, they share a look I can't understand. Did it have to do with the war? With moving countries?

"What was going on then?" I ask.

"Well, hard to explain." Khala Mojgan puckers her lips. Her words are measured, as if she's bound to the limits of a pact made by her teenage self. "Your grandfather had been sick, diagnosed with a rare and slow-growing cancer. It . . . was after a particularly bad scare that we decided to give each other some time to be normal. Even if only for one night."

"And that night was my turn." Madar closes her eyes while letting out a troubled sigh. Her hair dances across her temples. "I walked down the street to your father's house. We were neighbors back then."

"Really?"

Madar hums while she nods. "He moved down the road from us about four years after we moved to New York." She squeezes Khala Mojgan's hand tighter. "When he showed up at my dad's store that day, it was like after the universe had taken everything away, God wanted to let me have one good thing."

Like you were always meant to be. Only—I fiddle with my nails—*the fairy tale didn't seem to last.*

"Your grandmother wasn't herself in those days. Well, to be honest, she hadn't been herself since before leaving Kabul, so the responsibility to care for your grandfather fell on all of our shoulders," Madar recalls. "That night, we made a pact that we'd get through whatever would happen to him. And that night, dancing under the lights of a high school gymnasium that we didn't even go to, we knew we could make it through anything. Well." She paused. "Almost anything."

"Why couldn't you just let grandpa know you wanted a night out?" Ayesha scrolls through her phone. "I'm sure he would have understood why you needed time to rest."

In all the stories they told us, our grandfather was a strict man, but also a compassionate man. A better man than my father. I try to hold on to that image of him, but in between blinks are lingering remnants of smoke, clinging to the picture of his memory as I remember Memory Bibi fleeing in the night. He didn't understand my grandmother then, so would he have understood his own daughters?

We arrive at a small park in Northport. The water laps against the grassy shore. Khala Mojgan drops stunning information as she parks. "We never told him that he was sick."

"You *what*?" I ask in disbelief.

"We hid it from him," Madar whispers as she stares at herself in the passenger mirror. "Dada's English was okay, but when it came to work, business meetings, the doctor, he needed us to translate. He took us with him and when the bloodwork came back with the news, our mom decided it would be best to say it was something else. Something minor."

"You mean you lied to him," Ayesha says.

"Protected him," Madar corrects.

"Wow." Amena's eyes widen as we shuffle out of the car. "But isn't that cruel? I would want to know if I was . . . potentially dying. Right, Sara?"

Would I?

The correct, logical answer would be yes, of course. But as I'm eyeing the tiny threads of dark smoke winding and swirling around the crumpled legal papers in the front seat, I'm not so sure. I blink and the smoke disappears. Khala Mojgan walks around the car and links arms with Madar. I wonder what other teenage secrets linger between sisters, if any of them wrap around and protect Baba jan in other ways.

"He would have worried himself to death," Khala Mojgan says. "He beat it that first time. Your grandmother was there with him, every day. Cooked his favorite foods, smiled through the lies when she sorted his medication. Though there was always something that never quite made sense about that year."

I want to say that a lot of things don't seem to make sense about those years, but I keep my mouth shut. "Why's that?"

"I don't know." Khala Mojgan and Madar's sneakers crunch under the tiny rocks as they walk. "It's like holding that weight from him took something from her. When he got better, she was never the same."

I turn her words in my head. If Baba jan got sick when Madar was in high school, that had to be around five years after Bibi jan left Sumner. Around the same age Malika has been when I've seen her in the house.

"And you have no idea why Grandma would be . . . acting weird after that?" I press. "Nothing at all?"

"My mother was a private woman," she says matter-of-factly. "She rarely shared with us how she felt about these things."

"So you never asked? Not *once* in all these years?" I'm getting tired of these non-answers, these platitudes to gloss over the messy parts of our histories. "Or is this just another version of the truth for our *protection*?"

"Chill, Sara, it's not that serious," Ayesha interjects.

"Not that serious? Are you—"

Madar clears her throat in a way that hints *watch your mouth*.

"It's okay, Nargis. It's been a tough day." Khala Mojgan smiles weakly at me and waves us away. "Why don't you girls sit by the water and enjoy the afternoon. We'll be over here for a bit." They bow their heads together and walk in unison. I can't help but feel that ugly feeling again as they grow smaller against the afternoon sun. The longer I stare at them, the more the edges around them start to darken. Red and black smoke nips at their heels. A chill goes through me.

I don't buy Khala Mojgan's explanation.

"Glad that weirdness is over," Amena mumbles while leading us toward a dock. "It's always such a headache talking to our moms." We sprawl out onto the splintered wood. Amena's green dress fans out under her as she props her legs up on one of the stakes. Her phone is in front of her as she scrolls through it. I lie down with my legs dangling off the edge. Slowly my feet sway to the breeze while I count, turning the beads on my bracelet as I go over the new details. Something happened, something significant, and it has to be linked to Malika, I just know it. Ayesha sits cross-legged next to me, leaning against a pole and shielding her forehead with her hand. She squints.

"You know what I don't get?" she asks.

"What?"

"Why our moms don't just tell us the truth."

I snort. "What happened to *it's not that serious.*"

"You were in a losing battle in that conversation, and you know it. Talking to our moms is like talking to a wall. It's impossible to get a straight answer out of them for anything." She winds her brown hair in her fingers and works it into a braid. "Like, look at them. They're just standing there, walking in circles. The moment we ever get something from them that shows that they're remotely human, they shut us out."

"I don't know why you guys are getting so worked up over this. It's old news that everyone in our family has the emotional intelligence of a pea," Amena grumbles. She never stops scrolling. "What do you expect? They lied to their own father when he was *dying of cancer* but you think they'll tell you whatever you want to know? Please. We're just collateral damage to them. The sooner you accept that, the sooner you can move on and focus on something that matters."

"Like what?" Ayesha stares out into the sky, like she wants to step into it.

"Like a future where we call the shots." Amena continues to scroll. "Where we're as far away from our shitty home lives as possible."

Khala Mojgan's separation was nothing like my parents'. Where Madar and Padar left a hurricane, Khala Mojgan's husband left like a whisper in the night. It wasn't until six months later, when Khala Mojgan hosted a family dinner at her house, did we all find out that he was gone. Six months of pretending everything was fine, through sleepovers and shopping dates and movie marathons.

In all that time, Amena and Ayesha never spoke a word. Not until their mother opened the floodgates.

I glance at Ayesha's scowling face. The sky is a perfect shade of blue, the kind of sky you could get lost in. I wonder if, whenever she looks at it, she thinks about that one-way flight—if it reminds her of her dad. I want to ask her if she thinks the blue of the sky and of the ocean feel one and the same—infinite and impossible to pass through to get to him. If this idea of family I'm chasing is just that: infinite and impossible.

She catches me staring. "What is it?"

"How did you deal with it?" I finally ask. "When your dad left?"

"I didn't. I don't." Ayesha lets out a short laugh. Her dark green eyes grow glassy. "It's embarrassing to admit this, but it really felt like we woke up one day and he was gone. No warning. I didn't even know anything was wrong.

How messed up is that? It wasn't like with your parents, you know? They never fought, never once argued."

"Yeah." I'm not really sure though. Maybe to the outside world, the hurricane that was my family felt obvious, but it hadn't been to me. I hear that's what it's like to stand in the eye of the storm.

"He left all his stuff. If I walk into my parents' room, it feels like he's still there, even though he's been gone for so long." Ayesha sighs.

"Your mom didn't clear out his stuff from her room?"

"Nope." Ayesha picks at her fingers. "She hasn't even moved his prayer mat from his side of the closet. Its corner is still folded over, as if he'll be back any minute to pray Maghrib."

"Do we really need to be talking about this?" Amena glares at us. She wipes sweat from her brow and shakes out her dress before getting up. "Our parents suck. End of story. Now, if we're done talking about depressing things, I'm going to see if there's a decent place to eat in town." She walks off, a swish of perfume and hot air. She keeps her eyes glued to her phone as she goes.

"She still can't talk about it?" I watch her angry back until she turns out of view down the sidewalk.

"She's just like our mom. Just keeps on pretending nothing's wrong. It's annoying." Ayesha eyes my bracelet. "Though she refuses to touch anything our dad got her. Threw it right out, said it had bad energy or something."

We fall silent, just staring out at the Sound and watching the sway of anchored boats. There's a few people kayaking. My legs keep swinging as I keep thinking, keep counting, keep turning what Ayesha said until I can't help it, I have to let this out. "Do you think she doesn't want to touch them because . . . I dunno, maybe she thinks history lingers in places?"

"What?" Ayesha arches a brow.

"You said that Amena threw everything away because it felt off. Maybe there's a reason for that. Maybe it brings back the connections to those moments for her. Maybe—" The memories come back for her too. Like Sumner. Like how they do for me.

I am bobbing with the memory of the ripped dress, the spark between Bibi and me in the darkness of her closet, the gold-and-sapphire necklace that I can't seem to find, the flickering lights and the smoke that lingers and curls like shadows around the people I love.

"Are you having a hard time with keeping your dad's things? Is that why you're bringing it up? Because of the divorce papers?" Ayesha asks.

Round and round my fingers go as I think. What if I grill everyone and still get these roundabout answers? What if Bibi jan had spun a secret so tight, there's no other way to uncover it except through the things she's touched?

"Sara?"

What if the only way to get to the truth of what

happened to Malika isn't to investigate my family in the present?

Ayesha waves a hand in my face.

What if the only way in is . . . through yesterday?

"Hey!" Ayesha grabs my wrist and pulls my hands apart. I startle and flinch away from her. Her brows are knit together when she lets go.

"Sorry," I mumble when Amena's name flashes on her phone. "Looks like we're being summoned."

"Where do you go when you do that?" Ayesha helps me up. I walk away, but she's rooted to her spot on the dock.

"What do you mean?"

"You seem to . . . drift. Get lost in that head of yours," Ayesha says. "One second you're asking me a question, the next you're just . . . gone somewhere."

"I—" I clench my hands at my sides. I want to tell her. Her face is open, ready to listen.

I want to tell her that we're cursed, that maybe we're destined to follow in our mothers' footsteps, who followed in their mother's footsteps, who spun a tale so tight it hid the real story of the Amani family. A story our grandmother felt we needed protection from.

In so many ways, we are our mothers' daughters, but in this fleeting moment, I don't want to be.

"Well?" Ayesha stares at me, expectantly.

"I'm just having a hard time with this family history project," I hedge. "And . . . it feels like the more I dig, the more I'm questioning who we are, if that makes sense."

"Like what?" The sky darkens around Ayesha's shoulders, as a red shadow glints along her hairline. "Maybe I could help you talk it out. And, to be honest, I could use a distraction."

Dark, angry eyes reflect in the water when I try to say, *there's something in that house.*

I pause and watch as the eyes watch my cousin, watch me. My heart speeds up, just a tick.

"Later. I'll tell you everything," I say instead, leading Ayesha away from the water. The shadows only grow darker, trailing in my cousin's footsteps. "I promise."

That familiar fog settles heavy in my head, coaxing me once more. *Just one more night.*

Okay, I can do that. One more night. And then I'll tell her.

CHAPTER FOURTEEN

KI ASTI?

My grandmother rattles this question a dozen times a day. *Who are you* when I wash my face in the morning. *Who are you* when I pour her a cup of tea for breakfast. *Who are you* when I watch her carefully draw her eyebrows in the mirror. Her eyes never leave me. They watch as I struggle to answer her.

Who am I?

I am Sara Rahmat and not.

I am American and not.

I am Afghan-Uzbek and not.

I am the product of a grand love story and not.

I am and I am not.

My baba jan used to remind me, *history is what makes us,* and without it we are doomed to lose our way again and again. But as moonlight from my bedroom window scatters my thoughts, I realize it is this history that has set all of us spinning so far off course.

Not for long, though.

I will get us back on course. I will undo Padar's *for the best*. I will uncover what my grandmother hid, and maybe it will be enough to erase this cursed broken feeling that lingers in this house and turn it back into a home.

I blink, and then I am standing in front of a glass cabinet in my living room, staring down the rows and rows of precious antiques encased inside. A fog settles in my head, sprinkles along my shoulders and down my fingertips, coaxing me to slowly open the glass door.

There are bowls, cups, and platters filled with greens, golds, and designs written in a sprawling Persian script I can barely make out. My hands shake as I trace a gold-and-white teacup. The night presses in on me, making the walls feel like they're peering closer, waiting for me to choose. I hold the cup in my hands and hug it. When I was younger, I would stare at these family relics in awe. I wondered what stories were encased in them.

Now, I no longer trust the speakers. Because they lie.

A small knife gleams in the moonlight. Embedded in its handle are gems along with script I can't read. It looks etched, as if by hand. Irina put it here when my bibi jan nearly cut her cheek during a fit. She cried for an entire day when she found it gone from her room.

The fog guides my hands, helps me carefully wrap it in a towel.

I blink once more, and I am back at Sumner.

Sumner winks in: *Hello, welcome back.*

My bike clatters to the ground, and I wiggle through the broken garage window. I wander around the sprawling halls, hoping for yesterday to show itself.

"Bibi?" I call out to the stillness. The chandelier sways in familiar greeting. "Malika?" I kick a piece of plaster. Right. I need to make an offering. I'm on my knees in the kitchen, rummaging through my bag. I stand up and grip the knife.

Okay. It's now or never.

I throw the knife as hard as I can. "Aargh!" It hurtles toward the glass doors leading out to the deck. "Oh, wait, no! Not there!" I brace for the shattering of glass, but as the knife sails through the air, little specks of stardust shimmer through the night, as if it is cutting through to yesterday.

The knife makes impact with the glass. Instead of shattering, thin tendrils of gray smoke weave around it. I cough and cover my eyes. The room grows hazy with it until it swirls all around me. It pushes me out through the doors with a roar.

Then it's all gone.

Out on the deck there is a sound of chopping and humming. "Hello?" I see a girl chopping something. There are stalls, rows and rows of them everywhere. I take a tentative step on the creaking deck. "You can do this." I breathe a quick bismillah, because you never know.

The deck seems to stretch on infinitely as I walk directly across, past stalls that are encased in flickering shadows of people going about their shopping. They don't seem to notice me. But there is a tingle, a pull on the threads in my chest that take me where I need to go. I hit the final stall and I am face-to-face with a girl who looks to be about fourteen, with wavy hair barely dusting her shoulders. Her loosely wrapped white scarf slips off her head and onto her collarbones.

She is holding the gemmed knife and chopping dried fruit furiously.

"I can do it, I can do it, I can do it," she mutters to herself, like a mantra or a prayer, I can't tell.

"Can I help you?" The breeze blows my hair in front of my eyes as I take a step toward her. Her eyes are glued to the cutting board.

The girl looks up, her face half obscured in shadows, but I recognize her instantly. Bibi.

"Is there something you need?" she asks, not looking at me as she worries her lip. "My father will be back in a moment, if you're looking for something we don't have out."

"No, I'm just . . . looking." The backyard, as if lost in a dreamland, stretches and swirls. The wind carries with it a touch of creation. The more it blows, the more the scene changes. The pool disappears. The deck transforms into a road, where old cars drive past. I can no longer see Sumner. It really feels like I'm elsewhere. A hazy blood-orange glow shines down on us. "H-how long has it been?"

"Has what been?"

"Since your nikkah?"

Bibi's hand stills as she finally looks up at me with sharp, dark eyes. "Who are you again?"

"I—" *need to know what happened next.*

"Did someone send you here?" she snaps.

"No. I—"

"Then why are you here bothering me when I told you my father is coming soon and I need to, I have to—" At this, her small face pools with tears. The knife clatters and falls to the ground. She quickly swipes at her eyes. It isn't until she turns in profile that I notice the tiny swell to her stomach through her loose dress. "Is it that obvious?"

I look away in embarrassment. Okay, logically, I know what often comes next after marriage. But here, in this place, a part of me had wondered, had hoped for a different outcome.

"You never went back home, did you?" I whisper

quietly as I reach for her tiny hands. I try to hold tight but her hand slips past me like an illusion. "You stayed here."

"What choice did I have?" There's a fire in her, but it's suffocating. As if we both know one day, it will go out. "I'm too old to hold on to childish dreams for myself." But the fire still burns when she walks away from her stall and looks out to the busy road.

"I haven't told anyone yet." She sucks in her lips. "I'm too afraid to."

"Why?"

"Because once I do, it means—" *It's real.*

I reach out for her hand again, and hold on to the way her heart breaks as tears splash down her lashes and onto her round cheeks. "You can tell me." This time, the smoke latches on to me and I can feel the tremble in her hand as she keeps looking forward.

"At night, I wonder if somehow, it'll all go away. This feeling in my stomach that won't let me sleep. I wonder if this baby keeps me awake to snatch away my dreams. At least I had my dreams. At least." Bibi looks at me and her face is a picture of perfection against the blood-orange glow. "Does it get better when you get older? Do these feelings go away?"

"I don't really know. I'm only fifteen." I see how much she's changed in a year. What would another do to her? "But, maybe we can find out together? If you'd like?"

Something like hope blooms in her face. I wish I had my camera to capture the moment and keep it for always. There are so many things I want to ask her as the scene falls away and the stalls around us lengthen and loom taller and taller until there are only splinters of red light weaving through our shoulders and hair.

"You understand the way I feel," she whispers, holding tighter to me. "The way I wish I could dream again."

My throat is too tight. All I can do is nod.

Slowly, she slips away from me and rests her hand on her stomach. She makes the walk back to her stand, but with all the shadows it's hard to know where to go. "I hope it's a boy," she whispers, reaching down to pick up the golden knife. Its blade is stained red when she sets it down. "At least that way he'd have some choice over his destiny." She continues chopping again. The blade cuts so close to her fingers, I want to warn her. "At least it would make my father happy. He deserves to be happy again."

Her eyes dart up for a moment as she chops and her finger slips. The knife comes down, it's going to—

There's a horrible crash behind us.

The knife stills.

Bibi and I whirl around to where the road is. A car has crashed into a stall. There is a figure, facedown in the road, with limbs strewn at horrible, bent angles.

"Oh m—Bibi, no, come back here! Don't go near!" I reach to grasp her, but she's screaming like I've never heard. A wail erupts from her lips as her knife skitters to the ground. The shadowed silhouettes from the other stalls come together and swirl around us, muttering in languages I can't understand. They hover and loom over the crushed body as Bibi throws herself on top of it.

"Dada," she wails as she turns him over. His face is swollen, crushed beyond recognition. "Someone, please help us! Please! Who could do such a thing to my father?" Her hands are shaking as she grips her hair, covers her face. When she looks at me, in the orange light, streaks of blood slash across her face.

I can't move.

I am rooted to the spot, unable to see past Bibi calling for my great-grandfather to wake up. The stalls disappear, one by one, as a hazy pink sunrise begins to loom on the horizon. Little pieces of Sumner come back into view. The deck. The sliding back door. When I look through the glass, I nearly fall backward. Inside Sumner is a ghostly silhouette of my great-grandfather, shadowed and standing, staring at the scene in front of him, staring sadly at his daughter. Standing next to him is Malika. He looks at me, his dark eyes intent before they both become nothing in the morning light.

"Hey!" I call to them. "Don't go, please! How will this help me find you? Why are you showing me this? What does it mean?"

The smoke nips at my ankles and winds itself tight as Bibi pleads, "Please, help me save him. Please, he won't wake up. I never told him. I never—" She starts to dissolve into smoke. I sprint toward her, but she only gets farther away. I run past the hazy sheen of yesterday, but with each step, I am hit with this broken part of her heart that will never become whole. I am hit with the icy rush of loss that steals the air from my lungs, that burns as I fall and trip over the knife and cut my knee.

"You can't leave me, Dada. Not yet," she cries again and again. "Not yet."

I scream Bibi's name as the eternal night only gets lighter. But Bibi is no longer here. Nothing is. I am alone on this deck, and my leg has slipped through the wood.

Pain drums up my legs as I get up. There is a pounding on the front door.

And then: "Sara! Sara, are you in there? Hello?"

I am in a cottony haze as I stumble in the darkness of the house. The banging gets louder and, for a moment, I am afraid of who it could be. I scream when the front door swings open. The spots happen, and I can't breathe. Can't think. Can't count. Can't.

Everything shutters out as a looming shadow stoops in front of me.

Everything goes quiet when it says, "Stay with me."

CHAPTER FIFTEEN

"PLEASE, WAKE UP."

Warm liquid splashes on my face. In the darkness, I see Sam and a half empty Gatorade bottle clenched in his hand. He's thrown his arm over his mouth and nose, too afraid to breathe.

There's an ache in my knee. I cradle my face in my hands. "What's happened?"

"I should be the one asking you that." Sam crouches next to me. I flinch at the harshness in his voice. He clears his throat, softer now. "Why are you here all alone? Covered in—"

He inhales sharply.

Because there's blood. All over my legs, but mainly from my right knee down. I am suddenly hyperaware of the scene that has unfolded.

"It's not what it looks like."

"So you didn't sneak into a house being treated for black mold, lock yourself out on the deck, and literally cut yourself with glass trying to get back inside?" His face is stricken. "Sara, I heard you screaming *why did you leave me* from the road."

"I was screaming?" I whisper softly.

"I couldn't break down the door fast enough to come get you." Sam falls on his butt and pulls me close, envelops my cold body with his arms. "Come on, let's get you out of here."

He throws my arm around his shoulder and hoists me up. We walk slowly, but there is the fog again. It settles into my legs, locking them in place.

"Sara, come on, you've gotta walk."

We are in the kitchen. Everything is still, except, from a distance, there are two angry little eyes peering around the corner staring at Sam's back. And then they are gone.

"Wait . . ." I try to speak. But I'm so tired.

"If you're not gonna walk, then—" Sam hoists me into his arms and rushes out the front door. The shadowed chandelier is spinning. All I can hear are Bibi's wails. What is Malika trying to show me in this memory? What is it the house wants me to know?

How is this going to help me find her?

Sam gently places me in the passenger seat of his car. He jogs to where my bike is and throws it onto his bike holder on the back of the car. Little red footsteps chase his feet, like bloody gumdrops. They move where he moves.

"I think you stepped in something," I hear myself say.

"What are you talking about?" Sam looks at his shoes

and then sighs. "Be honest with me, Sara. How many times have you come here by yourself?"

"Just once." I glance sidelong at the little car light. The sun is still so low, the stars still fight to be seen.

"Stop lying." Again, hurt stabs Sam's face. "You can tell me. Please. Whatever this is, please just trust me with what you need. You haven't been you in so long. All I ask is that you tell me the truth."

"I—" Just say it, Sara. Even though my mouth works to speak, the ache in my chest squeezes, like a threat. The red footsteps pace around Sam. "I will," I finally say, "but not here."

"Okay." Sam's voice is warbled against the fog in my head. My eyes are open, but I see nothing. The car door slams shut. "Okay." Sam blasts the heat, but I can't feel a thing. As he pulls out of the driveway, I want to tell him about the squeezing and the choking and the cold. The cold that has burrowed its way under my skin for a long time now.

The last thing I hear before everything blips out is, "We're never setting foot in this house again. Not at night."

Once, when I was twelve, Sam and I tricked our parents into a double date. It was Sam's idea to do it. At the time, it was the perfect escape.

A night away from the war.

It was mid-January and a fresh layer of snow coated the streets. The neighborhood lights flickered on, and our twin footsteps littered the ground like bread crumbs as we walked down the winding road.

We had nowhere to go and nowhere to be, yet in that magic hour where the world was silent, it felt like we were headed *somewhere*.

Our breaths swelled up around us, wispy and magical, in the way we always imagined the world might one day be. I laughed and readjusted my puffy snow hat when Sam bellowed into the night and quickly tried to swirl his breath around his hands like fire. His boots crunched in the snow when he blew toward my face again, progressively twirling closer until we were both out of breath and giggling and surrounded by our own bubble of magical make-believe.

Snowflakes had clung to his eyelashes as we stood under the shining light. I glanced up at him and I wished for time to keep us this happy.

It's here, in this gauzy moment I find myself, that has Sam saying, "You sure you want to keep looking for magic?"

I push him in the chest, laughing. "Don't tell me you're scared."

"No, it's not that. Just." His wide blue eyes flit away to the shadows lurking outside our bubble. "With magic comes monsters."

I shiver when he shrugs, curl my coat tighter when he rubs his head with an embarrassed laugh. He extends a hand. "We should get back. Our parents will probably be home soon."

I memorize the halo of light around us, try to fight the cold that has settled so deep in my bones. But when I reach for his hand, the little halo around his glowing hair bleeds crimson red, like a dark sun has risen behind him. A shadowed silhouette looms above.

"What's wrong?"

I jerk back because I can't stop the shadow or the snow around his feet as they bleed red, as it snakes its way toward me. When I look back up, I shriek, because instead of Sam, I see Malika. Her tiny face mottled as she screams at me.

I wake up.

Sharp shards of sunshine stab through the darkness of my room. My head is cottony and I moan slightly when I push back my dark burgundy comforter and throw my legs over the edge of my bed. They dangle, unable to touch the floor. The smell of Old Spice body wash clings to my skin.

Wait.

"It's still early. You've got a few hours before people start to wake up." Sam lingers in the doorway, his shoulder pressed against the white-trimmed frame. His face is absolutely wrecked.

"What are you do—"

I look down. I'm wearing bright red flannel pajamas, gifted to Sam a few Christmases back. The smell of Old Spice is coming from me, my still-damp hair. That's when it hits me. I'm not home. I'm in *his* room. And it's daylight. Which means . . .

"Shit." I jump out of his bed, narrowly missing a pair of headphones carelessly thrown on the carpet. I was out all night. Madar is going to murder me. "Shit. Shit. Shit."

"It's barely seven A.M. I wouldn't have let you sleep much later anyway." Sam stands in front of the doorway, his palms out, like I'm a cat he's trying not to spook. "You've got time to rest a bit more."

"Why am I *here*?" I screech. This is beyond inappropriate. I try to move past Sam's shoulder. My knee catches against the doorframe, and it's like someone dumped a bucket of last night's memories over my head. I'm drenched in embarrassment, in the fear as I rode to Sumner, as I screamed, as Sam burst through the door. "Oh, wait."

We lock eyes.

I notice patches of something red in his hair. Is that from when I cut my leg? I look away. His mouth twists downward, ugly and raw. Finally, he shuts his eyes and says in a wobbly voice, "Sara, we need to talk. For real."

"I know last night was weird, but I'm *fine*." My heart thunders in my fingertips, itching to call upon my battle armor and hightail it somewhere so very far away. "Really, I just was spooked by—"

"Stop deflecting," Sam says. "The lies have to stop now, Sara. Last night was not weird, it was *terrifying*." I see it for the first time, the bruises that linger under his eyes. "And I'm not the only one who is scared for you. Your cousins are too. We all are."

"My cousins?" I jerk back toward the stairs. "Why are you even talking to them?"

"You know that the twins and I play flag football on the weekends—anyway that's not the point." He taps his hands on the sides of his elbows. "You haven't been fine, not for a while. And I've sat back and watched and waited for you to get better, but—"

His voice breaks the same moment my heart does.

I take another step back when he reaches out.

"If you could have seen how I found you last night, Sara. It was . . ." His worried gaze burns into mine. "I could never forgive myself if something bad were to happen to you."

"Nothing is going to happen to me, Sam."

"How can I believe you when you won't talk to me?"

"I don't know. You'll just have to."

We're caught in a staring match, waiting to see who backs down. The more I hold his stare, the more I'm drowning in those chilling waves, in the infinite ocean of his eyes. I see a thousand memories of me and him, of that ruined night, and the many nights after that I kept to myself this past year and a half.

"Mattin is right. If not me, then you need to talk to

someone. Let one of us in, Sara," Sam practically begs. "Because when I saw you in that house last night, after those divorce papers came, I knew I should have stayed with you. I knew there was something up with you and your dad. But we've been in such a weird space, I didn't know what to do, if you even wanted me around."

"So why do you keep trying if it's so hard?" I ask. "Maybe the universe is telling you to take the hint and give up."

"Because contrary to what you believe, you don't need to make a martyr of yourself. You don't need to keep punishing yourself for yesterday or the past year—for any of it," he says. "And I will never stop trying to make you see that."

"I am not punishing myself," I say quietly.

"Then tell me I'm wrong, tell me you're not pushing me away because I know what you did that night, tell me that's not the reason why our friendship is dying right now."

There's a loaded silence.

Something snaps somewhere deep inside me.

Sam continues on. "And instead of dealing with what you're feeling, you've become obsessed with that creepy-as-hell house and chasing a freaking ghost. For what?"

"For answers," I snap back. "For the truth. My family deserves to know what happened to their sister!"

"Says who?" Sam says in exasperation. "Why are you the one who gets to decide that? Have you thought that maybe it isn't your story to tell? That you should respect the choice your grandparents made? Or, and here's a wild thought, maybe there *is* no missing daughter."

"Of course there is." Sam's words feel like a slap in the face. "You saw her yourself. You drove all the way out to Queens to confirm it. Remember?"

"Oh, I remember. I wasn't going to mention this right now, but since you brought it up, I might as well air it all out." Sam takes a deep breath. "After you left me stranded to deal with your dad and the police, I did my own searching. I searched every online record for a Malika Amani. I even searched your grandma's maiden name. I checked out the records of the old owners at that time. And I found *nothing*. Absolutely nothing to show that she ever existed. And I think that maybe . . ."

"That maybe what?"

"You're chasing someone who, I'm sorry to say this, isn't what you thought. And after last night, I think that no one should *ever* go back inside that place." He fixes his gaze somewhere down the hall. The little footsteps are back, leaving their bloody marks on Sam's floor. They walk quickly from Sam until they stop right in front of me.

"*You're* the one who saw her in the picture," I say shakily. "*You're* the one who dreamed up this plan with me."

"I'm not denying that. I did, but now, I'm beginning

to think this has less to do with a missing daughter and more to do with that house," he mutters, still looking away. "It's doing something to you. Can't you see it?"

"Oh, so now it's the house? Or was it my self-punishing guilt that's changed me? You seem to be changing your story now." I refuse to use sticky words to placate Sam. He doesn't understand that the truth—my truth—is that I'm not going to let go of where Malika wants to take me.

I *will* find her, and it will fix everything. This is the wrong I must make right. It's the good karma I need to put into the universe to fix everything else that went wrong.

"I'm not trying to fight with you, Sara." Sam rubs his temples with his hands. "I just wish you'd hear me out."

"And I wish you'd hear me out, so here's some advice, Sam. Don't follow me again if you don't like where I lead you." I walk stiffly past Sam, avoiding the red footsteps, even as they trail behind me and match my stride, step by step, out the door.

I try to ignore the shiver that settles in, but no matter how many times I try to count, try to blow on my frozen fingers, the cold never leaves. And if I can't make what happened to Malika right, I fear it never will.

CHAPTER SIXTEEN

I DON'T SLEEP WELL IN THE NIGHTS THAT FOLLOW.

There is always smoke following my every step.

A shadowy figure lingers by my grandmother's bedroom, watching her through opaque glasses as she sleeps.

Little red footsteps gleam in circles around the porchlight of Sam's front door.

Our pool glimmers dark with Ayesha's reflection as she braids strands of red smoke into her hair.

My dreams, relentlessly, take me to the gates of Sumner, past the mirrored walls, down into the dark basement, staring at a shadow curled up on the couch that I am too afraid to identify.

So I stay awake and lie on my roof. Count the stars and wait for dawn and pray the cold can't reach me here.

CHAPTER SEVENTEEN

IT IS TRADITION THAT ON THE THIRD SUNDAY OF every month, my khala Firoza hosts afternoon tea in her backyard. I'm holding my grandma's hand as we slowly shuffle down the neighborhood with Madar and Irina in tow behind us.

"Can't I stay home?" I beg Madar for the fourth time on our five-minute trek. "I can barely keep my eyes open." I try to blink away the shadows that twist around our feet and the hulking smoky figure that trails behind us, always watching.

"Well, if you weren't up all night watching Netflix, maybe you wouldn't be so tired, hm?" There are bundles of Tupperware in Madar's arms. Peace offerings for Madar's mercurial moods these days. "Thank god Sumner has gotten back on track. Work there a few days and your sleep schedule will work itself out."

"Sounds great," I mutter under my breath.

Bibi walks steadily forward, with her wispy hair pulled

elegantly into a bun. The edges of her sheer black scarf pool behind her shoulders. She's unusually quiet as we walk. I want to ask her about what happened to her father.

If she too can feel the shadow of his presence following her.

If she thinks we are all destined to lose our fathers too soon.

A slew of white luxury cars are parked haphazardly in my khala Firoza's driveway. The music is blasting, even from here. Madar's mouth quirks up in a smile as she hustles into the backyard.

"Come on." She grips Bibi's other hand. "We're missing the fun."

I let go of Bibi's hand and watch the three of them plow on ahead. Ever since she was served those divorce papers, she's thrown herself wholeheartedly into *having fun*.

We still haven't actually talked about what happened.

I doubt we ever will.

My sneakers squish in the grass as I enter the backyard. There's laughter and kisses and clinking of glasses. Khala Firoza, with her perfectly swept-up hair, settles the contents of Madar's Tupperware into glass serving dishes. Khala Farzana, Gulnoor, Maluda, and Zenat crowd around the deck on the second floor. Amena and Ayesha are lounging in a porch swing under the deck. The pool sparkles and sloshes with waves of sun-kissed kids treading ruby-red water.

That can't be right. I blink and rub my eyes, but the water remains dark.

Ayesha waves when she sees me.

Maybe it's a sign, that's all. A film settles over my thoughts as I glance up to where the majority of my khalas are. Maybe Malika is just giving me a push to ask the right questions this time, and it will all go away.

"One sec," I call out, and make my way up the stairs.

In true khala fashion, Khala Farzana thwacks my shoulder. "You should really stand up tall. Posture is everything, you know." The teakettle from inside the kitchen shrieks and she tsks while hurrying to stop it. "And stop scrunching your face like that." She sighs dramatically as Madar leans in the sliding doorway. "Youth is truly wasted on the young."

Madar laughs while helping Khala Mojgan bring out bowls of pistachios and dried apricots.

Don't lose your temper, I chant as I cross my arms inside the vast tent of my hoodie. *Don't freak out over the fact that our entire family origin story is based on lies.* I let out a long breath. Okay. I can do this.

Khala Afsoon's palm plops on my forehead. "You feeling okay? You're so pale. Ghostly, even." I know this is khala code for *you-look-like-poo-poo*. I swat her hand away from my sweat-soaked hairline.

"Here, sit, sit." She steers me to the metal deck chairs and forces a cup of steaming lemon water in my hands.

"If you don't drink it, your insides will only continue to breed spores of bacteria—"

"Thank you, khala jan, for that visual." I gulp the bitter liquid for courage. It's now or never. "So . . . I was wondering something." Everyone continues to bustle about, laughing and fussing over frown lines and muttering over the never-ending wedding season gossip.

I knuckle the mug and try my luck inside. Madar, Khala Farzana, and Khala Gulnoor are settled around the quartz kitchen island. Madar's phone is buzzing off the hook—probably Erik calling with a housing crisis—but uncharacteristically, she switches her phone to silent. I watch as she frets over the chip in her manicure.

"Do you need something?" Khala Gulnoor looks sidelong at me.

"Yes." I fuss over my bracelet. I don't know how to say it. How to say that I've lately been staying awake to avoid dreaming horrible dreams. Of tragedy following our family members, and how we're cursed to lose our loved ones too soon, whether it be a father, or a grandmother, or maybe even a daughter. As I stare into the warm, concerned eyes of my aunts, I decide I need to ask. "I wanted to know about Baba Kalan. For my project."

"My grandfather?" Khala Farzana stirs a pot of rice on the stove. Ayesha slips in through the sliding glass door. Dark, wispy smoke trails through with her.

"How did he die?"

The entire room stiffens. Madar nearly chokes on a pistachio. "Sara, that's not an appropriate question to ask."

"*How did he die?*" I ask again.

The smoke thickens and whirls around their ankles, but no one sees a thing.

Khala Farzana and Khala Gulnoor share a look and, quietly, Khala Gulnoor mutters to Ayesha, "Shut the door please. Firoza jan hates when we discuss this. It's . . . a very sensitive topic."

Ayesha's eyes widen as she shuts the door and scoots next to me. "Am I going to regret coming up to save you from the khalas?" she whispers.

Khala Gulnoor smooths the wayward curls around her ears and gestures for Ayesha and me to sit by the island. "What would you like to know, Sara jan?"

Her face swims in front of me, and I have to blink away the shadows that grow around her. To be honest, I'm a little bit shocked that they're not doing their usual hedging and skirting around it. Looking at my aunt, it isn't until this moment that I realize why I need to ask. "We never talk about him. No stories, nothing. Right, Ayesha?"

Her brows knit together as she thinks. She looks at me and nods. "I don't think we've ever talked about Grandma's dad?" Which is odd because if there's one thing my family loves to do, it's tell stories about the people we descend from.

"Like I said, it's a sensitive topic for your grandmother and for me too." Khala Farzana swallows and gently takes hold of my hand. "You see, we never knew our grandfather, your bibi jan's father, not like you knew yours. He left this world long before any of us were born. All the stories I know are from my elders. And the story you want to know is a sad one."

"Why is it sad?"

"If we tell you, you both have to promise this stays in this very room. Understood?" Khala Gulnoor levels us with her stare. "I mean it. Not a single person."

Ayesha and I nod.

"Our grandfather was the kindest man you could have ever met. He came from a lineage of scholars and poets, but he was a businessman. He sold a little of everything—dried fruits, books, and rugs. Things that were essential. Items people needed. He had a way about him, how he always led with kindness, that made him a favorite among the people of Mazar-i-Sharif. In a short span of time, he became powerful and influential. His business grew to be very successful. He knew all the right people. His reputation is what attracted our father's family. It was no surprise that our father's family would ask for our mother's hand in marriage."

"Seems like a fairy tale," Ayesha says.

"It was and in a matter of weeks, our mother was sent to start her new life with our father."

If this was any other time, I would have lost myself in the romance of it all. It does sound beautiful, but it feels like an incomplete truth. Not quite a lie, but a glossed-over version to make this story sound like a happily ever after.

"Okay, and then?" Ayesha is biting at her cuticles, and I swear for a second I see the smoke creep its way up her forearm. Only, I blink and it's gone.

"My grandfather's kindness was both a blessing and a curse. While influence can make you powerful, it can also make you a target. There was a span of years where my grandfather's goods were blocked from entering the country. Without products, money was tight, and soon my grandfather started to accumulate debt. He kept going, though. He had wives to take care of, children to feed. But as the difficulties grew, the more it took a toll on his heart, his reputation." Khala Gulnoor looks past the glass doors to Bibi jan sitting comfortably on a swing chair on the deck, a heavy blanket wrapped around her. "Because of that, there was a lot of speculation about his death, about the political rivals that were afraid of his kindness, his influence. In the end, he was fatally struck by a car. Grandma saw the whole thing happen."

Ayesha gasps. "Was it an accident or . . ."

"Something planned by those who felt threatened by him?" Khala Gulnoor sighs. "I don't know, but what I would give to be able to ask him what happened in those days. There are rumors some political figures were afraid of my grandfather's popularity. Those people spread horrible rumors about him . . . rumors that he walked in front of the car himself."

"Why would he do that?" I stand abruptly. My stool squeals uncomfortably. The shadows have curled and warped around the kitchen. In the corner is the dark reflection of Baba Kalan, face shadowed, staring silently at me, at my aunts, at my mother. I settle my gaze on him. *Did you leave her, or did someone take you? What are you trying to tell me?*

My great-grandfather stays silent. A lone tear trails down his cheek.

"Hey, hey. Take a breath. It's okay." Ayesha rubs my shaking back as another three sets of worried eyes stay glued on me. "Maybe you need some air, yeah?"

"No." I shrug her hand away and rub my eyes. "I need to know exactly what happened."

"No one here is going to have that answer for you," Madar starts. "But what we're not going to do is give those ugly rumors power. If he could, he would have stayed with his family forever. He would never leave us like that."

"You don't know that for sure!" My hands are shaking as I pace. "What if the only legacy we really have is leaving each other behind, then—" *What's stopping it from happening to me? From what happened to Malika? From what happened to Bibi?*

The ugly doubt rears its head as I think a traitorous question: Could my grandmother have left her behind?

Is that what the memory is supposed to tell me? Is that the connection?

There's a knock on the glass door. Khala Mojgan raises a brow and gestures at all of us.

"I know it's upsetting, janem." Khala Gulnoor waves dismissively at Khala Mojgan with a smile. "A daughter should never have to see her father leave this world so young. It was so sudden, so unexplainable. And we didn't want the moment of his death to overshadow the great legacy of his life. It's why your grandmother doesn't speak about it. Maybe that was our mistake. Maybe we should have talked about him more when my mother still remembered."

"That doesn't bother you at all?"

"Why would it bother me?" Khala Gulnoor blinks in confusion. "It happened long before I was born. It didn't happen to me."

"But it did. It happened to your mother, who buried it, and then taught you to bury whatever felt hard, just like how *you're* teaching *me*." I am too overwhelmed by how they can't see what I see. "Horrible, painful things keep happening to us, but burying the bad feeling doesn't mean it's gone. It's warped us, warped the way we deal with grief, with everything—"

"Ayesha, I think you should take Sara for a walk out back." Madar's tired voice cuts off my rant. She raises a finger in warning, and looks at me. "If you can't speak to us calmly, then you need to go cool down."

"Fine by me." I don't wait for Ayesha to follow. I slide open the door and race down the stairs of the deck, ignoring the shadowy figure of Baba Kalan swinging next to Bibi, and stalk past the pool and down the stone steps so I'm on the lower level of my aunt's backyard. Green grass squishes under my sneakers.

"Hey! Wait up." Ayesha is running, her hair flying behind her as she gasps to keep up. "You know I hate exercise. You should be flattered that I'd sweat for you." She hunches over on her knees before standing tall and taking a deep breath. "Want to explain that freak-out back there?"

"No."

"Well, as I recall, you did promise you'd tell me. You should know that I consider you a woman of your word, so." She clasps her hands on my shoulders and steers me toward the trampoline.

"Ayesha, stop it. I am not going on that thing."

"Too bad. Until you loosen up and tell me what's bugging you, you don't really have a choice." I really don't know where Ayesha managed to get the strength, but she gives me one last push and I tumble onto the edge of the trampoline. She hops up and pulls my upper body up until we are both on our backs on the jiggly surface.

"I hate you." I cross my arms when Ayesha gets up and jumps. "I truly, truly—" She does a double jump and I go flying up with a shriek. "—HAAATE YOU!"

"That's right, let it out!" Ayesha laughs as she jumps

higher, the dark shadows wrap around her arms, causing her to slip. "Tell me how you reaallly feeeel, cousin."

"I am"—I fall face-first on another bounce—"going to!" I finally find my footing and reach Ayesha, suddenly very afraid for her as she goes tumbling down. "STOP IT!" I leap and catch her right before she rolls off the trampoline. We both go down and roll and bounce back into the center.

Ayesha manages to tickle me right under my ribs, oblivious to the shadows warping around her. Malika's angry face flashes again. I scream, but then Ayesha hits a particularly ticklish spot, and against my will, my face cracks into a huge grin, and I laugh and laugh and laugh through gasping breaths. My glasses go flying.

"FINALLY, A SMILE." Ayesha is breathless and whoops her arms in victory as she rolls off me to lie on her back, trying to catch her breath. Her tinkling laugh draws me away from the dark.

One, two, three . . .

I'm shrieking as Mattin, Aman, Amena, Ayesha, and I pelt each other with water balloons on my fourth birthday. Padar clutches his stomach in laughter, and Madar religiously records us on her phone.

Four, five, six . . .

Ayesha and I are on her bed, ripping up the latest birthday party invitation after our parents told us we couldn't go. Ayesha pirouettes in her room, assuring me it *isn't a big deal* and *she's not missing anything*. I nod with her and let her spin in circles, pretending not to feel like caged birds just watching the world go by.

"There you go again." Ayesha rolls on her side and props her head up with her elbow. She pokes my forehead. "Always thinking away in there."

I sigh and squint at the blinding sun peeking through the trees. The shadows are nowhere to be found. "I know. I'm sorry, I'm just . . . wrapped up in this family history thing. It's messing with me."

"I get that." Ayesha sits up and twists her hair into a messy bun. She hands me my glasses. "It's heavy stuff, so maybe now is a good time to make good on your promise and let me shoulder some of that weight with you. Besides, what's the rush? It's not like the past is going anywhere, right?"

"I can't slow down now. I said I'd finish by Eid-al-Adha. I promised." I keep looking up, keep counting my beads. I haven't been able to find Malika, but I'm sure the memories she's been showing me are all connected. If I can figure it out, figure out *why* Bibi left her, find where it all went wrong—

"Look, Sara. I get what you're going through, I really do. And I know that with our huge family, it's easy to feel like a drop in an ocean of people. Which is why we've got to stick together. You said it yourself, our moms bury everything, but that doesn't mean we have to do the same thing, you know?"

I sit silent.

She takes my silence as encouragement. "Plus, we're all we've got. Americans don't get us. And our parents seem to be living in their own realities." Ayesha eyes my bracelet. "I need to let you know that *I'm* here. I'm never leaving you. Never."

I hate it when she's right.

"I did say *I promise*, didn't I?" I mutter under my breath.

"You sure did," she chirps brightly. "So why don't you lean on your dear old cousin Ayesha and seek out her wisdom and support."

"Okay. So. The question about Baba Kalan wasn't random." I give Ayesha a measured look. "I was testing our aunts because I . . ." I swallow. "I *saw* what happened to him . . ." Shit, how do I say what I saw. ". . . in a vision."

"A vision?" Ayesha looks at me thoughtfully.

"It's the best way I can explain it," I say uncomfortably. "But ever since it came to me, I can't stop . . . seeing him."

"Is that why you get quiet sometimes?" There's no judgment in Ayesha's tone. Just curiosity. "Because you're seeing . . . him?"

"That. And other things." Little alarm bells are ringing when I see Ayesha turn what I said in her head. I know how it sounds. My face is burning in embarrassment, but there's no going back now. "I know it sounds—"

"Thank you for telling me." Ayesha holds on to my hands and squeezes. "I know that must have been hard."

I nod.

"Will you tell me the next time you have another one?" she asks. "If you want, maybe I could help you understand them?"

"That would be—" The cold seeps in, violently, just as a red haze shines against Ayesha's shoulders. A trickle of blood trails down one of her nostrils. "Ayesha, you're bleeding."

"Oh my god." Ayesha jerks back, her hands go straight to her nose. We wobble on the trampoline. "It's going to ruin my shirt." She rolls off the trampoline and runs back toward the pool.

I am rooted to the spot, breathing hard. What just happened?

Up above me, on the deck, Bibi jan swings. Baba Kalan's glasses glint against the sun in warning, as if to say *Leave the present out of the past.*

"Leave them alone." I stare at him in challenge, and then I blink and blink and blink, but he never disappears, never stops swinging, never stops watching.

I am suddenly very afraid of what will happen if I fail to solve Sumner's message.

CHAPTER EIGHTEEN

THERE ONCE WAS, AND THERE ONCE WAS NOT A list of possessions:

A handmade Persian rug;

A pink-and-gold china tea set;

An emerald ring;

A carefully tucked-away prayer rug.

I feel the stars peeking through the windows as I circle each floor of Sumner like a ritual, throwing each item like an offering in exchange for the missing link of what happened to Malika.

I pace the basement, the main floor, the second floor, the deck, until I find a new part of the house to set up my offering.

Each item, delicately placed, swirls in fragile smoke until a new hazy scene breathes life into this house of yesterday.

Bibi, at fourteen, rolling up her father's rug as she and Baba jan pack up his belongings. They move to Kabul and never look back.

Bibi, at sixteen, clinking a delicate teacup with her first daughter, Khala Farzana.

Bibi, at twenty, in the middle of the night, pulling out her mother's ring, wishing for her words of comfort.

Bibi, at twenty-three, praying with cupped hands, bargaining with God to take the ache out of her chest, to smother her never-dying childhood dreams. Her four daughters' distant cries lying forgotten as she locks herself in her room.

Memories, full and bright, fill Sumner. Bibi's life plays in stolen moments I've thrown to the house, unraveling the early image of the Amani family. And yet, there is still nothing about *her*.

The more items I feed to the house, the more I am afraid there will be no more left to find.

And if I run out of Bibi's past, then where does that leave me and the shadows that refuse to let go?

CHAPTER NINETEEN

MY HEAD IS POUNDING AS I TRY NOT TO FALL asleep on the job.

"Pull yourself together," I mutter while leaning back on a faded pink vanity in the upstairs master bath of Sumner. The construction crew chatters and laughs through the fuzz of a stereo downstairs. My head droops and I shiver into my hoodie. It's harder to stay awake, to keep the frost out of my numb fingers and toes.

My replacement phone (purchased from Costco as an early Eid gift from Madar) buzzes nonstop in my front pocket.

Padar: Don't forget, 4th of July is my turn
Padar: Dress nice
Padar: It's important

The mystery woman takes precious real estate in my thoughts again and I groan while I sprawl out dramatically on the dated tiled floor of this bathroom. The popcorn ceiling stares back at me. There are waves and waves of conversations that play out in my head. Random scenarios where I actually text Padar back, where I hold Padar accountable for the hurt he's caused—not only to Madar, but to me.

The thing is, I can control the conversations in my head. It's real life that's the problem.

There's rustling as a trash can gets knocked over. Sam grumbles when he sees me. I immediately sit up and nearly pass out from the head rush.

"I didn't realize you were working in here." He scans the master bedroom and picks up a toolbox. "Was summoned for this. Then I'll be out of your hair."

"It's okay, I was just taking a break." I stall for an excuse, slightly embarrassed I was caught slacking. Sam is drenched in sweat from the July heat. He bunches his shirt and uses it to wipe his face. "Do you need help carrying all that, 'cause I could—"

"We both know that helping me is the last thing you want to do," he responds. "So unless you're ready to do some real talking, there's nothing you can do for me right now."

I don't like the way he is looking at me. It's the same look Madar would give Padar whenever their dance pushed them apart.

"Then I guess you can just move along."

He hesitates, chews on the bottom of his lip. There's a

war going on in his head too. I hate that I know that. The thing about Sam is, he always breaks.

"Why do you keep doing this, Sara?" he finally asks.

"Doing what?"

"This." He gestures between us. "This back-and-forth dance we have going on. One second we're joking in my kitchen, and the next you're freaking out at me for finding you in this house, covered in blood in the middle of the night.

"And after that, to top it all off, you ghost me. Again. But like an idiot, I gave you space, hoping you'd stop what you're doing, stop coming to this house every night. You know I see you slip out on your bike, but still, *still* you pretend that nothing is wrong. That's not what I deserve, Sara, and you know that. So why can't you just be honest and tell me what the hell is going on?"

He's furious. Sam is never furious. I am alarmed at the way his words make me feel, all twisted and bent up and misunderstood. Even more alarming is what he left unspoken, but I've gotten good at reading between the lines, seeing the glossing over. I realize that he wants to say *I need you* and *don't you need me too*?

It almost slips right out of my mouth, the whole truth: I am afraid to need him in that way.

The words stick in my throat when I see the shadows that dance behind Sam. The red aura that seeps slowly from the master bedroom, reaching for his ankles. The little footsteps that run in circles around him. The darkened silhouette of Baba Kalan stands in the corner, shaking his head. Suddenly I am very afraid for an entirely different reason.

"You're right."

"I'm—what?" Sam deflates a bit in shock.

"I'm a jerk." Red haloes Sam's glowing hair. The ugly bent-up feeling is pounding relentlessly in my chest.

"And?"

"And what?" My eyes dart to the floor. The tiled walls shrink in on me, and I can feel the weight of something else in here with us. "I can't change how I am."

"So that's your excuse?" Sam scoffs. He waves his hands. "You say that, and you don't have the courage to even look me in the face?"

I am tense when a breath dances across my neck just as Sam stands up.

The red recedes as he takes a step back.

"Can you please just look at me?" He waits for me to look up. I don't. "Okay. Message received, captain." He heads out of the bedroom, the toolbox banging against his knee. I wince at the sound, but it isn't until I hear his stomps down the stairs that I finally let out a breath. The presence is still looming, but it's relaxed.

My phone is buzzing again. Padar's name pops up. I send him straight to voicemail.

"Keep him out of it." I don't know who I think I'm

talking to, if there's even someone or something that's listening, but I say it anyway. Just in case. "He won't be a problem anymore, I promise. Just leave him alone."

Then I get back to work.

⌁

It's like I blink, and suddenly it's the Fourth of July.

I'm in a daze at my Fariba amma's house. My aunt is currently helping my dad string up lights in her small backyard. Her freshly manicured lawn is coated with red, white, and blue. Balloons cheerfully wave in the breeze. The air reeks of salt water and car exhaust.

I am sitting on the grass, staring out at the busy parkway and Little Neck Bay, staying as far away as possible from the tinkling of music coming through the expensive Sonos speaker system. My fingers wind around my bracelet in a desperate rhythm to stop the chill that's spread to my elbows.

For whatever reason, Padar has chosen to make this year's Fourth of July a formal affair.

"It's going to be a night we won't forget." Padar had said when he kissed the top of my head this afternoon. His energy was palpable. There was pure joy literally radiating off his body. I was (and still am) 100 percent weirded out.

"Why?" I asked when he shooed me away to get ready.

A grand smile was the only hint he gave.

I squint at my reflection in my phone screen. Staring back, I don't recognize myself. It's not because of the makeup and contact lenses. Or how I've set my hair in long dark waves against my blue-and-white cocktail dress.

It's because I can't see myself at all. Instead, I see little shadows of Malika and Bibi, of Baba Kalan and Bibi Kalan and Khala Farzana. Little shadows that only have led to more questions and one simple request: to go back to Sumner.

It is like a drum in my head that I can't turn off at night. *Go back, go back, go back.*

I sigh. Not tonight. I stand shakily on my feet. Tonight, I need to be here. I need to know just how far Padar has spun off course. And because I don't want Ayesha to worry, I plaster a fake smile on my face, even though I can't remember what joy feels like. I snap a picture and pass the time in my cousin group chat.

Sara: Rahmat family 7/4 pics incoming
Mattin: Looks fancy
Amena: Is that my dress?
Ayesha: thumbs up
Aman: hahahaha someone photo bombed you

"Are my eyes playing tricks on me?" My cousin Eman glides in, arms linked with Maha. "Or am I seeing a ghost?"

"Given her lack of a tan and that we're halfway through summer, seems pretty plausible to me." Maha giggles while wrapping me in a hug. My arms could wrap twice around her slender frame. Though I'm not what your average American would consider tall, the girls on my father's side of my family are what one would call petite, code for very, *very* short.

"I've been at my mom's." I shrug. "You know how it is."

Eman's inviting face never falters, but I notice the flicker of uncertainty in her eyes. "Well, I'm glad you're here now. We miss you around here."

"Yeah, and maybe after the news tonight, there'll be more of an excuse to see you more often."

Under the glow of string lights cast through the canopies of planted trees, I stop. "What news?"

Eman and Maha share a confused glance.

"You do know why we're here, right?" Eman asks.

"It's the Fourth."

Eman takes a step closer to me. "You seriously don't know?" she whispers in my ear.

"Obviously not." I give her my best deadpan stare. "What do you know that I don't?"

"I—"

Loud bangs erupt behind us. Padar's eldest brother has ignited a series of small celebratory fireworks. The entire Rahmat family—all eight of them—whoop and clap as the music is cranked up and blares through the entire house. Eman and I cringe as they all form two lines with sparklers lit at the backyard entrance. Their arms are extended in an arch.

"What is going on—" My dad's sparse family has always felt stark compared to my mother's sprawling clan, but they do share the same tight-lipped secrecy. In this moment, they feel like an army stacked against me.

My aunt's trilling echoes against the music. It's a cacophony of sound as two people emerge from the backyard entrance—Padar and a woman dressed in a long blue gown.

Everything goes quiet when I see Padar's hand clasped in hers. The world tilts, and it's the kiss on her cheek that brings everything crashing back in—sound and color and all.

My fingers grasp on to my bracelet, whirring round and round. I try to catch my breath, try not to pass out. I hold on to the count.

One, two, three . . .

It's Madar, Padar, and me, ready to take off on our flight to France. Madar leans into Padar's shoulder, their hands intertwined. He kisses her hair. We are happy.

Four, five, six . . .

It's Madar and me, standing in Sumner. Her shrieks as she sinks onto her knees, letting the divorce papers spill from her hands. She is staring at the wedding band she has yet to take off.

Seven, eight—

"No," I whisper as I sink to the ground, suddenly losing

all feeling in my legs. All memories of who my family used to be shatters mercilessly in front of me. "No, this wasn't how it was supposed to be." Papers could always be burned, words could always be thrown away, forgotten, forgiven. But this?

"Sara!" Maha's and Eman's concerned shouts float somewhere nearby. I can barely feel them as they pull me up. I can barely see anything at all.

As my eyes fill with tears and Padar's shining face emerges from the blur with his hand outstretched for me to come join them, I know. I rip my arms away from my cousins' grips and glare at Padar's smiling face.

I send an S.O.S. text to the cousin group chat. No amount of counting can keep me here.

CHAPTER TWENTY

ONCE THERE WAS AND ONCE THERE WAS NOT A boy and a girl. Separated by time and war and an ocean. But despite the odds, they found each other, in a little suburb in Long Island. Destiny came for them in the form of a daughter.

They were meant to live happily, three together. They were meant to ride into their American Dream, and start a new life away from hardship and fighting. But maybe the daughter was a fool to believe in peace and destiny, when war was always looming over them. Always.

My Fariba amma hustles toward me and hoists me up. "Come now, there is no need to cause a scene," she says sweetly as she smooths my hair out of my eyes.

Her words detonate something inside me. I can feel my battle armor creaking from its slumber. It clinks into place and unleashes a well of dormant rage.

"Someone should," I shout. Someone has cranked the music even louder. Classic. I throw my aunt's hand off me. There are resounding gasps from Eman and Maha.

Eman, the eldest cousin in our tiny family, falls into her role of damage control.

"I understand how you feel, but can we just get through this night? We can talk about it later." She's radiating warmth, and she nudges my shoulder as the rest of my family embraces this new woman. Threads of *congratulations* and *so lovely to finally meet you* make me want to vomit.

"Is that supposed to be a joke? What's there to talk about?" I shout, throwing my hands in the air. "When? When I'm forty? Did we not grow up in the same family?" A laugh bubbles through my lips, and I can see uncertainty in Eman's posture.

"*Biz qitaylig na'aram bolmasin bizdan,*" Maha says to Eman.

"*Khai salom aytip kegan qitaylig,*" Eman shoots back.

It is here, in this moment, that I feel the wall of separation between my father's side and me. Even though we are all mixed—not all Uzbek, but also not all Afghan—it's obvious my mother's language and customs dominated our household. Maha and Eman know this. They know I can barely manage a few words in Uzbek, a language that has dissolved from my DNA, but that doesn't stop them from the language switch.

Looking up into their perfect faces, and perfect reactions, and perfect well-raised calmness, I feel like a fish out of water.

"I don't belong here." I stare at the group of people who feel more like strangers than blood. "I don't—" My grasp is slipping on my anger, and I try to hold on to anything to keep the flame burning.

"Fariba apa, Maha jon, Eman jon, *bize tana qoyasala-rma.*" Padar's cool voice. "*Gapim bor qizimga.*"

The women nod and fall away, leaving Padar and me in the eye of the hurricane.

"You know I don't like it when you language switch on me," I mutter as I scroll through my phone. I can't bring myself to look at him. "How is this supposed to be any better?"

"Sara, you knew there was someone new in my life. I have been trying to explain to you, but you won't pick up my calls, and you know how your mother is about reading texts. This isn't a big surprise, I thought you understood from our talk." Padar sighs again in exasperation. "At least say hello to her. I didn't raise you to act this way."

My cousin group chat glows like a beacon on this shitty night.

Aman: Your chariot arrives to whisk you out of hell

"Actually," I say, "this is exactly how you raised me to behave. Rashly and without warning."

⸎

"Who are you and what have you done with our cousin?" Mattin hollers from the driver's seat when I slink into the middle row of Khala Nazaneen's SUV. "I guess Uzbeks really know how to party."

"Ha ha," I mutter while throwing off my heels. Amena casually hands me a pair of white sneakers before tying her hair up in a ponytail.

"Sooo, where to?" Aman twists from the front passenger seat and wiggles his eyebrows at me. There's a glint of knowing in his eyes.

"Anywhere that isn't here." We peel out of my aunt's driveway just as Eman and Maha emerge, searching for me.

I let the sound of my cousin's chatter take me away from the pent-up feeling that is choking me. I drift with each bump of the road somewhere else, back to when I could feel something other than the haunting cold that has taken hold of my arms and legs, from the chill that is seeping closer still to my heart.

Fireworks shimmer faintly in the tinted windows. With my forehead pressed against the glass, I wonder if whatever is broken inside me will pass. Or, if I've learned anything from Bibi's memories, that this is just another moment I'll have to bury. Forever.

Mattin parks, and I stiffen when I glance at the worn, familiar sign of Centerport Boathouse and Marina. I tuck my hair behind my ears.

"What are we doing here?" I glance at Ayesha. She gives away nothing but a secret smile.

"Come on." She reaches over me and opens the door, nearly pushing me out of the car and into the summer air. "We don't want to miss the fireworks."

Everyone shuffles out, slamming their doors.

"Mattin, right here, the lighting is perfect." Amena tosses her phone at Mattin as she hops up on the wooden fence overlooking the marina. There are dozens of flash-lights and phone lights dotting the background behind her. Little pedal boats inch out as people chatter with snacks and light-up necklaces and sunglasses.

I pause on the rocky trail to take it all in.

I've always wanted to come back to do this, ever since I can remember.

This marina.

The lights.

The water lapping at our pedal boat's edge.

Madar and Padar's tinkling laughter as they laid me in their laps. The rocking of water lulling me asleep under the twinkle of stars. And then the magic began.

Colors shot across the sky in explosions that felt like they covered the whole wide world.

The warmth of us filled my very soul.

My earliest memory.

Ayesha catches up next to me. She leans against my side, entwining her arms with mine.

"Hey," she says softly. "We'll get through this, okay?"

"If you say so," I mutter.

"You will. I will. Amena will." Ayesha holds on tight to me. "I promise." She winks and laughs when Aman stumbles in.

"Feels like we're not on Long Island anymore, right?" he laughs and motions to the line. "Let's get a spot before they run out of boats." He zips on down the trail, slipping and sliding when the rocks turn into prickly sand.

"Your mom's gonna kill you for messing up those shoes!" Ayesha laughs. "Hard to believe he's in all honors classes, right?"

"Can recite all the past U.S. presidents backward, but can't dance a basic attan." I shrug as we take our place in line. "I'll never forget his face-plant at Sana's wedding."

"Hey, that was *one* time," Aman defends himself. "It wasn't my fault Mattin let go of his handkerchief."

"No one else slipped on it," Ayesha teases through laughs.

"Whatever." Aman's face turns red as he smooths his hair back. "I think I'm reconsidering my pedal boat partner. Where's Mattin? Bro, save me!"

"Too bad he's still taking pictures of Amena." Ayesha pushes Aman's hair back in front of his face. He rolls

his eyes horribly. "You're stuck with me on this ride."
Ayesha jumps into her side of the boat and pats the seat
next to her for Aman. "Let's goooo."

"Wait." I notice all the boats are two seaters. "I can't
go by myself."

Aman snorts. "Who said you'd be riding by yourself?"
He kicks off the dock and waves conspiratorially at me.
Ayesha hasn't stopped smiling.

"Hey!" I jump in the next empty boat and point at
them. "Some friends you are!"

"Look behind you!" Ayesha cups her hands over her
mouth as Aman pedals away. "We're too far away for
you to kill us now! Get over yourself and make up so you
can be friends again."

Someone clears their throat behind me.

I look up at the dock.

It's Sam.

"Hey, neighbor," he says in a low voice.

"Hey."

Sam jumps in without another word. The hem of my
dress snags on the edge of the boat as Sam pushes off and
slowly pedals away from land.

The awkwardness from our last conversation feels like
a third person in the boat.

I turn away from him. "Must you torment me, neighbor?" I watch the other dozens of boats milling around.
Lights reflect every which way, and I am even more upset
at how breathtaking the scene is.

How can this place still be so beautiful when I feel so low?

Minutes pass, and I absentmindedly find myself counting the seconds until Sam breaks.

Because isn't that the trick between us? I want to say when five minutes turns to ten of absolute silence. *Laugh. Fight. Repeat. Laugh. Fight. Repeat.*

But why should it be? a small voice whispers as I hold myself tighter.

We stop moving. Sam stops pedaling. I can feel the weight of his stare, and the weight of something new—his resolve. I keep looking out into the dark water. The stars ripple back at me. I realize I'm holding my breath, waiting for the telltale shadows to appear, but they don't.

"I can play this game all night, if that's what you want." The boat shakes, and Sam leans back so he's got his hands behind his head as he looks up (so I imagine—it's not like I'm looking at him from the corner of my eye). His feet prop up against the edge of the boat.

I can't help it. I look, and something gaping unfurls in my chest.

Our eyes catch each other for a nanosecond. *Ah, shit.*

For the first time, I break.

"I was wondering how they knew to come here." I lean over the side of the boat until my fingers glide along the dark reflections of Madar and Padar and me. I was three then.

Reality blurs into memory as we float gently in the water. This moment has been locked tightly in the vault of my childhood since forever. They are from the Before, back when Madar and Padar never argued. I did it to preserve them. In psych elective, our teacher told us that memories are like ripples. We imagine them to be solid, tangible firm objects we can hold and touch at will. But really, the more we go back to them, the more they warp.

The less reliable they become.

So I locked them away and forgot. I only gave one person the key to this memory.

"Mattin sent out an emergency S.O.S. Who am I to ignore the plight of a comrade?" Sam stretches and scratches the tip of his nose. He's pretending to be relaxed, but the strain in his jaw gives him away. "And . . . to be honest, drastic times call for drastic measures, don't you think?"

"Like drastic speeches in haunted houses," I mutter while propping my elbow up on the side of the plastic boat.

"Or drastic escape plans from surprise girlfriends." Sam raises a brow. "Did you even get a look at her face?"

"No." I wipe my hand on my dress and frown. "But I imagine her to be hideous."

"Why?"

"Because only an ugly person could pursue a married man and not feel bad about it." I kick off my shoes, and swing my legs around so my back is facing Sam. I kick my legs and the warm water feels like a balm.

"How do you know she doesn't feel bad about it?"

I twist and glare at Sam. "Whose side are you on?"

"I'm an objective third party." He rubs his head. "I'm just saying, how would you know if you've never spoken to her?"

"Because if she *did* feel bad, she wouldn't have showed up tonight," I say uncomfortably. I twist back toward the water and fiddle with my bracelet. "That's not what I wanted to happen."

"What would you want to happen?" The boat rocks again, and I can feel Sam shift closer. "In a perfect world, of course."

I suck in my lips and puff out my cheeks. There are lone fireworks whistling up in the air all around us. Everywhere I look, there's a 360-view of light followed by curling smoke. In the wisps, I see Sam and me, sitting knock-kneed in the cold, watching my parents' arguing silhouettes across the street. I feel Sam's parents' warm embrace as they whisk us away for a round of hot cocoa and donuts. I blink away the vision just as the ugly feeling rears its head.

Because what I want is too far gone.

In my earliest happy place, I say, "I'd do anything, give anything, trade anyone to go back." I hunch over myself, and my hair forms a curtain around my face as my legs still in the water. "I'd stay there forever if I could."

"But that's not reality, Sara." Sam lays a warm hand on my shoulder. It's light and unsure. "You can't just live in your head."

"You think I don't know that?" I blink back the tears and wipe under my eyes. "You think I don't feel ridiculous even saying it?" My nerves are shot, and I'm a jittery mess. Adrenaline is running all over me. The full-body shakes won't stop. The melancholy squeeze won't stop. The thoughts never stop. My fingers never stop.

"Sara." Sam leans over and stays my hands. So softly, he turns me so my legs are back in the boat. His large, worried eyes are glued on me. "Stop."

"I *can't*," I whisper back.

"You *can*." Sam leans closer as he holds our hands. "If you just let yourself lean against someone, lean against *me*."

There it is again.

The unspoken truth hidden in protected words.

The message bottled tight.

I cannot need you, the words jam in my head, *I cannot love you*.

I glance up, knowing my mascara has smeared hopelessly. I flinch. Because I see wisps of red peeking through Sam's hair, see it seep through his earnest expression and into the veins that color his eyes, cheeks, neck, arms, wrists. I feel the twist of anger, the screaming reflection of Malika, in his pupils.

"I'd only pull you down with me." I stiffen and snatch my hands away. "I don't need you to be my Majnun. I don't need anyone to save me."

"Then why do you keep holding on to that?" He nods at the bracelet on my wrist. His words hit me hard. "If our friendship means nothing to you, then why are you always clutching that bracelet I gave you like it's the only lifeline you've got?" He stands up and nearly shouts the last part.

Heads swivel near us. We've drifted right into the middle of the lake. Other pedal boats swivel out of our way.

"Everything okay over there?" Ayesha's tentative voice calls out in the darkness. "Aman, can you pedal any slower? Come on, move it!"

"You act like you don't have a set of feet that could help get us there faster," Aman retorts.

"Where is your sense of chivalry?" Ayesha asks.

"You just had to get them involved," I mutter while hastily putting my shoes back on. "Couldn't just keep this to yourself."

"And be like you? A stone wall after that night?" Sam rubs his head, like his mind is running a mile a minute. "It's like you flipped a switch. One second you were my best friend and then the next, you were gone. And I—stop acting like you're going to run right out of this boat!" Sam grabs my wrist just as I have half a mind to jump out, newly replaced phone and all.

"Let go of me," I hiss through clenched teeth.

"No. This one time you can't run, you—" Sam's voice breaks, and I stop trying to yank away from him. His eyes go real glassy. Oh shit. I've really done it. "This past year and a half, I've needed you too, you know. My dad's company collapsed during the pandemic and we're broke. I've been helping with the houses, but it's not enough, and I'm afraid we're gonna lose every . . ." His voice putters out.

"Shit. Sam." I feel like such a jerk. "I didn't know."

"You never once asked, but the Sara before that night would have." His stare burns every inch of my skin. I feel like we are on the precipice of a mountain, teetering on the edge of our tug-of-war, with the rope wearing thin. "I've made excuses for you. I've waited. Because you've been my best friend since I was six years old. I told myself I could stick it out. What's a rough year or two when we've had eight awesome years of friendship? But I don't think this new you is temporary. I need you to let me in. I can't keep letting you break my heart over and over again like this, Sara."

"Incoming!" Aman announces as his boat bumps not so gently into ours. I grip the edge to keep myself from going over.

"Oh khar, you trying to capsize us?" Ayesha swats at Aman as they bobble back five feet.

"So what you're saying is, after this colossally shitty night, you brought me here to—" I can't get the words out. Can friends even break up? Is that a thing? It's getting so hard to breathe, and even though I'm in wide open air, my lungs are on fire. It feels like breathing fire and glass all at once.

The world shifts and tilts.

Maybe the bent-up feeling is more than just friendship. Little dots litter Sam's face, and the scene seems to be narrowing. My breaths come shallower, faster. My heart is slipping in a way I don't quite understand.

"I can't keep doing this anymore, Sara." Sam's eyes steel over as he wipes a tear from his cheek. "I'm sorry."

My battle armor malfunctions—already overused from earlier—and my hands are itching to move, to keep busy. So I push Sam.

"What are you doing?" he shouts in panic as I shove him again and again and again.

I am consumed by this feeling.

"I hate you," I cry through gasped breaths. "I hate that you've ruined this place for me."

"That makes two of us," Sam mutters as he steadies himself.

"Whoa, calm down, guys." Aman grips our boats together.

"Just leave me the hell alone!" I am beyond mortified.

Without thinking, I dive into the water.

"Sara, have you lost your mind?" Ayesha calls out. "Sam, you were supposed to make things better, not *worse*."

I let the water wash over me and, with my eyes squeezed shut as I swim, I hear the song pulling me to the only place that won't hurt me.

Maybe I'll never learn. Maybe this is all I'll ever hope to be—cursed to loop the same mistakes. Over and over again.

CHAPTER TWENTY–ONE

ONCE THERE WAS AND ONCE THERE WASN'T A GIRL who wore flowers braided into her hair and danced in the mirror to the song of *happily ever afters*. To the lyrical love of her grandparents, star-touched and windswept in their kingdom of sapphire and gold. Their magic seeped into her parents' skin as the world tore them apart and brought them back together thousands of miles later. And before they lay in their beds, each generation whispered their magic into ever-blooming flowers.

The girl fed herself on this dream of flowers in her hair.

Until, one by one, they were plucked, leaving the truth bare in shattered reflections that made the girl scream, *how could I ever understand love when love can't understand me?*

"Why can't you just show me what I want to see?" I scream into Sumner's empty halls. The house, now bare and exposed, feels larger with the layout entirely rearranged and walls blown wide open. I throw one shoe down the stairs of the basement, and then another, drowning in this anguish. "I've had enough of your game! Show me so I can be done!"

I sink down onto my knees and hold my stomach, trying to ignore Sam's words, forget the feeling of being erased from Padar's and Bibi's stories. If only I could rinse and erase this feeling from my body.

In the grand living room, with walls filled with fractured mirrors, I sob.

Big, ugly gasping breaths.

"Why do you have to leave me alone here, too?" My sopping-wet hair and dress cling to my skin as I cup my face with my hands. I whisper my questions to the empty halls, wishing for the walls to mist and smoke, for someone to listen to let me escape.

"It's easy, janem," a familiar voice whispers behind me.

I startle, and see Memory Bibi—the one from that very first day—standing quietly behind me. A little ways off, Malika peeks from behind the finished banister. She makes a move to come closer, but Memory Bibi holds up a hand.

"You . . . you're here." My thoughts scatter and whir when I see them. "I thought you'd never come back."

Young and beautiful Memory Bibi swoops down and stills my shaking hands. She holds my twitching fingers. I flinch, expecting more of the cold. Only, warmth blooms. Sensation that I haven't felt for weeks returns to the tips of my fingers.

"A beautiful girl shouldn't cry so." Bibi's musical accent is like balm for my ears. She wipes the tears from my nose.

"Everything is all wrong." I drink her image in as I pour every ounce of this shitty night into her. "And I can't make it stop. I can't control any of it."

"There is something you can do." Bibi smiles so wide as her touch continues to warm me. Her hands pass over my temple, and I nearly sob all over again. I had forgotten what it was like when Bibi was normal. "You already know it," she whispers into my hair as I collapse into her.

"What do you mean?"

In Bibi's transparent hands is my bracelet. When did she even slip it off? She turns the worn beads round and round, a line forming between her brows, like she can feel each worrying thought.

"This has so much weight to it." She folds it into my palm and squeezes softly. "Why bear it when you can let it go here?"

"Because I'm afraid," I confess.

She laughs. "Of something that's already happened? Nothing in there can hurt you. But keeping it in here"— she nods toward my chest—"will consume you if you don't let it out."

I look down at the beads, each a different shade of blue— my favorite color—with hand-etched pieces of armor drawn on each bead.

"How do you know it'll wo—"

She's gone.

With shaking hands, I curl in on myself and finally let the bracelet go. It clatters to the ground. Smoke snarls and twirls from my knees and winds round and round me until I am encased in a cloud of blue and gray. It stings my eyes, but I keep them open, unsure of what I'll miss if I blink.

When the cloud clears, I am at Sam's house. I stand up in a panic. His Lego couches are covered in tinsel and boxes of ornaments. It's a tradition at Sam's house to pack up the Christmas tree on New Year's Eve. A sort of symbolic message: out with the old and in with the new.

There is a fire gently burning in their living room. Sam's parents are laughing, joking with one another as they take down the star, while listening to the countdown on the TV. I stand in the middle of their living room in my sodden state, but they don't seem to notice me.

"Mom! You didn't take the lights down outside, did you?" Sam's panicked face shoots out from the top of the stairs. He bolts down, skipping steps, with something gripped in his fist.

"You've only told me twenty times to not touch your little setup back there," Sam's mom mock complains as she winks toward her husband. "Don't you look nice all dressed up, hm?"

"I-it's not like that." Sam's face goes tomato red. "It's a nice, friendly gesture—"

"We're just kidding, Sam." His father, all crinkly eyed, jokes. "We're busy in here. Just holler if you need anything."

"Right. Okay." Sam takes a deep breath and smooths out the front of his collared shirt. He's got it tucked into his jeans, and I realize I don't remember the way he looked that night, a year and a half ago.

But that's exactly where I am.

Back during that night, only I never made it to Sam's house.

I follow Sam as he treks into his kitchen. He fiddles with the bracelet, grips it tight in his hands, and says, "I know it's been a crappy year, and I know how much you hate gifts, but you've given me a gift that I—no, that's gross, Sam. She'd hate that." He sighs and leans against his kitchen island, tapping his knuckles against his forehead.

"Sara, you're right. I won't ever know how you feel, but as your best friend, I want you to know you're the strongest person I know. And whatever happens with your parents, I don't want you to ever feel like there isn't a place you can come home to. You're—"

I am shell-shocked and transfixed as he sucks his teeth in uncertainty and stares at the bracelet, turning over each bead of armor.

"A helmet to protect your determination," he mutters, "and a chest plate to protect your heart so you never lose hope that things will get better." He wanders to the patio and opens the door. I step through, not wanting to lose him from my line of sight. The smell of snow and wonder hits me like a wall as I step through and let my bare feet crunch on the patio. It smells of hope and new beginnings. Sam turns, haloed by the strings and strings of lights he's strung all around so it looks like a tower of light, cocooned from the rest of the world.

Like a cage of glowing armor he's constructed just for me.

Everything falls away when I stand in the heart of it all.

In front of the Sam I forgot existed, once upon a time ago.

The memory comes back in snippets. I remember our plans, a tradition born of my parents fighting. I was going to come over to watch the year turn, like I had for the past three years. Only, Madar and Padar's fight was different that night.

It was the beginning of the end when it went too far. The bursting glass. The blood from Padar's cut hands. The marks on Madar's neck. My crying screams as I broke the one promise I made to my parents—*no matter what happens, don't call the police.*

But I did and when the blue and red lights came, I ran.

I ran far, far away because maybe, deep down, I knew what it would mean.

That call.

That night.

"It's all my fault," I whisper to Sam. "If I hadn't called,

maybe Madar and Padar would still be together. If I wasn't weak, if I just held the course."

"You did the right thing, Sara." Sam tilts his head to the side. His dirty blond hair flops to the side. This was before he cut it all off. "If I had seen what you saw, I would have done the same thing."

"The divorce is *my* fault. Our ruined friendship is *my* doing. All of it." I take a step toward the light. "Don't you see that?"

"What are you talking about? There's nothing wrong with us." Sam looks confused as he takes me in. If he finds my sodden clothes or ruined make up alarming, he doesn't show it. "In fact." He takes a deep breath and crinkles his eyes while jutting out his hand. "You're just in time for the surprise."

I take the bracelet with shaking fingers. "What surprise?"

"You'll see." Sam's face lights with glee as he steers my shoulders. "Just stand right here. Yes, okay perfect." He runs to the edge of the patio, to the ends of the lights and there on a table are sheets of lights strung together like walls. Four walls actually. He hangs each one around me until I am encased in a fort of bright, white light.

"Here we go." Sam crawls under and sits right in front of me, his face illuminated with anticipation.

"What is this?" I raise my hands to touch the walls. "What's this for?"

"For you, obviously." He playfully rolls his eyes before nudging the bracelet. "So that when you're feeling like you can't see the light at the end of the tunnel, just come back to this moment, this place."

"But why would you do this? All of this effort?" I look around and remember the resigned hurt in Sam's face. "I don't deserve it."

"That's simple," Sam answers so earnestly as he levels me with his stare. "You're my best friend, my most trusted confidant. And it's just what you do when you love someone. You're there for them, no matter what."

I blink in surprise. "You . . . love me?"

"Don't make it weird." Sam rubs the back of his head in a laugh. His ears turn pink. "And it's love with a lowercase l. Not *love* love. Just, good ol' neighborly *I'll always have your back* love."

I look up and around, anything to not have to expose my own tomato-red face. But the longer I sit here, the more today's shit show melts away, as if the lights are keeping the monsters at bay.

"I wish we could stay like this forever," I confess as I memorize this feeling of Sam and me. Before everything got bent and twisted and ruined. Before my heart warped into a thorny battleground. Before I hurt him. "I wish it could have played out differently."

"Who's to say we can't?" he asks with wide, happy eyes. "Who's to say we can't stay?"

There's a hazy heaviness on my eyelids as I lean back in cozy warmth. "You're right. I guess I don't have to leave just yet."

Because I know this will all fade come sunrise, I stare and stare and stare at who we used to be before falling asleep in the halo of light, with Sam looking after me, wishing this vision were reality.

Before the fight.

Before the dementia.

Before I lost sight of *happily ever after*.

CHAPTER TWENTY–TWO

IT'S THE SOUND OF SHOUTING THAT WAKES ME.

I sit up with a raging headache. There is so much sun. Too much light. And noise. I rub my burning eyes and startle when I can see perfectly clearly without my glasses.

"What the?" I look down and immediately panic. "What am I doing here? What time is it?" Sumner's looming halls look innocently on as sunshine and a breeze from an open window perfumes the stale air. I stand up, and not only am I absolutely drenched in paint from my waist down . . . I managed to walk around the entire newly sanded floors, leaving a trail of paint behind me.

"Oh fuuuuuuuuu—" My dripping footsteps circle all over the main floor to the kitchen and out to the deck. I clutch my head and try to remember last night.

I can't.

Not a single thing.

Fear flits through my cold arms as I try to hold on to my beads, hoping for the familiar motion to whir the moment back into my brain. The bracelet is gone.

"Check the backyard, near the pool." There are voices. A lot of them. I scramble on my hands and knees, crawling until I'm under the nearest window.

If I could shrivel up and die in this very moment, I would. Madar, Khala Nazaneen, and Khala Mojgan are scanning the perimeter while Mattin and Aman stomp up the deck steps. Soon, the front door jiggles, and I am suddenly faced with three options.

Option 1: Pretend to be dead.

Option 2: Attempt to escape through the cracked window in the basement garage.

Option 3: Own up to being out all night and ruining the floors.

Yeah.

There's only one viable option.

I bolt for the basement.

"Sara? If you're in here, open the door!" Ayesha bangs on the front door before I hear a thud of something heavy hitting the wall. "Please, answer us!"

I'm down the stairs in record time. Chills vibrate all up and down my arms and legs when little whispers float through the darkness. Like tiny eyes are watching, flitting from left to right.

Baba Kalan, with his opaque glasses and bloodied shirt.

Bibi jan, clutching her necklace around her throat like a noose.

Malika, sitting between them with her hands kept patiently in her lap.

And Sam, hiding in a corner with one eye shyly peeking at me.

My heart stops.

"What are you doing here?" I whisper.

"I think the real question is, why aren't *you* here?" he whispers back.

I am confused. "I am here?" I want to ask him what he means, but the moment I blink, they are gone.

All that is left is the whispering.

"She's not upstairs!" Amena's voice grumbles. "Holy sh—"

It's Madar's shriek, "Who did this to the floors?!" that breaks the spell and I move like I've never run before.

Oh, shit, shit, shit, I mantra over and over. Relief comes when I throw open the door to the garage.

There's blinding light. The garage is already open. I cover my eyes with my forearm.

"Hello, neighbor," a cold voice greets me. "I had a feeling I'd find you here."

"Sam." I rush toward him. "Is that really you?"

"Of course it is." He scowls, and the purple bags under his eyes aren't lost on me.

"I need a favor." The words rush out like a flood. "Please, please, *please* don't tell my family I was here. Let me just slip away and we'll call each other even."

"Even like when I took the fall for you taking my car?" Sam steps aside, with his arms outstretched as if to say *after you*. "Even like how you left us looking all night for you?" His expression is cool.

"I-I can explain."

Sam grips my hand and pulls me close enough to quietly say, "I wasn't lying when I told you I was done."

My knees knock together when he lets go. "Sam, you wouldn't—"

"After last night?" He raises a brow. "No more excuses."

"Last night . . ." I rack my head for a snippet, a shard of what happened. Bits and pieces, like looking through fractured underwater light.

Fireworks. A blue-and-white dress. Padar. *Her*. A boat. And then nothing.

"I found her!" Sam calls out. In a matter of seconds, I am facing the angry stares of my cousins and aunts.

"What the hell were you thinking?" Ayesha's tear-filled accusation twists my heart as I take a step back. "I thought you'd drowned or gotten hurt or—" Her face crumples as she bursts into tears on Amena's shoulder. Deep bruises shine under Amena's eyes as she shakes her head at me and steers Ayesha toward their mom.

"We're ready to go home," Amena says.

Mattin's look is scathing. "We were up all night looking for you."

"I'm sorry." I don't sound anything like myself. To be honest, staring down at my paint splattered hands, I don't feel like me either. I can't recognize the girl who is missing time.

"You're sorry?" Madar finally catches up. "You don't know what it means to be sorry. Not yet." Her small body crumples in on itself as she shouts, "Get in the car now. I am so *sorry*, Nazaneen."

Khala Nazaneen winds her arms around Madar. "Don't worry about it. It's what family does," she whispers, holding Madar tight. "Go easy on her. It's been a long night."

⌀

The car ride home is the quietest it has ever been between Madar and me.

"I'm sorry—" The words are tangled on my tongue. I try to force out a small *for last night, for Padar, for ruining everything.*

"Save your apologies, Sara." Madar is terse. "I don't know who you are anymore, who took away my shirin girl."

I stiffen.

I try to grasp for my battle armor, for the familiar strength of steel to wall me in its protection. No matter how much I will it to come, it doesn't.

I don't say another word for the next three days.

I don't know who I am right now either.

CHAPTER TWENTY-THREE

BIBI JAN JIGGLES MY LOCKED DOORKNOB. "WHO IS in here?" her halting voice grumbles. "This is my room. My room. Why is this door locked?" She bangs against the door.

"Bibi jan, your granddaughter lives there. Come, your room is here." Irina's sweet melody guides Bibi away.

I sink deeper into my bed, watching the little stars on my ceiling. My memories, no matter how hard I try to recall that night, keep slipping away.

It feels like it's right on the tip of my tongue.

It's right *there*.

But I can't reach it.

And then there's an echo of something. The hollow of an unknown ache. Something I should feel. But I don't. I don't feel anything except a crater of emptiness blooming wider and wider. It's colder than I expected, feeling this empty.

I know I need to message Ayesha or Amena or Aman or

Mattin. Hell, even Sam (maybe not Sam). But I can't face them, can't say the words *I don't remember.*

And, if I'm being really honest, I can't risk the chance they don't respond.

After that night, I'd hate me too.

CHAPTER TWENTY–FOUR

I AM GROUNDED FOR FOUR DAYS.

On the fifth day, Madar waltzes into my room like a hummingbird.

"When I said you were grounded, I didn't mean you could mope in your bedroom like a vampire child." She turns the lights on. Her dewy face wrinkles in disgust. "We need to let some air in here. Come on, bekhaiz, now. *Get up.*"

"Why can't I just sulk in peace?" I groan when Madar rips the blanket from my naked legs. I give myself a sniff under my arms, and okay. I get it. I might smell a little.

"Come on. You're better than this." She opens the windows just as Bibi jan shuffles in the hallway. "You are going to get up and face the day. Because that is what we do in this family."

I scoff. "What family?"

Madar's smile at Bibi freezes. "What did you just say?"

"Nothing," I mumble.

Can we call ourselves family when I can't even remember what once made us family? I watch Bibi's gaze glaze over us. Her hand moves absentmindedly toward her neck.

I imagine all of us as ships on an elaborate board, sailing in opposite directions in silence. We are all too proud to admit that we are sinking, drowning in the dark, and all we want, so desperately, is to find a way back to the light.

And then there are more pressing, worrying matters going on.

Why aren't you here? Sam's voice rumbles as I stare at Bibi's shrinking back.

What did he mean? I rub my face. What does it mean that he's there and I'm not?

"It's the strangest thing," Irina mentions to Madar. "Bibi's necklace and some of her jewelry has gone missing."

I beeline it to the bathroom.

Madar looks perplexed. "Sara, would you know where they'd be?"

"Why would I keep track of junk?"

"Sara!" She knocks against the bathroom door. "Don't think I haven't noticed the way you ignore me and your grandmother! This behavior canno—"

I ignore her and splash water on my face. My knuckles grip the edge of the counter as I stare at my pale reflection. Gaunt and sunken and swollen all at once.

Haunted.

I am filled with the weight of Bibi's past and with no clear answer regarding Malika.

The more time that passes, the more I'm starting to question if Sam was right: Was it Malika calling out to me all this time . . . or the house?

I avert my gaze from the mirror because I can't look at the resolve that is crumbling in my reflection and the thought that maybe I am running out of burdens to bear.

$$\sim$$

Padar: I'm trying a different approach, okay?

Padar: Let's have lunch this afternoon.

Padar: Just the three of us. Give her a chance.

I stomp through the grass since Erik's team is getting the driveway repaved. My camera swings against my neck as I crane to find a good shot of the exterior. I aggressively take as many pictures as I can to not think about Padar's texts.

As I snap away, I can't get over how different Sumner looks in daylight. Clean. Inviting. I walk through the doors, snapping progress pictures. A slight shiver rolls down my spine. The paint has been cleaned up as if it never happened. I try to ignore the glares from the crew. Yeah, even I can admit that must have been a pain to clean up.

On the inside, Sumner feels crowded. When I turn a corner into the grand family living space, flitting images reflect in newly hung mirrors and tiles. Faces I've grown accustomed to—Bibi jan, Malika, Baba Kalan—but also new ones. Sam and his parents glow in a bathroom mirror. *What?*

"Watch it." Sam barrels through the hallway, holding a box as big as his body. His neck strains as he rushes past me, toward the back wing where there is a bonus den, bedroom, and mini kitchen. He trips over a misplaced hammer on the floor.

Without thinking, I rush to help him hold on to the box.

"Close call there." I groan, and we both waddle until he abruptly lets go. "Hey, a warning would have been nice." I also let go of the box.

"What would you know about nice?" he bites back.

"Okay, I deserved that." I keep out of Sam's way.

"Good." He storms off. I watch his back shrink until he's out of sight. I tinker with my camera to ignore the prickling in my throat. As I'm adjusting the settings, something catches my eye.

Dark hair.

Angry eyes.

And the sound of laughter.

Malika.

"Hey!" I scramble toward her. "Hold up." She bolts into the den where I first saw Bibi all those weeks ago. Only, now, the parquet floors have been ripped out and replaced with smooth, dark hardwood.

She turns her head and smirks at me. "You're almost too late."

"Too late for what?" I burst into the room. I am alone. I scream in frustration.

"What are you keeping from me?" I sink on my knees. "I can't take it anymore. I can't—" I bury my face in my hands, but there is no peace in the dark. I can't escape Bibi's burdens, can't escape the longing of dreams that scream in the night. Can't help but feel like all of this is in my head.

A little voice whispers, wafting, "Give me one more night, and it'll become clear."

"It's always one more night," I say to no one. I grasp my shaking wrists. There's a soft haze in my head still adrift from the Fourth of July.

Looking around, I feel their eyes. Watching. Waiting.

I want to scream, *for what?*

My phone keeps buzzing, and I swallow the knot.

Padar: I'm here.

Guess I can't avoid it any longer.

───────⟡───────

Padar's apartment smells of tomato sauce and baked cheese. Which, after our streak of disastrous visits, can only mean one thing.

A peace offering.

Padar strides into his bedroom to wash his hands. I

notice the dastarkhan is out where we normally watch TV. The table is pushed to the side along with the couch to make space for us to sit. Seeing the three place settings makes me nervous. Even though Padar gave me advance notice this time, it still feels weird to know the third place setting is not for Madar.

A head pops up from the galley kitchen. Padar's someone. She has soft brown hair that spills over her shoulders and kind eyes that crinkle when she sees me.

"Oh, you're here early." She pulls out the tray of baked lasagna and places it on the stove. "I'm Sahar. It's nice to finally meet you." She smooths the front of her blouse, nervous.

"Yeah." I can't say the same, so I say nothing at all.

We stare at each other awkwardly until Padar strides out of his room, swinging the door wide open. "Mmm, that smells good. I can't tell you how long we've been surviving on ramen." He smiles hopefully at me. "Isn't it nice to have a guest here for a change?"

I shrug my shoulders and try to keep the fluttering nerves in check, when I notice a pile of suitcases in Padar's room.

She's not a *guest*.

Something about that image makes me freeze up. I clutch my head in my hands. "I wasn't ready for this." This peace offering is starting to feel a lot like an ambush.

A headache is coming on as shards of that night burst through.

Padar punching the mirror, glass shattering all around his bloodied hands. Madar screaming, *I'll die without you.* Padar's handprints around her neck, *you'll kill us both with this madness.* Me, floating out of my body, watching the beginning of the end. Fluttering, fretting, *I can't survive if they both go.*

Your fault. Your fault. Your fault.

I try to block it, but it keeps playing on repeat, like it won't let me go.

Padar wraps an arm around Sahar's waist, unsure of how to deal with my less than ideal reaction.

"After the Fourth of July fiasco, I thought it would be better to have something a bit more . . . private to talk, and for you two to get to know each other." He beams while gazing at Sahar. "I never thought this day would come. The moment Sahar jan fell into the picture, after being unhappy for so long, I felt like music had re-entered my life."

Sahar blushes and swats at him. "Don't exaggerate."

Somehow, the levity and calmness of the moment is only making me feel worse.

"I know we still need time for the dust to settle and all." Padar turns to look at me; his Adam's apple bobs as he hesitates. "But if all goes well . . . we'll start discussing engagement planning. Wouldn't that be nice, to plan something happy, Sara?"

"You're"—either my brain is having a total meltdown or I don't understand the English language anymore—"getting remarried as an already-married man?"

Now Padar looks surprised. "What do you mean?" He adjusts the collar of his shirt. "I received your mother's signed divorce papers from her lawyer the other day."

"Her *what*?"

"Maybe we should cool the future talk, dear," Sahar butts in, looking concerned. "Take it one step at a time. What do you say, Sara?" I give her credit, she's really trying. "Your dad tells me you like anime. I do too. Maybe we could watch some tonight?"

Padar agrees. "That's a great idea." He waits a beat for my reaction, but I'm still in shock. Seeing Sahar fret over things I might like just takes me over the edge. Everything is too normal, too *nice*.

"I need a minute." I shuffle into my room and shut my door softly. I don't know what's worse: Padar announcing a maybe engagement or Madar signing the papers and never telling me. I try to keep the tears at bay, but this . . . is it. With no warning, no sit-down, no *Sara, I'm sorry, we tried, but it's just not working out.*

I get on my hands and knees and search under my bed for a dusty box. Sitting on the warm carpet, I open the top. There are little tiny trinkets that really aren't worth much. A broken yo-yo. A paper with glued noodles and yarn. Some old fortune cookie notes. And a picture.

I take it out with shaking hands.

I must have been five or six. My parents had taken me to Uzbekistan for the first time, to expand my worldview. I am mid-twirl in a traditional dress. Madar is hiding a grin behind her manicured hands while Padar is sitting playing his tablas, singing into a microphone. The beat of the drum and their laughter speaks to me, even now.

Back to who we used to be.

Little tears blur my face. I had gotten so used to our dance these past few years, so used to being the rope that held my parents together, I never gave time to the idea we wouldn't make it. In some weird way, the way we fought with each other gave me hope. Like we were always meant to come back to one another because we cared, because we had the passion to lash out and scream and fight.

Because family doesn't give up. Isn't that what all the stories tell you? About enduring love?

Except.

Now we've given up.

I throw the photo on the ground.

I guess the story of my family is over now.

I guess there's no reason left for me to keep hanging on.

CHAPTER TWENTY-FIVE

GROWING UP, WHEN I WAS CURLED UP IN BED, I was never swathed in *once upon a time*s, like how most English fairy tales go. My nightly routine was a little bit different. In Farsi, stories always began with *There once was, and there once was not.*

Without knowing anything more, I learned from the very beginning that all beginnings, and most ends, were bittersweet. Even if the princess lived happily, even if good vanquished evil, even if the boy became real, there was always something that was lost along the way. Be it a friend or a book. A voice or some shot at freedom. *Happily ever after* never quite felt as *happily* as I'd like to believe.

Not then, and not now.

Especially now, as Padar drops me off in front of Madar's house. I can't help but focus on *there once was not* and how my family's story went all wrong. My

parents. My grandparents. My great-grandparents. I
thought that by undoing the wrong, by finding Malika,
there'd be some cosmic balance restored, some reward
I could cash in.

Now I see differently. Our story was never going to turn
out any other way. Not once I opened Pandora's box.

I'm unbuckling my seat belt when Padar clears his
throat. His fingers drum on the steering wheel as he looks
at the house. Khala Mojgan's car is in the driveway. "I
think it's for the best if you don't tell your mother that
Sahar is visiting. I'm not sure she'd . . . handle it well."

"'Kay." I try to brush my way out of the car.

"Hey," he says softly, "look at me, bachem."

I really, really don't want to, but for some stupid, silly
reason, I do. "What?"

"I know change is hard. And I know Sahar will never
replace your mother, but this new normal is going to be
so much better than the past few years were, I promise."

Flashes of cupcakes and wishes choke me.

"If you say so." No matter how hard I try not to, when
I look at my dad, all I can see and hear and feel are the
hazy images of the family I lost, of being tucked away
under the stars of my bedroom with a steaming mug of
chamomile tea and his stories of Laili and Majnun, of the
fairy tale of what it meant to be loved unconditionally.
And how it was a lie. All of it.

The stories. My grandparents. My parents. Me.

"Your secret is safe with me." I reach in my back pocket because of course I took the photo. "'Night." I watch as Padar drives off, stare up at the sky. Sam's driveway is full of cars and even from here, I can see the shadows of his family lounging around on their Lego couches. *Time to face the music, Sara.* It's not like I can stay out here all night.

The scent of steaming pallow and gosht waft through the house. Madar is helping Irina in the kitchen. I scratch my cat's ears when Madar perks up.

"You're home, Sara?" Madar wipes at her eyes and clears her throat.

Khala Mojgan is chopping carrots into tiny slivers. I pretend not to notice the small smile she throws her way. Or the red smoke that is so thick, I can barely make out Baba Kalan's figure sitting in the kitchen nook, watching it all.

"Yep." I stand awkwardly in the living room. Amena and Ayesha are sprawled out on the couch, the TV on some random channel as they scroll through their phones. The red threads of smoke are still bound and woven in Ayesha's hair. I've gotten so used to the shadows, I barely bat an eye at them now.

I choose the lesser of the battles and head toward the kitchen.

"Coward," Ayesha throws quietly my way.

"How was lunch at your dad's?" Khala Mojgan makes small talk. "Anything new?"

I feel like a traitor when I say, "Nope."

I take a seat next to Bibi jan, who stares vacantly toward the window. She sways gently, leaning back in her chair. "Salaam, Bibi jan." She doesn't hear me. I wave my hand in front of her face, wondering if she can see the thick shadows too. A little nugget of guilt peeks out of hiding. I can't remember the last time she and I have had a moment together.

Bibi's eyes bob over me as I let down my hair and take off my glasses. I take a deep breath and count as her brow furrows.

"Who am I?" she asks.

I nearly fall over. "W-who . . . are *you*?" I look at my mom incredulously. But she continues making salad, a stiffness to her shoulders as she works.

Bibi jan smiles at me, so painfully sweet, smoothing her thin hair back. Her weathered hand holds mine. Her bell of a laugh. "You know my name?"

I put my glasses back on. My throat is scratchy. "Your name is Sara khan." I squeeze her hand back. "Like mine, don't you remember?"

"Sara khan." She tests out the sounds as if tasting them for the first time. She sinks back into her chair, her knotted fingers resting on her neck. "Sara khan."

Baba Kalan continues to watch.

"She's been getting worse lately," Irina calls out while washing dishes. "Like it happened all at once. Ever since her necklace went missing."

"She must have hidden it somewhere and forgotten

about it." Madar strides over to Bibi jan and smooths her hair while giving her a hug.

"And you didn't think to tell me this was happening?"

"Well, if you didn't lock yourself in your room all the time, you'd have realized Bibi's condition," Madar snaps.

Ayesha peeks up from the couch, her arms resting on the divider that separates the living room from the kitchen.

"Well, do something." I stifle the sinking feeling as I blink the smoke away from my eyes. It's getting so dark, so hard to see. Baba Kalan's figure floats closer to us. "Maybe you're just not asking her the right questions, that's all." I point at the photo hanging right above the mantel. Of her and Baba jan. "Who is that?" She knew less than a month ago.

She stares vacantly.

"How many kids do you have?" I try again.

Bibi blinks. She stares at her fingers. "I have—I." Her face remains impassive as a deep dread washes over me. I scoot so close to her and whisper in her ear, "What about your father? Baba Kalan?" I glance over at the darkening figure. He is even closer now. Tears fall down his cheeks as he watches. "Do you see him here? What about Malika? Your dreams, Bibi jan. You . . . the night you were married, don't you remember anything at all?"

But Bibi only smiles serenely at Baba Kalan, as if who she was had been plucked out of her. Like someone had scooped out what made her *her* and put it somewhere else.

Like she's missing time.

Like—

My missing night.

No. There's no way. I back away slowly as a seed of horror grows in my gut.

The smoke is so thick, so dark, so red, I can barely breathe. Barely see as it swarms all of us.

"What's wrong, Sara?" Khala Mojgan puts down the knife and looks worriedly in my direction.

All I see are the suffocating shadows that bloom around my grandmother, a darkness that envelops the kitchen, swallowing us whole. And by the fridge. A little girl, with sad eyes and a sunflower dress, hiding.

A mantra blares like nails on chalkboard. *My fault. My fault. My fault.*

I scream to drown it, but it only rings louder.

"Sara, what's wrong?" Madar is alarmed as she strides toward me. I bump my way out of the kitchen, the corner of the table jabbing my hip.

I was supposed to help my grandmother, find Malika, be the one who brought us all together. The items I took—it was to save us. Undo a wrong by making it right.

Wasn't I?

I breathe fast, too fast, and it's hard to see correctly. It's like my lungs are shrinking and my heart is growing too quickly, so big that my fingers and toes go numb.

Hands reach for me, but I fight back. I swat them away.

"Breathe in slow." Ayesha is on her knees, holding my

shoulders. When did I get on the ground? "In through your nose. Yes. Good. Now let it out. Again."

Amena is in the kitchen, holding on to an extremely startled Bibi. A little hospital bracelet has fluttered to the ground. Amena tries to calm her down, but doesn't know the right words in Farsi.

This chaos is all because of me.

My lost family, Bibi's lost memories.

"Maybe it might do Sara some good to be away from home tonight?" Madar looks at Amena, begging her to extend an olive branch. "Maybe a night at your house would take some of the stress off?"

"Um. Yeah, if she wants . . ." Amena trails.

"Nothing is going to get better." I clutch my throbbing head. "Because I just made it worse."

"Hey. Bibi's dementia isn't your fault." Ayesha gently pries my hands from my face, and she squeezes tight. "It's shitty, but you can't put that blame on yourself."

"You don't know the truth. If you did—" There are no words to catch me, no counting, no drifting into moments of before. Because I can't shake this naked truth that I won't be able to undo this.

"Well, how about you stay the night and tell me? You promised you'd be honest with me, after all." Ayesha guides me up. Amena takes her place and wraps an arm around my shoulder.

"We can call a truce for tonight, and resume being mad

at you come daybreak, what do you say?" She has the hospital bracelet in her hand. "Weird, this thing is super old. It's Baba jan's." Amena cranes toward her mom. "Didn't you say Bibi never told him that he was sick?"

I take the bracelet. The year *1985* is written in faded letters along the plastic.

That year, Bibi was never the same. Like the weight of that time took something from her.

I glance, searching for Bibi's stare, but Irina has already shuffled her back to her room.

Baba Kalan locks eyes with me. His tears never stop falling. Then he fades away too.

"Come on." Ayesha steers me away. "We'll even drop by 7-Eleven. Amena's treat." Ayesha winks.

"Hey!" Amena swats at her.

No amount of Sprite and Hot Fries will erase what I now suspect is the reason Bibi jan's memory is deteriorating. No cajoling from Amena as the three of us curl up on her queen bed, under twinkling lights and the glare of a self-installed tiny projector, can erase the dark that won't go away.

Because how can I tell them there is a clawing inside me? A craving so powerful, all I can think about is *one more night*? Even now.

"I'm getting a refill, anyone want anything?" Amena crawls out of the bed and stretches in her oversized sweatshirt. "Let me guess, Sprite Zero?" She points at

Ayesha, who enthusiastically nods. Amena waltzes out of her room.

Ayesha is lying down with her legs up on the wall, careful not to ruin any of the hundred photos taped on Amena's wall. "I can't believe she's almost out of room. There's like no space anymore."

"Yeah." I'm in half the photos, my ever-changing face littered across the wall with Amena and Ayesha and Mattin and Aman over various vacations and holidays and masjid classes. "Feels like it was yesterday." My fingers twitch on my bare wrist.

I can feel Ayesha's inquisitive stare.

"Are you ready to tell me what I don't know yet?" Ayesha is careful, like she's talking to a spooked bird. "Because a promise is a promise, you know. I expect you to be a woman of your word."

"What are you talking about?" I blink. "I already told you about the visions."

"Visions?" Ayesha's eyebrows crinkle.

"At Khala Firoza's house? The story about Baba Kalan?" I say, but her blank stare continues. "The trampoline, you got a noseblee—"

No.

"I don't . . ." Ayesha rubs her wrists and shivers, almost like she can see the tiny whirls of the dark circling her. "Are you just trying to get out of telling me? I expected better from you."

"I—" There are a million things I want to say to her. About the cold and the counting. About the numb that has taken over every feeling I used to feel. About the secrets our fragile family history is built upon. About Madar and Padar and Bibi jan and Baba jan and Baba Kalan and Malika.

But telling her *was* my mistake.

I won't let that house take any more pieces of her, of anyone. I can protect her in this way, at least.

Because the danger is me.

So instead, I tap at their photo wall and say, "If you knew your family was going to end, would you . . . want a redo?" I wave at the cluster of photos of Amena and Ayesha with both of their parents. "Do things differently the second time around?"

"I know what you're doing, Miss Let-Me-Stall-and-Redirect." Ayesha sits up and tucks her legs under her. "But I'll take the bait, temporarily." She picks at a worn photo right by Amena's pillow. "If you asked me last year, I'd probably say yes." The photo shows the four of them. Her father's face is beaming as he holds Amena, who is holding infant Ayesha. "It was . . . confusing when my dad left. Because it was so unexpected, you know?"

I nod. "But now?"

"Now, I'd say no." She lets out a deep breath and leans against the wall. "Don't get me wrong, it still sucks. Last week, my dad sent Amena a really long email and invited us to see him for Eid."

"That's a good thing, right?"

"He emailed *Amena*. Not me." For the first time, I see Ayesha wince. "I mean, I get it. They've always had a closer bond. And his leaving really hurt her, not like she'd let it show. It's something I've always been jealous of."

"Well, it's not all it's cracked up to be." I glance out the door. Khala Mojgan and Amena are talking somewhere. "Maybe you're luckier this way."

"Doesn't make it hurt any less," Ayesha says. "If anything, I think it makes it worse. I know it's awful to say, but sometimes I think Bibi is lucky for not remembering all the terrible things she's gone through." She lies back down on the bed, picking at her fingernails. "Maybe she's the luckiest of us all."

I don't know what to say to that.

"Am I a horrible person?" Ayesha asks. "For moving on and actually starting to be happy again?"

"No."

"All right, make room for me. That is my spot, Ayesha." Amena wiggles her way between us and hands Ayesha her glass. She takes a tentative sip as she shuffles over and resumes watching the movie. Amena snuggles closer to Ayesha, her chest leaning close to the photo of what their family once was.

For the first time, I wonder if my cousins had felt the

same cold when their family fell apart, the numbness that seeps in almost undetected.

I wonder if Ayesha would understand that I'm her a year ago.

I wonder if she could forgive me for what I have to do next—to eliminate the danger, once and for all.

CHAPTER TWENTY–SIX

IN THE END, THERE IS ONLY ONE CHOICE.

The halls of Sumner expand and stretch, yawning to life as I sit at the edge of the grand entryway stairs. They gleam, freshly polished, under the rainbow cascade of a modern, geometric chandelier. I click photographs of everything. The polished floors that gather and seep into each room, leading me through the grand entertaining space. Winding up from the fireplace is a wall of mirror, and in it I can see everything behind me, see the flickers of Memory Bibi, neck choked and dancing, Baba Kalan's dangling legs from the top floor, peeking through. Little kid Khala Farzana sipping a tea set with an older Memory Bibi jan, marveling at the sleek shape of the newly installed light fixtures.

I capture all of them.

They smile and wave as I turn away. I make my way to the kitchen and freeze in the middle of my steps. Sam is leaning against the doors, hidden in shadows, staring out at the deck. There is a peaceful expression to his face, something I haven't seen in a long time. Very quietly, I take a picture of him too.

His head turns as the sun shines through, catching his long, glowing hair. He smiles.

"Hey, you're blocking the hall."

I startle and jump out of the way just as Erik, Sam, and two other guys come barreling through with a gas range. Wait. "Weren't you just—"

"I can't believe it's finally coming together." Madar claps a hand on my shoulder and squeezes. "I think if we push through, this could go on the market as early as next month. How are the pictures coming along?"

"Take a look for yourself." We watch the photos together, a reel of empty space.

"These are beautiful." Normally, I'd drink up Madar's praise, but when I look behind me, I see what's missing. "Who wouldn't want to wake up in the morning and eat breakfast overlooking this view?" She shows me the picture of the kitchen, with the French doors closed. There is no Sam. "Keep up the good work."

I take the camera back from Madar and scroll through. There is a sinking, almost fearful feeling rising up in me. Why is there a version of Sam here? What did I give up for him to be here?

Most importantly, what did *he* lose to be here?

Light of my heart. I wander down the original hallway, lulled by the sweet melody. I walk past the bath and bedroom and turn right. At the end of the hall, there is a huge mirror hanging. In its reflection, there is Malika.

"You finally made it," she says.

"How are you here?" I run up to her, almost nervous to touch the surface. I've only ever seen her in the dark.

"Because you're ready to see the light." Her eyes zero in on my phone in my pocket.

"This?" I handle my phone delicately in my hands.

Malika only continues to stare.

I pry the waterproof case off. Hidden within are the old photo of Madar, Padar, and me and Baba jan's hospital bracelet. I stare hard at them, and the syrupy fog filters through me. It isn't understanding, but something close to it.

"Is this the answer?" I toy with the aged bracelet and my heart skips a beat. After all these nights, is the truth behind what happened to Malika hidden within faded plastic?

Or is it a trick? Was there never any missing daughter at all?

I grip it tight and squeeze my eyes shut, let the feeling of the house wash over me. *If all else crumbles, let me know this. Trade one truth for the others. Give the other memories back.* I feel the bracelet dissolve between my fingertips until it's gone.

When I open my eyes, the hall doesn't change. There is no smoky haze, no gauzy moonlight like the many nights before me. I choke when I see my empty hands. My chest is stretched tight.

"Why didn't it show me?" The words are stuck in my throat as I look at Malika's reflection. "What am I doing wrong?" I think of Bibi jan and Ayesha and Sam. I was supposed to fix them. Instead I have sunk them to the bottom of the ocean, too far away from the light of the surface.

Malika's hand is outstretched. "If you want to know, you know what you have to do." The hospital bracelet dangles on her small wrist. The tip of her finger touches the mirror. A little crack webs from her touch.

I hold her gaze and allow the fog to settle into my forearms and wrists. I raise my hand closer, transfixed at the darkness that pools in her eyes. At the anger that wraps protectively around her like armor.

"Sara?" Sam's voice comes from the hall. "What's going o—stop! Sara!" His crashing footsteps come down the hall, but I never turn to look at him.

Instead, I bend down and pick up the crumpled photo, my last memento of Yesterday, and stand tall.

I take a deep breath and do what I should have done all those nights ago.

I take Malika's hand and step into the mirror.

Haze spirals all around us as the smoke swoops up and around my neck and shoulders and ears, as the lullaby grows louder and the beat of Padar's drum echoes deep in my heart and Madar's laughter chimes all around us and Bibi jan is singing in her sweet Farsi.

I know. In this moment, if I cannot undo the damage I've done, I can at least remove myself from causing any more harm.

I make the ultimate offering to the house.

Myself.

Part Three

THE TRUTH

"If you could hold on to one memory, which would it be, Bibi jan?"

"Your question is wrong, janem. What you should be asking me is . . . when will these memories stop holding on to me?"

—A conversation with Bibi jan
Five months after diagnosis

CHAPTER TWENTY-SEVEN

WHEN I STEP INTO THE MIRROR, A MEMORY PLAYS.
Only, this time, it is solid and bright. Too bright.

I'm in Sumner, but it's like Sumner as seen through a time warp. All the modern fixtures are gone and the waves of white marble and walls and cabinets are replaced with dark wood and deep beige walls. The gothic chandelier sways overhead in warning. Traditional furniture in orange, tan, and brown is placed elegantly in the rooms.

I walk toward a side table in the foyer. There's a little calendar next to a picture of Malika. *1985.*

There are three sharp knocks at the door. I turn, about to open the door from habit. A woman walks right past me, her messy black hair in a bun. She wipes her hands on her apron and, after quickly checking her reflection in a small mirror by the door, she opens it.

"Yes?" Her hands shake and slip on the door. "Can I help you?"

I peer around her, and on the doorstep are Bibi and Baba.

"We are so sorry to bother you," Bibi's voice in Uzbek wafts. "But we were in the neighborhood and, well, can we come in?" Her words waver, but Baba jan holds tight to her hand, his little hospital bracelet peeking through. He smiles encouragingly at her and then at the woman at the door.

Strangely, I understand them, word for word, like the unfamiliar sounds have flipped into familiarity in this place.

"I was hoping I could get some answers too, if you'd let me." Baba jan's voice feels like a scratchy wool blanket wrapped so tight around me. It's a feeling I forgot had felt like home. I walk toward them, but they don't notice me. Not when the woman with her unsure face ushers them in to the living room separated from the kitchen and busies herself with boiling water for tea. Not when Baba jan sits rigidly and inspects his wife walking around the room as if greeting an old friend for the first time. And most definitely not when I walk right up close to Baba jan, so close I could touch him.

He looks so *real*, so present. Everything does.

"It's been so long since I was last here," Bibi jan murmurs. Her fingers dance lightly on the wood-paneled wall where pictures are hung of the woman, her arms wrapped around a man and other photos of a baby—a little girl.

"Almost six years," Baba jan agrees, gripping the solid armrests. His gray eyes stay on his wife, who stops at the photo of the baby girl. "And look at the life we've built in that time. No need to clean other people's castles when we have our own now."

But Bibi jan is floating away. It's strange, the way I can feel the thickness of the clouds in her head as she drifts back into her thoughts.

"Ahem." The woman comes back in, along with the man in the pictures—I spy their plain wedding bands—and everyone sits in tense silence, sipping tea.

"We haven't seen you in quite some time," the man says with a tight smile after a moment of silence. "And I apologize for being so abrupt, but I don't recall hearing that you were planning a visit. If you're in need of work, I d—"

"It's not about work. I . . ." Her knuckles flush against her teacup. Her perfectly curled hair flutters against her shoulders. "It's more personal than that, I'm afraid."

"Go on," the man urges.

I sit down on the rug next to the entrance, lean against the wall. Through the flourescent light, all eyes are glued on Bibi jan as a delicate tear shimmers down her cheek.

"I don't quite know where to begin," she says while looking up at the photos. "Or how I got to this point from all those years ago. I remember being here like it was yesterday, dancing to records to keep the loneliness away. To keep what little remained of who I was from falling apart. This house reminded me of a time I had buried so long ago."

I hear a rustle next to me. Malika, in her sunflower dress, with two yellow bows in her hair, peeks through.

"There was so much uncertainty when I was here. And I was filled with so much fear and grief, the only thing I had left to cling on to was the hope that one day, I'd get through it all. I just needed to wait and one day it would come. But it never came . . ."

Baba jan takes Bibi jan's cup when tea sloshes onto her floral skirt. "It's okay. Take your time."

"When I realized she was coming," Bibi jan whispers her confession to all of us, "I was so close to broken. I couldn't handle another. I couldn't stomach the thought of doing it all again. I couldn't—" *Keep her.*

Malika stiffens next to me. I . . . am in shock. Because my bibi jan, my sweet, loving bibi jan, gave her up.

"Sara jan, we know all this already." The woman is tense even though she is smiling. "And we understood your reasons. We gladly welcomed Malika into our home. She—"

"You must think me a terrible woman," Bibi interrupts with her fingers knotted together. "A woman with so many children already, who was so . . . empty. What was one more child?" Shadows flit all around her. There is thirteen-year-old Bibi with her legs folded, leaning against the chair. Fourteen-year-old Bibi, belly swollen, standing with her hand on her shoulder. Each iteration of Bibi's girlhood crowded around her in solidarity. "But it wasn't just one more girl, it was all of them. Seeing them, here in this house . . . they overtook me.

"I thought that as years slipped away, after I left this place, it would get easier. I'd forget, or remember that she had a better family, a better mother who needed her. That she wasn't mine to worry about or stay up all night thinking after. That she would be loved in a way that gave chance to hopes and dreams. Something I could not give her." Bibi looks up, and she shares an unspoken conversation with the woman. I wonder if the feeling, if the syrupy fog got to Bibi jan too. "But this secret has eaten me alive. No matter how hard I try, I cannot forget her."

Malika scrambles on all fours, and moves closer, her eyes wider, hungrier as she lurks behind Baba jan's chair. I tamp down this feeling of unease. So this is the truth. I found Malika, but there is still a lingering question.

Why isn't Malika running down to her? Why is it that no one knows her *now*?

Why is she still nothing more than a figment of my grandmother's recollections?

Why can't anyone here *see* her?

See us?

"Please don't ask," the woman's eyes are wet with

tears. Her husband slumps in his seat, his face covered by his hand. "Please—"

Bibi leaps up from her seat and falls on her knees. In front of the woman, she begs, "I need her back. I don't deserve her, but I'm better now, I swear. I would give anything to be her mother again. To have a chance to raise her now that I have love to give."

"Again? You were *never* her mother," the woman chokes back a sob, and her face crumples in on itself. "You will never know her. The sweetness of her laugh. Of her wit and curiosity." Waves and waves of sorrow push past my shoulders, knocking me off balance.

"There's something you should know." The husband looks at Bibi and Baba jan. He motions to the basement and slowly, we trek down each step. Here in the dark, Malika stays at the foot of the stairs.

"Are you coming?" I ask.

She shakes her head.

In the basement, there is the same couch, only now it is pristine. Toys are scattered about, as if just played with. The television is blank with a layer of dust, the only indicator that no one has been down here in quite some time. It reminds me of an old dream.

"What is it?" Baba jan asks.

"It—" The man takes a deep breath as his wife curls in on herself. She lays a hand on the couch. "It started with a fever. We didn't think anything of it. But then she was covered in red bumps. The doctors said there wasn't anything to do except keep her home and wait for her to recover. Only, she . . ."

"Don't you dare finish that sentence." Bibi jan flushes as her panic rises. "Don't you dare!"

"I came down here to check on her; she used to love to sit and watch old movies. She was just taking an afternoon nap. But she never woke up." The man looks at the ground when Bibi jan's wail pierces the air.

"You died." I look at Malika from the bottom of the stairs. Realization knocks me back as the scene begins to dissipate, and Bibi jan collapsing into Baba jan fades into a blanket of smoke. The room shifts and bends until we are back in the foyer, Malika and me in the bright sunshine. A knock comes from the door.

"Yes?" The woman's hands slip and shake on the door. "Can I help you?"

Baba jan and Bibi jan peer hopefully in the doorway.

I understand why they can't see Malika.

It's because she isn't a part of this memory. She isn't a memory at all.

"You knew I'd never be able to find you." I turn on Malika. "You knew all along what happened to you. You never left this house. So why did you bring me here? Why not just tell me what happened?"

I can't unsee Bibi jan's vacant stare, or unhear her wail of despair, or unfeel her dreams slipping through my fingers. It is all burned so horribly in my mind that I can't begin to untangle where she ends and I begin. It is all rage and fury and sorrow and loneliness and fear.

"It wasn't my choice. I warned you." Malika looks up at me from her dark eyes as the memory replays itself. For the first time, her sad smile sends chills down my spine. "When the house wants you, it's only a matter of time before it takes you."

CHAPTER TWENTY–EIGHT

"YOU...KNEW WHAT WAS HAPPENING TO ME, TO the memories." I suddenly feel very sick. Malika turns on me. Every hair on my body wants to run out of this house and away from her. I realize too late that I am the girl who has ignored every warning sign, who has fallen down into the basement, who has ruined her relationships with everyone she has ever cared about. And for what?

"I want to leave. Now." My knees knock as I bolt for the door, only to find myself running back into the house. The eternal sunshine never stops beaming, nor do the three sharp knocks. The woman slipping on the door. Bibi jan floating in her thoughts. Baba jan trailing to keep up with Bibi jan's secrets. All of it is suffocating. "What are you doing? Let me out now."

"I'm not doing anything." Malika sits neatly at the bottom of the stairs with her hands clasped together. "I'm stuck, just like you." Her serene expression only makes the panic worse. My fingers are tapping on my wrists as I run to each window, bang on each door, scream as loud as I can.

"Help!" I burst through the living room, but the memories don't even bat an eye. It's as if I don't exist. "Someone get me out of here! Madar! Sam! Erik!" I run through the kitchen, down the hall, toward the mirror. In far-off reflections, I can see the construction crew, flickering in and out of view. But it doesn't matter how hard I try to go through. Everywhere I go, I just meet cool glass.

"It's too late." Malika hesitantly trails behind me. "Don't you understand yet what happens when you give things to this place?"

"I didn't disappear." I whirl on her and startle when she startles back. There isn't anger in her eyes anymore— just a clawing loneliness.

"Of course not. You've just been erased," she whispers. "Like me."

"Someone must know what to do. Where's Memory Bibi? Where is she hiding? She'll have answers, she'll help me." There must be a way out. If Malika won't tell me, I'll find someone else who will. "Where are you?" I run up the stairs into the master bedroom where I first saw her crying. Into the master bath. Mirrors coat every wall while I spin around and turn.

In every wall, there is a reflection of Bibi. Each stolen moment, staring back at me.

"What is going on?" I whisper as they walk closer, growing larger in their reflections. Malika comes into the room. Her wide eyes grow hungrier as she steps next to me.

"You asked for her, so the house is showing you. She's always been right here, silly." Malika stretches on tippy toes and places both hands on my chest. Her dark eyes widen even further. "I was so lonely before you found me. I waited so long for someone to find me. It's been better. The house is less lonely with your memories, but it's not enough. Not yet. I need more. *Show me more.*" She digs her fingers into my shirt and I scream at the ice that channels and rips through me. So much worse than before. It steals my breath away as the mirrors and bathroom around us populate with more. "*Let me see all of them. So they can see me.*"

"Get off me!" So much light bursts through as I shove Malika off. But the memories don't stop. They flood all the mirrors. For the first time in a long time, I face the smiling faces of Madar and Padar, arms looped around one another. Baba jan is blinking in wonder as if waking up from a decade of sleep.

"It's about time you got here."

"Amena?" I whirl and see Amena and Ayesha leaning against each other, glowing phones in hand. Ayesha peeks up at me. "Ayesha?" Behind them, lingering in the master bedroom I see Aman and Mattin caught in an intense arm wrestle match. Sam is between them, keeping watch.

"I remember this day," I mutter while stepping toward them. The bedroom transforms into home again, two years ago. The last Eid we had as a family. I am back in my living room, sitting in between Amena and Ayesha. Sam's parents are crowded in our kitchen with Madar, Padar, and too many aunts to count.

My heart is impossibly full as shouts and cheers raise up when Mattin overpowers Aman.

"Cheater!" Aman jumps up as Mattin and Sam high-five each other. "I demand a rematch!"

"Oh, give it up," Amena jokes. "We're tired of watching you lose."

Hiding in the hallway near my room, I catch a glimpse of dark hair and angry eyes.

"Where are you going?" Ayesha asks when I get up.

"One sec." I'm in the hallway. A little shadow wiggles its way right toward my parents' room. No, Bibi jan's room now. Right? I try to remember, but it's getting so foggy.

Malika is exploring the room. Her body whirs as she opens drawers, searching for something. I wander into the closet with her when she clambers up the shelving unit, knocking down pairs of shoes.

"What is it you're looking for?"

"This." Her tiny fingers extend for the photo albums, but they are just out of reach for her. I stretch up, and there is tingling in my fingers when I bring the albums down. I sit down next to her, under the shroud of hanging St. John's pantsuits and sweaters and the smell of Bibi's and Madar's perfumes.

Pictures of before splash in front of us. Malika's fingers trace each and every one. Of Madar in a dark blue-and-white one-piece bathing suit tangled with Khala Nazaneen and Khala Mojgan at a public pool. Of Baba jan gazing pensively at the camera at a family dinner. The convenience store. Madar and Momo Ali posing in front of cash registers.

Malika's eyes fill with tears as she drinks it in. She no longer looks angry. Just lonely.

I think I understand.

"You wanted to know them," I say under the blanket of clothes protecting us. "It was never about me finding you, but you finding *them*."

"Can you blame me?" she whispers back, her eyes still so hungry.

"No." I look down at my tapping fingers, searching to hold on to something. "Not when I've been doing the same thing."

Malika covers my fingers with hers. I can't help but keep staring at her little face. "So does that mean you'll stay with me? With all of us, forever?"

"Forever?" That can't be possible. "Wouldn't I . . . have to die eventually?" After all, I am still alive. Doesn't everything have to end, eventually? Isn't that the truth of life we can't escape? That all things, even good, must end?

"Not if you don't want it to." Sam stands in the doorway. A younger Sam with floppy hair and goofy smile. He extends a hand to lift me up. But there's something else hidden in the palm of his hand.

"My bracelet," I murmur. It all comes flooding back. That night. The fight. Sam. "I almost forgot it all." I look at him as he perches on the side of the bed. The fuzziness clears. "I put you here."

"Duh." He crosses his arms and laughs. "It only took you forever to get here yourself. We've all been waiting."

Laughter erupts from the living room, causing me to look back. I actually feel . . . happy. A little light of hope blooms in my chest as I thumb through the worn beads of armor. "Do you think . . . it could really last forever?"

"Only if you want it to." Ayesha is now sitting where Sam was. Her hair is carefully braided back as she kicks her legs on the bed. There is no smoke. No red swarming her hair and wrists. In the mirrors, I catch a glimpse of Erik and Madar, calling my name.

"Sara, don't do this," Madar's voice is hoarse. Her hat slips off her head as she flits out of view.

"But you always seem to be floating somewhere else." Ayesha frowns when I touch the mirror. I startle at my own reflection. I am twelve again. "Why would you ever want to go back where it's *horrible*? Where your own mother lies to you? Where your father moves on without warning? Where your grandmother can't even remember her name? Where your best friend can't bear to speak to you?"

"How do you know all of that?" My stomach drops. Ayesha stutters and looks around a bit before regaining her composure.

"Because we've seen it!" Ayesha paces, undoing her braids. "I mean, it's in every wall you've touched, those moments, those feelings. They exist everywhere here."

"So then why am I like this?" I look closer into the mirror. My hair is shorter and tied half up into a double Dutch braid. There are streaks of pink littered through my hair. A past me who wasn't afraid to take risks. Who knew her parents would catch her if she fell.

"Because this is your happy place." Padar's voice is sincere as he wraps his arms around me. His aftershave cocoons me, and it's no use, everything gets blurry as I blink away tears. "Because, in this world, life can be anything you want it to be. Don't you want to be happy again?" He brushes back my tears and takes me into his arms.

I am back in my childhood bedroom, bundled up in my favorite blanket. A cup of chamomile tea sits on my nightstand as Padar and I look up at the glowing stars on my ceiling, ready for my bedtime story.

"Don't you want to see our family together again?"

Yes, I think as smoke, hazy and thick, curls around us. I shut my eyes and will it so deeply. I never want to forget it. Not one second of it.

"Even if it means us forgetting you?"

My eyes snap open. Madar is sitting on my bed, her hair a tangle around her shoulders. Her eyes look haunted, but she doesn't reach for me. "Even if it means losing who you'd become?"

I already know who I've become. A daughter who can't speak to her mother. A cousin who hurts her cousins. A friend who can't see how her friends are struggling. A granddaughter who is so wrapped up in her own hurt, she can't see how her actions harm those around her.

A girl who has made so many mistakes. Who is a danger to everyone she touches. Her family. Her friends. Herself.

"But what if I don't like who I'll become?" I whisper to my mother. I see in her the girl sprawled in a bathing suit, the girl who never knew sadness, but now it's the only thing she feels.

"How will you know if you never give yourself the chance to find out?" Madar holds on to my hands. "Janem, don't you see? Life, itself, is a memory. That is all we are. Past, present, future—all memories. But don't you want to know what could be?" Her question lingers like a fresh breeze that wafts through the smoke until she, too, fades and I am left alone.

Holding my blanket, I walk down the hall of memories and watch the same scene replay over and over again. Mattin beating Aman. Sam cheering. Padar and Madar wrapped up in one another, but with smiles that never quite reach their eyes. Not in the way Padar's smile glowed when looking at Sahar, when Madar beamed as we sat together, with my laptop open, tracing our histories together.

Somewhere along the way, I've learned to see between the lines, see what's unspoken.

"This isn't real." I watch the cheers, smell the buttery sweetness of sambosa and cream rolls, and take a step back. I drop the blanket. "I love everything about this moment, but that's all it is. A fantasy." This isn't real happiness because if it were, then why do I suddenly want *more* than this?

I want to see what happens next.

What happens when we graduate, when we, one by one, go off to college.

I want to see who I could *be* after this moment has gone.

"I can't stay here. Please let me leave." Panic flutters as I run. Halls meld from house to house. My home. Bibi's home. Sumner of before and after. My fingers whirl and whirl around my bracelet as I look for a way out, away from the flood of the past.

"Wait." Malika's little voice floats.

I fall on my knees, a few feet away from the mirror that started it all. In its reflection, I can feel Madar shouting, feel her fear, how she gets smaller and smaller with each passing second. I can feel the house reaching for it too. Using it. Coaxing me to keep looking back at Malika.

I sit up with a start and instead of looking back at her, I keep my eyes trained forward on the mirror. I do the only thing that feels right. Thumbing through my bracelet, I count, but this time, I hold myself firmly to where I want to be.

One, two, three . . .

I am seventeen and graduating high school, with Padar, Sahar, and Madar cheering for me, happily in their seats as I walk across the stage.

Four, five, six . . .

I am twenty and studying screenwriting, and spending countless nights chipping away at a script that could be my legacy.

Seven, eight, nine . . .

I am twenty-five and sitting in a new city, across the world, with Amena and Ayesha and Mattin and Aman and Eman and Maha and we are all together, laughing and wondering at where life will take us next.

I keep going. I don't stop until the future is all I want to see. I make it feel real, until there is nothing else left to feel. Smoke and light whirls around me as Malika runs and shouts, "No, please don't!"

I don't look back. I cannot afford to look back.

I stand up and keep walking until I am right in front of the mirror, staring at the me I could be.

"Hey," she says, extending a hand. "You sure you're ready for this?"

"More than ever." I don't even hesitate. Just smile into her light.

Our hands clasp together.

The mirror shatters.

"We've got her!" Hands—so many of them—reach and pull for me. I tumble and fall onto the wood floor. Cuts scrape my knees and elbows but I don't care. Madar crushes me into her embrace, and I breathe her in and hold on tight right back.

"Don't you dare leave me like that again," she breathes into my hair.

"I'm sorry," I say back. And without hesitation, I say, "I promise I'll never leave again."

"What is that?" Sam holds on to a hammer and launches himself at the mirror. It's already cracked, but in the missing pieces, there is Malika, with her sunflower dress and her yellow bows and her dark eyes.

I hold on to Madar when Sam swings.

The last thing we all see is Malika lunging, yelling desperately, *Don't let me go!*

And then all is silent.

CHAPTER TWENTY-NINE

CLARITY IS A FUNNY THING.

How all the little pieces meld together to form an incomplete picture. I sit in my grandmother's closet under the hanging clothes and imagine Malika sitting next to me. Her tiny face. *Don't let me go.*

It's weird. I thought knowing what happened to Malika was going to feel different. I thought solving the mystery was going to fix everything. Like it would be some big, grand finale. But that's not how I feel at all.

If anything, it makes me wonder more.

After Sam smashed the mirror, Madar rushed me to the hospital.

"You just collapsed when the mirror shattered," Madar had said in the waiting room. "For a moment, your heart skipped a beat and then stopped."

The doctors ran tests, but there was never an explanation of *why* or *how*.

They chalked it up to stress and sleepless nights. An electrolyte imbalance.

I tried to tell Madar that knowing wouldn't make a difference. It won't happen again.

"No, it won't." Madar held my bandaged hands in hers. "Because things are going to be different from now on. No more hiding. I'm going to tell you everything you want to know. Starting with the divorce."

I used to think Nargis Amani was too headstrong for her own good.

Now, I think I understand her a little better.

"I'll just be glad to put this house behind us," Madar muttered as we drove home. "With any luck, this will be off our hands soon enough."

Glancing out the window, I asked, "You saw her too, right?"

"Saw what?"

"Nothing." I shouldn't have been surprised, but a part of me was disappointed.

Will all of this be forgotten? Pushed under the rug, never talked about, just . . . erased? Just another casualty behind the gates of Sumner? And yeah, I'll be the first to admit that maybe holding on too tight might not be for the best *either*, but still.

I don't think running is the answer.

Not anymore.

I bravely pad down into the kitchen, where Bibi jan is sitting vacantly in the little reading nook. Sunshine sweeps all around her shoulders and neck as she soaks up the warmth. Her severe and gaunt face gives no sign of recognition when I bend down and squat in front of her.

I hold on to her knee as she stares at me. A question in her eyes.

Bibi jan had tucked away her memories of Malika. All those years ago. Maybe at first, it was the only way she knew how to deal with it. To run, like me. Run from the horrible truth that bad things happen without rhyme or reason, and we don't always get a chance to make them right. And maybe I'll never know if she ever told her daughters. Maybe she did, and it was plucked from them. There are some moments, no matter how hard we try, we can't get back.

But maybe, for my family at least, there's one way to get us out of Sumner's clutches once and for all.

"We can't run anymore, Bibi jan," I whisper to her. "Not when it means losing you."

Bibi jan keeps drifting. I stand up and grip my laptop to my chest.

"Madar, are you ready yet?" I knock on the door to her room, where she is sitting and curling her hair. She looks up at me and smiles.

"Almost. What are you planning?" She quirks a brow.

"Just . . . something I should have done a long time

ago." I think of Malika. "A promise I have to keep." I only hope it isn't too late.

⁓

Sumner looms before us as ten cars park alongside the driveway.

"Are you sure you want to go back in there?" Madar hesitates. She parks right in the middle of the driveway, past the gates and my family's curious stares. "I think it's too soon, jan." Bibi jan drifts in her seat as she looks out the window.

"Trust me on this." I reach back and hold on to Bibi's weathered hand, a hopeful smile on my face. Ayesha taps on the window. "Just corral everyone inside, okay?"

"Yeah, yeah." She gives me a thumbs-up and waves at Khala Nazaneen's army of children and makes big sweeping arm gestures. "Iiinsiiiide. Yes, let's go, kiddos. No, I will not carry you, Madina."

Holding Bibi jan's hand, we walk up the newly paved driveway and wind up the stairs. The columns on the front porch sparkle and shine as we approach the doorway. Bibi jan halts right before. Her watery eyes search, and her hand gets tight in mine.

Don't, the little voice whispers.

"Together." I squeeze her hand, and we walk on

through. My hand glides along the doorframe and onto the wall as I turn left into the grand entryway. "Tell us the feeling."

The feeling is this:

Crowded in the living space are ten sisters, one brother, and too many children to count. Madina and Harun, along with a flock of others, are running around, exploring what secrets a house as big as this one could hold.

"So, you got us all here." Amena slides out a chair for Bibi jan by the fireplace. "What's the big surprise?"

So many sets of eyes are glued to me, and I take a shaky breath. It's now or never. I scan the sea of family, for the one set of eyes that's missing. When all is quiet, I begin.

Not quite from the beginning, but in the only way I know how.

I pull up the file, where I spent the past week typing down everything I could. Every stolen memory that does not belong to me, in hopes to make things right.

"First, thanks for coming here on short notice. I know it's kinda random to be here and at first, that's what I thought too, when summer started and Madar dragged me to this place." I think back to the peeling wood, the cabinets filled with cockroaches, the sadness that clung like a scar. "But nothing about this house is random. Not even a little bit. And especially not for Bibi jan."

"No, Bibi." Amena tries to corral Bibi, but she swats her hand away and on her wobbly little legs, she takes in the empty space. Khala Farzana whispers something to Khala Firoza.

"You know I've been collecting stories, trying to piece together some fragment of who Bibi was, something we could all hold on to when Bibi won't be around to tell us anymore." The lump in my throat stops the words, and suddenly Madar's hand is on mine.

"Go on." Her eyes are glassy. Her eyeliner is all messed up. I am reminded of the Madar I saw when I was trapped in the past. This gives me the strength to continue.

"The story I ended up finding wasn't the one I wanted, but it's a story that needed to be heard." Little smoky wisps carry around Bibi jan as flickers of a girl packing a small bag flits through. A girl cutting dried fruit with a jeweled knife. A young woman sipping tea with her first daughter. A weary woman making a choice she could never take back.

"And that story begins and ends with a little girl. Bibi's eleventh daughter. Malika." I recall each and every moment, each stolen item in hopes of seeing something. A flash. A flicker of recognition in Bibi, something to restore what I had taken.

"Her *what*?" Khala Zenat looks shocked. My aunts and uncle look at one another, unsure about what to believe.

"That can't be possible . . ." Khala Afsoon rubs her forehead.

296 &ᶜᵉ DEEBA ZARGARPUR

I half expect Madar to rip her hand from mine, to call me crazy again. She doesn't.

I scan past the doubt and hope and wait. There's nothing left for me to say now.

The silence that sweeps across the room sinks my hopes.

"Sara honey." Khala Mojgan looks nervously at me while coming close to Madar and me. She is flanked by Momo Ali and Khala Firoza. "I know you've been going through a hard time, and believe me, I'd want to get lost in stories too. Sometimes it's easier that way to—"

"I'm not making it up." I curl in on myself, but my battle armor has long gone away. People are muttering and sending me worried looks as they start to shuffle out.

"Come on, we'll drive Bibi home." Khala Firoza moves to grab Bibi's arm. "And maybe have a long talk, Sara? Maybe a professional . . ."

An icy cold feeling grips my chest, as a familiar longing stirs from the shadows of the hallway that started it all. And a tinkling melody.

Madar's brow knits. "Do you hear that?"

From the shadows, something faded emerges. The rustle of a sunflower dress. And two dark eyes. She hesitates before finally stepping out into the light.

Khala Firoza and Bibi freeze when they lock eyes with Malika.

Malika shimmers into the room the way I first met her. Like stardust as the light pierces through her tiny steps.

"That's . . ." Madar blinks. "From the mirror."

"A jinn?" Khala Maluda yelps while threading her prayer beads through her fingers.

"No." I shake my head. "She's nothing like that."

Tentatively, Malika stands in front of Bibi.

Bibi is transfixed—all she does is stare and stare and stare.

Then, she reaches, her knobby fingers outstretched. They touch for a second. When I blink, Malika is gone.

"Where did she go?" I panic while striding over. Ayesha and Amena have their jaws hanging open.

"I'm not the only one who saw that right?" Amena asks.

"Holy shit." Aman runs a hand through his hair. "Did anyone get a video?"

"Seriously, Aman?" Ayesha hits his shoulder.

"What?"

I look around the hallway, the kitchen, but Malika isn't anywhere to be found. Nor are the items I thought would somehow come back. "It's time," I demand the house. "Give it all back." Yet nothing happens.

"*Light of my heart, dance.*" Bibi jan hums a melody very quietly. "*In melodies without worry.*"

I turn.

"*In hopes without regret.*" She continues to hum to

herself, softly swaying, circling the floor, her fingers touching everything as she goes. Her humming fills the air, and when she reaches me, she smiles a real, *I'm here* smile.

"My father used to sing me this song." She leans against me and says in a breathy whisper, "You know, I have twelve children. One son and eleven girls." She looks up at her children, who have frozen still as she counts for the last time.

"Farzana, Firoza, Gulnoor, Afsoon, Maluda . . ."

Madar comes closer and holds on to Bibi's other hand. ". . . Zelaikha, Zenat, Nargis . . ." Soon, everyone else comes together and our voices echo grandly into the air, finishing the count.

". . . Mojgan, Nazaneen, and Malika."

I don't know what will happen when we step out of this house. If this yesterday will be plucked and smoothed over from our minds, but that's okay.

Because we remember *now*.

I laugh through my tears while hugging Bibi jan and feel, somewhere deep in my heart, a hope that Malika can now find peace.

For a moment, we are complete.

CHAPTER THIRTY

"SARA, CAN YOU TAKE THIS TRAY AROUND, PLEASE?" Madar bustles in our little kitchen with Irina as they brew tea and pour almonds and dried figs and chocolates into little gold-and-blue bowls.

I wiggle past Bibi jan in her chair, sitting in the little nook filled with sunshine, a smile on her face while she watches her home fill up with people. Eid has snuck up on all of us, and I am happy to finally have a time to celebrate.

I take the tray of tea and head to the living room, where there are at least a dozen folding chairs out, filled with aunts and uncles and cousins and other extended family.

"Thank you, jan." Khala Farzana winks at me while taking a steaming cup. Her eyes twinkle in secret camaraderie as I circle back to the kitchen.

It turns out, Sumner was giving us one last parting gift. We ended up tracking down that Uzbek couple's records and finally found Malika's resting place. I think the shock that she was so close, for so many years, was a hard pill to swallow for Khala Farzana, especially when she found out Malika was born the same week as her own daughter.

"I feel like I've failed her in so many ways," she admitted when we put flowers on her grave. "Like I should have known. That a part of me should have felt her." She turned to me. "But maybe that's exactly what you were meant to do all along to bring us together."

I blushed and covered my face with my hair. "Yeah, anytime."

"When is your dad going to pick you up?" Madar wraps an arm around my shoulder and squeezes tight. "It's getting late, isn't it?"

"I've still got time. He's coming in a bit." I swallow hesitantly.

"Good, okay." Madar smooths her hair back. "And Sahar?"

"She's okay." I fiddle with the gold bracelet on my wrist. Perhaps the most surprising development was the bouquet of flowers I woke up to in the hospital. Sahar was sitting very quietly next to me—Madar must have ducked out for a moment—and she held my hand. *I don't want my presence to make you suffer*, she said. *If you don't want me with your dad, I'll accept it. Your feelings matter too.*

After everything I went through in Sumner, I shook my head. It was time to break the cycle. It was time to move on.

Stay, I had said back. *Let's see what could be.*

It's still something to get used to, this weird in-between honesty our family is going through, but we're trying. I can admit it makes me a little uncomfortable. But I don't run from it. I let it sit and try to understand it.

I've let my heart get bent-up and twisted for too long.

"Give her my regards," Madar says, and kisses my head. I slip out because she just reminded me. Before I go, there's still one more thing I need to do.

I knock on Sam's front door.

There's a FOR SALE sign stuck in the grass.

My mind is racing a mile a minute. I try to suppress the need to throw up and run off.

"Oh. Hey." Sam tenses, and he makes an awkward half move to cross his arms, but then decides to keep them by his sides. "What are you doing here?"

"Can I come in, neighbor?" I peek past him at the boxes that are open.

"I don't think that's a good idea." Sam swallows, and

his stare is hard. "It's a mess. You'd probably trip and end up making more of a mess for me to clean up."

"Ouch." I wince and rub the back of my head. "I guess I deserve that." My fingers fiddle with the gold bracelet on my wrist, like they're trying to reach for some fuzzy, familiar feeling.

"Shouldn't you be out celebrating?" Sam opens the door a little wider and places a hand in his back pocket. "Considering you solved the great Sumner mystery."

"I had some help." I offer him a smile. He tries to keep his face straight, but there's a ghost of a smile he's fighting. "Took an army, as they say."

"Well, I'm glad for you. You seem . . . happier." Sam shrugs his shoulders and I can't read his face. But I do understand that this is the signal for goodbye. He moves to close the door, but I put out my hands.

"Wait." There's still so much left unsaid between us. So much I couldn't let go of that got in the way of me seeing Sam for who he is: my very best friend. I still don't remember the Fourth of July, and maybe I'll never remember whatever Sumner took from me, from him, but I get that I can't keep doing the same thing to Sam and expecting a different result.

"Look, I know our friendship can never go back to how it used to be. I get that we aren't those people anymore." I try to be brave as I lay my heart bare for the first time. "And I know shutting you out was wrong. I'm not asking for you to forgive me right now. I know it's been a one-way street for too long, but . . ."

Sam raises his eyebrows, as if to say *go on*.

"But, if you want, maybe we could . . . start over?" I suddenly feel very shy.

"Start over?" Sam tests the words.

"Yeah, like." I stick out my hand and blurt, "Hey, I'm Sara. I live across the street, and I'm known to be an asshole, but I'm currently in recovery. And you are?" I hold my breath when Sam doesn't move.

A part of me is screaming, *Good job, you idiot, you think you're in some kind of movie?*, and my hope falters.

"Right." I glance away, tuck my hands around my arms. "It's probably for the best to not." I turn around and trudge down the porch and toward the driveway.

"Hey, wait up," Sam calls out. His hair is glowing in a way I've always liked. "Let me know when you're out of recovery."

"Might take a while." I sniffle and scream mentally, *Don't embarrass yourself, keep the waterworks in!*

"I can wait." Sam shrugs and smiles wryly. "Just don't take too long, neighbor." He pauses before shutting the door, taking one last look at me. He waves.

As hope blooms, I wave back.

I know we can never go back to who we used to be. The little kids who used to knock knees and watch the stars and play make-believe in the snow.

304 &C DEEBA ZARGARPUR

Maybe that's okay.
Sam shuts the door and my phone buzzes.

Padar: On my way. You ready?
Sara: Waiting right outside

I look up and smile.
Maybe we could be even *better*.

ACKNOWLEDGMENTS

WRITING *HOUSE OF YESTERDAY* FELT LIKE A FEVER dream, something hazy and slippery in my mind, yet also painfully solid and real. This book would not exist without the support of so many people, and for that I am forever thankful.

Thank you to my fantastic editor, Trisha de Guzman, who saw the potential in Sara and the Amani family from the very beginning. I will never forget that first phone call and the way you saw right into the heart of this book.

To my agent, Elana Roth Parker, who tirelessly fielded so many emails, plot rewrites, title changes, and emergency texts. Thank you and the LDLA family for taking a chance on me and this sad-yet-hopeful story.

Thank you to Melina Ghadami for bringing Sara to life with your stunning artwork and to Trisha Previte and Veronica Mang, for the haunting yet beautiful design—I keep pinching myself, I still can't believe this fantastic cover is mine. Thank you to everyone at FSG for all that you do for my book and all the incredible books on FSG's list: to Chantal Gersch, Eleonore Fisher, Lelia Mander, Allyson Floridia, John Nora, Elizabeth Clark, and Mallory Grigg. It has not been easy to work during these uncertain times, and I am so thankful for all that you do.

Community plays a huge role in Sara's world, and I would be nothing without the mighty army of my family (I would name everyone personally, but alas, this book would go on for another fifty pages so know that I love all of you!!). I owe so much to my aunts and uncles, cousins, and extended family for teaching me what it means to be part of something greater and that home isn't a specific place, or a country—home is where you are loved, and I am so blessed to be loved by so many.

Another community I would be nothing without is the incredible kidlit writing community. Thank you to my word warriors—June CL Tan, Swati Teerdhala, and Roseanne A. Brown—for keeping me sane during stressful deadlines and for always lending an encouraging ear when doubt started to creep in. I will always treasure our friendship. To Alexa Donne, for your constant praise and friendship. To Kat Cho, Rebecca Kuss, Emily Berge-Theilmann, and Alexa Wejko for those very early days when *House of Yesterday* was only an idea. Your support kept me going when I was ready to give up on this writing dream. To Judy I. Lin, for being a wonderful mentor very early on in my writing career. To all the writer friends I made along the way, whether it be a passing conversation or a tweet, I would be nothing without the encouragement of this wonderful writing community.

Thank you to my very first writing friends, Laura Pohl and Dana Nuenighoff. I will forever be so grateful to have found you all those years ago. Thank you for being the very best of friends and for reigniting my passion for writing.

To my Afghan writing community, thank you for your kindness and patience, for your words of praise. To Nadia Hashimi, for always having the best advice. I am in awe of everything you do and feel so blessed to know you. To my fellow word nerds, Zohra Saed, Zarena Aslami, and Leila Nadir. Thank you for your friendship and support. I still can't believe how lucky I am to have met you. You inspire me to keep growing, to keep learning.

Thank you to my Madar jan, for always encouraging me to pursue my (many) dreams, and for being my very first reader and my number one supporter (also my number one critic, haha). There aren't enough words to express how much your support means to me, not just with this book, but through my entire life. You've been the one constant, cheering the loudest, and I will never be able to thank you enough for all of it. To my brother, Aman jan, for all the late-night talks, where I'd make you listen to all my road blocks and half-baked explanations.

Thank you for the laughs and logic breakthroughs. Please be prepared for more of these brainstorm sessions in the future.

I would not be here today if it wasn't for the courage of my grandparents and great-grandparents, who packed up and started over in a new country in the hopes of giving us a brighter future. Thank you for always putting family first, and for loving me with all your hearts. To my Bibi Khanum Gul, whom I love fiercely, and to my Baba jan and Baba Haji, whom I miss deeply. You inspire me to make your sacrifices worth it. I only hope to continue to make you proud.

And finally, to my Bibi Dil jan. I don't even know where to begin. There is so much to say, so much I wish I could say to you. When I started this story, you were there holding my hand. In many ways, you kept me steady, even when it felt like your mind was an ocean away. You were always my anchor in the toughest of times. Without you, sometimes I feel lost at sea too. I never thought I'd be releasing this book without you. I missed you then, I miss you now, and I'll miss you forever. I know you're at peace now, and I know one day, we'll see each other again. Until then, I'll meet you in my dreams, with my hand outstretched, ready to take yours.

Until then, Bibi jani qand, I love you. Always. Thank you for loving me, for holding my hand, for always having a smile ready, just for me. I will never forget your smile.